RIPPED APART

RIPPED APART

A RIPPLE EFFECT MYSTERY, BOOK FIVE

JEANNE GLIDEWELL

ePublishingWorks!
love what you read.

Book and cover design by eBook Prep
www.ebookprep.com

May, 2020
ISBN: 978-1-947833-45-6

ePublishing Works!
644 Shrewsbury Commons Ave
Ste 249
Shrewsbury PA 17361
United States of America

www.epublishingworks.com
Phone: 866-846-5123

To all of the victims of Hurricane Harvey——from the animals at the Aransas National Wildlife Refuge, whose home was severely damaged; to the resilient citizens of south Texas; to the folks in Houston——and everyone and everything in between.

ACKNOWLEDGMENTS

I'd like to thank Mother Nature for supplying the inspiration for this novel, although I would have preferred a gentle summertime shower. I'd have been more than happy to name this book *Rippling Streams* rather than *Ripped Apart*. A big thank you to my editors; Judy Beatty, of Madison, Alabama; and Alice Duncan, of Roswell, New Mexico. Another big thank you to Nina and Brian Paules, of eBook Prep and ePublishing Works, for their confidence in me, and for all they do to promote my work. An especially big thank you goes to Shirley Worley of Merriam, Kansas; Sheila Davis, of Fairway, Kansas; and Sarah Goodman, of Olathe, Kansas; who willingly, but possibly unwittingly, volunteered for the monumental, and yet, unpaid task of proofreading my manuscript and catching typos and bizarre errors that slip by my editors and me. I appreciate all of these wonderful people very, very much!

Samantha McCary
Rockport, Texas

FOREWORD

BY SAMANTHA MCCARY, ROCKPORT, TEXAS CITIZEN

On August 25th, 2017, my hometown of Rockport, Texas, got hit by a little storm named Hurricane Harvey. And it hit Rockport with a vengeance! Lives, cars, houses, campers, boats, and everything else in Harvey's path got turned upside down. What twenty-four hours earlier had been a quiet, peaceful little drinking town with a fishing problem, now looked like ground zero in a war zone. Houses, apartments, businesses, schools, and structures of every kind were just gone. As people made their way out of the rubble and evacuation locations and back to what had been their homes, the true desperation of the situation began to sink in. Hundreds, if not thousands, of Rockport citizens had no home to go back to and no place to turn. That is where my part of the story began.

I had a house and three acres at the edge of town, and although Harvey leveled *Mermaid's Kitchen*, my catering business, my house was nearly unaffected by the storm. As soon as we discovered we had a place to come back to, my family and I started a donation drive to bring back items we knew people would need. As a cook, I knew people would need to eat. What grew out of that first sixteen-foot trailer load of supplies, including twelve tents and two outdoor showers, is a story in itself. But I will tell you that in the following two years, I saw the very best and the very worst of humanity. At one point, there were at least one hundred and thirty-five people living in tents in my yard, some for a few nights and others for many months. Most were displaced locals, but at least a third were volunteers; people who came from as far away as Tennessee and Alaska to try to help get Rockport cleaned up. As to be expected, there were a few who just showed up to take advantage of the situation.

I watched lives change, a few for the worse, but so many more for the better. I don't consider myself a philanthropist or a home-town hero, as Jeanne Glidewell refers to me in *Ripped Apart*. I was merely following the golden rule, doing what I'd hope someone would do for me if our situations had been reversed. As the late

Canadian writer, Charles de Lint, said, "I don't want to live in a world where we don't look out for each other. Not just the people who are close to us, but anybody who needs a helping hand. I can't change the way anybody else thinks, or what they choose to do, but I can do my bit."

INTRODUCTION

Even though I have injected some humor into this fictional story, please do not think I am making light of an event that was both tragic and catastrophic. Hurricane Harvey was devastating to many of our family, neighbors, and friends. We didn't escape its wrath, either. Our waterfront condo was destroyed by the storm.

"Rockport Strong", "Houston Strong", and "Port A Strong", among others, were not just new mottos thrown about because they made good media sound bites. They were declarations made by the Texas citizens of those towns to persevere, to conquer whatever obstacles they were faced with, and to rise to the occasion no matter what. From the moment Harvey finally abated, the citizens of Texas vowed to make certain the recovery and renewal of their towns resulted in them becoming bigger, stronger, and better than ever before. From what I've witnessed in the past two-and-a-half years or so, those promises have been kept. Most of the businesses have reopened and are flourishing, the majority of damaged homes have been repaired or rebuilt, and even a few of the destroyed landmarks are being replaced.

Tourism, one of our primary sources of income, suffered a

crushing blow following Harvey. Amongst many other activities, there's great art-gallery browsing, tremendous bird and dolphin watching, delicious restaurants, unbelievable fishing, fascinating beachcombing, exciting boating, and every other water sport you can imagine. I could go on and on until I've used every complimentary adjective in the dictionary, but I'd rather you come and check it out for yourself. We are open for business once again!!! You won't be disappointed, I promise.

As always, I hope you enjoy my story and forgive me for the words I have made up in the telling of it.

Feel free to send messages to JeanneGlidewell@epublishing-works.com. I respond to every message I receive.

Happy reading,
Jeanne

CHARACTERS

Rapella Ripple - seventy-year-old amateur sleuth who's determined to discover the truth behind Reilly Reynolds's mysterious disappearance.

Clyde "Rip" Ripple - other half of the full-time RVing couple who's an unsung hero for not only putting up with his wife's impetuous actions and single-minded obsession to bring criminals to justice, but also for occasionally assisting in her often dangerous pursuits.

Regina Moore - fifty-one-year-old daughter of Rapella and Rip, whose home on Key Allegro Island has been damaged by the hurricane.

Milo Moore - Rapella and Rip's son-in-law who owns MC Hammerheads Construction Company and is in the business of remodeling and flipping houses.

Reilly Reynolds - Regina and Milo's newlywed next-door

neighbor who goes missing during Hurricane Harvey and is presumed dead, a victim of the storm.

Walker Reynolds - Reilly's husband, who reports that he watched her chase their dog, Scrappy, down to their pier in the midst of the storm. He's convinced she was blown off the pier by the high winds, never to be seen again.

Jessie Garza - general contractor who takes on the job of repairing his friend, Walker's, home following the hurricane.

Bruno Watts - diminutive and diabetic drywall sub-contractor hired by Jessie to assist with the Reynolds's home restoration project.

Anthony "Tony" Torres - owner of TNT Demolition and another one of the sub-contractors hired by Jessie to help restore the Reynolds's home.

Suzanna Pandero - the neighbor on the opposite side of Regina and Milo's home, who has two rascally creatures to contend with; one is a pet chinchilla, the other a straying husband.

Percival Pandero - the deceitful husband of Suzanna, who has even more immoral tendencies then she realizes.

Barlow Barnaby - another resident on the Moores' cul-de-sac who has a habit of "seeing things" and calling the cops on his neighbors. He's not well-liked among his neighbors on Flamingo Road.

ONE

"**Y**our daughter doesn't have the sense God gave a day-old boll weevil."

"*My* daughter?" I asked my husband, Clyde Ripple, better known as Rip. "I could've sworn you were present when Regina was conceived. I guess it *was* the milkman after all."

"Why would she and Milo ignore a mandatory evacuation order?" Rip was too tense to appreciate my attempt at levity. "It's not like Mayor Wax would issue one for no reason."

"When I spoke to Regina on Friday, I literally begged her to flee the coastal area." My mood turned on a dime and my eyes grew misty as I spoke. Rip and I were currently visiting friends in Rockdale, Missouri, and the news of a major storm along the Texas Gulf Coast had been disheartening.

"Well, at that stage of the game, it was probably best they stay put rather than risk getting caught up in the storm while traveling in their vehicle," Rip replied.

I swallowed hard at the thought Regina might have reconsidered my pleading advice and, in order to appease me, convinced Milo to evacuate too late, placing them at even greater risk. Our fifty-one-year-old daughter, Regina, and her husband, Milo Moore, lived on Key Allegro Island in Rockport, Texas.

Late in the evening on August 25, 2017, Hurricane Harvey had made landfall in our quaint little hometown of approximately ten thousand people, causing massive, catastrophic devastation, according to the latest weather report. Regina had informed me just hours before the storm hit that they planned to ride it out in their waterfront home. I saw no particular honor in their decision to "go down with the ship" if the hurricane was as destructive and life-threatening as anticipated, and I told her so. Three or four times, in fact!

But, unfortunately, my words appeared to fall on deaf ears. Just a few hours later, the hurricane came roaring into Rockport with all its pistons pumping, and wreaked havoc on everything in its path. It'd been reported that all of the town's utilities had been put out of commission indefinitely. This included cell phone and Internet service, leaving us no way to contact our daughter to see if she and Milo had survived the storm. If they did, I'd be tempted to strangle them both for causing us such angst by behaving so recklessly. Rip had just recovered from triple-bypass surgery. The last thing he needed was to be stressed out about Regina and Milo's safety.

Just after noon on the twenty-seventh, Rip and I were in the parlor of the Alexandria Inn with Lexie Starr and Stone Van Patten, who owned and operated the renovated Victorian bed and breakfast facility located in Rockdale, Missouri. We'd been glued to the TV for hours, watching *The Weather Channel* and anxiously waiting for updates on the progress of the still-churning hurricane and the devastation it was leaving in its wake. We gasped in unison as meteorologist, Jim Cantore, predicted Hurricane Harvey would inundate the Houston area with over fifty inches of rain. *Fifty inches of rain!* I couldn't quite wrap my head around the idea of over four feet of rain falling in one storm!

The magnitude of this forceful hurricane, which had strengthened for days in the Gulf of Mexico before making landfall in Rockport, was unprecedented and expected to become one of the costliest, if not *the* costliest, tropical cyclone on record. Through it all, we had no way of knowing how Regina and Milo were faring, or if their beautiful home was still standing. Rip and I were nearly a thousand miles away and felt helpless, knowing it was unlikely we'd be able to get to our daughter's side anytime soon.

The damage reports were not exactly encouraging, either. Local airports, and nearly every thoroughfare leading from Houston to south of Corpus Christi, were closed and were apt to remain so for days. Thousands of power poles had been snapped in two. Downed electrical lines, uprooted trees, debris, and various other hazards were making every road in the vicinity impassable.

I shook my head in despair. "Even if the kids survived the storm, I doubt their fancy-pants house did."

"Let's not borrow worry, Rapella." Rip tenderly stroked my back. "We need to hope for the best, even as we prepare for the worst."

Just then our cell phone rang. "It's Regina!" I exclaimed. Flustered, I grabbed the phone, accidentally disconnecting the call.

"What the– ?" Rip looked at me as if I'd just hung up on the Pope. When the phone rang a second time, he snatched it from my hand. "Sweetheart? Are you kids all right?"

I nervously watched as Rip strained to hear Regina's response. As usual, he'd left his hearing aids in the safety of his toiletry bag, a habit that was a constant source of irritation for me.

"Give me the blasted thing!" I snatched the phone back.

"Mom?" Regina sounded on the verge of hysteria. Her voice was cutting in and out. "I___ ___ one bar___ ___ ___first time___ ___get out all___."

"I can't understand you, honey. Are you and Milo okay?" I asked.

Her barely audible reply sounded like, "I'd prefer banana pudding on my radiator."

"Your what? Did you say radiator?" Between a terrible connection and her obvious distress, I was unable to make out much of what she said. I took comfort in knowing if she was able to speak, she was at least alive and conscious.

"All roads closed___ Milo ___ ___the roof___ ___ the terribly strong wind___ ___ ___ dead___ ___ ___ripped apart___ ___ the pier___ dog___ ___ big mess___ ___ ___what to do." That's all I could make out before the call dropped.

I immediately tried to call her back, but it was to no avail. Everyone who'd gathered in the parlor stared at me in trepidation. I was so choked up, I could barely speak. "I, um, I think she was trying to tell me that Milo's dead. And something to do with the dog making a mess."

"What?" Rip asked. He was clearly perplexed.

"Then again, maybe it was their dog that died."

"They don't have a dog!" Rip said loudly. "What exactly did Regina say?"

"I think she might've said Milo fell off the roof due to the strong wind." I was desperately trying to make sense of what few decipherable words I'd heard. "There was definitely something said about a dog, too. And something, or someone, was ripped apart."

"No doubt a lot of things were ripped apart, but even Milo's not foolish enough to stand on the roof in a hurricane. Did

Regina specifically say he'd been killed?" After a career in law enforcement, Rip was more focused on facts than emotions.

"I'm not sure. There was a lot of static on the line."

"I reckon all we can do at this point is wait for Regina to contact us again," Rip said after a heavy sigh. His voice was composed, but his expression was anything but. "So far they've only reported one death in Rockport related to the hurricane."

"Oh, good! That's very comforting." After I spoke, I looked around at the expressions on everyone's faces and amended my statement. "It's not good, or comforting, that someone lost their life, of course. I'm just thankful no other deaths have been reported."

Although I was extremely relieved to have heard Regina's voice, I remained distraught the rest of the evening. With all forms of communications down, it was possible something *had* happened to Milo, and Regina had been unable to report it to the authorities.

Just then my phone beeped. It was a text from my friend, Gracie Parker, who was in my old bunko club when we lived in Rockport. Gracie, a widow, lived just a block or two down from Regina and Milo. As I read her message, my expression must have been alarming.

"What is it?" Rip asked, a catch in his voice. "What's wrong?"

"It's from Gracie. It says 'I just heard someone on Flamingo Road was swept away in the storm and has been classified as missing and presumed dead. Have you heard from Regina and Milo? I know they live on that street. I'm sending you a text because I can't get a strong enough signal to call.'"

"That's not good," Rip replied simply.

"Hardly." I was surprised at how calmly Rip had reacted to Gracie's message that someone on Regina and Milo's street had gone missing. "Oh dear! Rip, you don't think maybe it was Milo who was swept away, do you?"

"I wouldn't think so. But who knows? Regina did sound very upset. Guess we'll just have to wait until she can contact us again. Try not to stress out about it, honey."

"All right." *Fat chance of that!*

Sleep that night eluded me. I lay in bed, staring at the ceiling. An uneasy feeling churned in my stomach, letting me know unforeseen changes lay just over the horizon.

TWO

It was three days before Regina contacted us again. Three long days of waiting for our phone to ring. We stayed glued to the television, hoping for any bit of optimistic news or encouraging information. Most of what we saw were photos of total devastation and piles of debris everywhere. According to Jim Cantore, the storm had moved on up the coast and was now dumping a record-setting fifty-one inches of rain on the Houston area.

When the phone rang, it lay face-down on the kitchen table. Rip and I nearly knocked each other over racing to the tiny kitchen in our thirty-foot travel trailer to answer it. I reached the phone first, but I'd been more fleet of foot than Rip even before his recent bypass surgery and hip-replacement operation less than two years prior.

"Regina? Is that you?" I asked. I sounded breathless, as if I'd sprinted to answer the phone from two blocks away. I decided to let her dictate the conversation. If she had bad news, I'd let her tell it in her own time.

"Yes, it's me. How are you and Daddy? Is he following the doctor's orders and recovering all right from his bypass surgery?"

"We're fine, sweetheart," I replied. "And, yes, your father is getting stronger with each passing day. He balks at having to go to his cardio rehab sessions, but I have ways of making him compliant with his physical therapy, medications, and healthier diet."

"I'm sure you do." Regina laughed.

"Okay, enough about us." Patience was not a virtue of mine, and I could no longer wait to find out how Milo had fared. "How are you and Milo? That's the most important thing right now. I assume he's alive?"

"Of course, he's alive. Why would you even ask such a thing?" Luckily, I didn't have to respond because she kept on talking. "We're doing okay, all things considered. It's been a rough week, for sure."

"No doubt. And your dog?"

"What dog?" Regina sounded confused at first and then concerned. "Are you all right, Mom? You haven't been cooking with sherry again, have you?"

"No, of course not. Been there, tried that, and didn't like where it led me."

"To the emergency room, you mean?" Regina laughed—at my expense—before continuing. "You know we don't have a dog. I'd tell you if we got a new pet. You probably misunderstood me when I told you that the next-door neighbor's dog got swept away in the hurricane."

"Well, that's good." I then realized how awful that sounded. I'd been speaking before thinking a lot in the last few days. I quickly corrected my gaffe. "I don't mean it was good that the poor dog got swept away. I feel for the pooch and its owners. I'm just glad it wasn't your pet that died."

"Oh, the Reynolds's dog didn't die. Scrappy survived

somehow and, with the help of social media, was returned safe and sound to his home yesterday. Unfortunately, Reilly didn't. She and Scrappy disappeared at the same time. We haven't heard any updates yet today, though. As of yesterday, Reilly hadn't been located or her body recovered. It's presumed she drowned after being swept away by the ferocious wind when she chased after Scrappy. The little guy got spooked during the storm and ran down toward their fishing pier in absolute terror."

"That's awful, honey. I'm glad the dog survived his brush with death, but I'm so sorry to hear about your neighbor. Maybe she'll show up yet. Keep the faith."

"I'm trying, Mom. The aftermath of this storm is so sad. I'm trying to stay strong, like the town's new motto—Rockport Strong—however, I still keep breaking down into tears at the thought of how many folks lost their homes, their businesses, their jobs, and even their schools. We suffered some loss too, but I swear, Mom, some people lost just about everything but their lives."

"Sounds like your neighbor might have lost even that!" I exclaimed. I could tell Regina was getting worked up about her neighbor. I didn't want her to collapse into a fit of sobbing again, so I changed tack on our conversation. "And speaking of being swept away by the wind, Milo wasn't hurt too badly when he was blown off the roof, was he?"

I watched Rip roll his eyes as I waited for a response from our daughter. I had half a mind to switch the phone off "speaker" so I wouldn't feel like I was being judged on my comments to our daughter, ridiculous as they might be.

"Where'd you get the idea Milo was blown off the roof? Is that why you asked me if he was alive?" Regina asked. If nothing else, her melancholy mood had morphed from sadness to astonishment at the flick of a switch. "Are you (bleeping) nuts, Mom? We weren't even convinced we should ride out the storm inside

9

our house. No way Milo would get up on the roof with wind speeds approaching one-hundred-and-forty miles-per-hour."

"I thought you said…" I realized how foolish it sounded as I began to put it into words. An exaggerated guffaw from my husband made me feel even sillier. *Dang it!* I thought. *I knew I should have taken the phone off "speaker" when the thought occurred to me that having Rip listening to both sides of the conversation would not bode well for me.* I watched now as he mouthed the words *I told you so.* "Oh, forget it. Just a misunderstanding, I guess. So you are both okay?"

"Yes, we're fine. Wish I could say the same about the house."

"Did it suffer quite a bit of damage?" I asked.

"Yes, but I think every structure in town sustained some measure of damage, and many were totally destroyed. All-in-all, we were pretty lucky. Our standing-seam metal roof held up pretty well, compared to the composition-shingled roofs on a lot of the houses here. And the tiled roofs took it the hardest. The tiles peeled off like dominoes in many cases. We had broken windows from flying debris, and the garage door buckled, along with some other damage. Fortunately, our house was built to hurricane code when it was constructed in 2005."

"That sounds like good news."

"Yes, for the most part. There's still a lot of water damage from all the rain that poured in through the shattered windows. We'll be adding hurricane shutters when we get everything repaired. The problem will be finding available contractors to do the work. The remodeling companies, electricians, plumbers, roofers, and framers will be in short supply, as will windows, doors, drywall, and all other building materials."

"But Milo owns MC Hammerheads Construction. Remodeling and flipping houses is his line of work. Shouldn't he be able to get your house back in tip-top shape in short order?"

"That's just it. This is a great opportunity for him to pick up some very lucrative jobs, and make some serious money. If he's concentrating on our house, he won't be able to capitalize on the situation. I don't mean to sound callous or insensitive to other people's plight. It's just that we're going to have to depend on Milo's business to get by for who knows how (bleeping) long. My income has just been dealt a real blow."

"I understand, honey." And I truly did see where she was coming from. As a realtor, Regina's livelihood had undoubtedly suffered a serious setback. There might not be more than a handful of homes in all of Rockport worth buying any time soon, and probably very few folks anxious to buy a place in the hurricane-ravaged area at the present time. The real estate market had undoubtedly just bottomed out in the area being called "ground zero" following the destructive storm. A lot of real estate agents would be looking for another line of work to make ends meet. Regina and Milo were luckier than most couples, in that Milo was a home remodeler whose skills and services would be in high demand. A realtor's job might not be since most houses aren't even standing let alone in any condition to be sold. "I agree you kids need to make hay while the sun shines, so to speak. Let us know if there's anything we can do to help."

"Thanks. I appreciate your offer." It was Regina's next remark that threw me for a loop. "In fact, we were hoping Daddy could come down and work on our house while Milo makes money hand over fist on other people's homes. Daddy's so handy, you know. Just like Milo."

"Well..." I began, stalling to come up with a good response. Three things troubled me. For one, Regina's remark about Milo making money hand over fist *did* sound extremely callous and insensitive, no matter how hard you tried to spin it. Secondly, I saw our plans to spend the fall and winter at a waterfront camp-ground in Gulf Shores, Alabama, fade away like cheap paint.

Last, but not least, I wasn't sure if I was even included in Regina's invitation.

Apparently, Reggie suddenly realized her comment might have sounded offensive to me. As an afterthought, she added. "And we'd love to have you down here too, of course. I'm sure you'll be a big help to us as well."

It was nice to hear Rip wouldn't have to find a place to board me while he and Dolly, our spoiled cat, traveled down to south Texas. This was one concern eliminated. Also on my list of concerns, and possibly the most critical, was that my dear husband was anything *but* handy. I'd watched him install a light fixture over our bathroom sink once. He didn't even recognize the fact that the light was too close to the ceiling until he was ready to light it up and admire his work. It was then he realized the glass globes could not be raised up in order to screw in the light bulbs. When he comprehended he was going to have to knock another hole in the wall to lower the light fixture, he said, "Looks like I might have to call our handyman, Bob, to patch the hole. I'm not as good with drywall as I am with electrical projects."

You can't imagine how tough it was for me to keep my pie hole shut at that point. I nearly bit a notch out of my lip as I tried to restrain from telling him I wasn't overly impressed with his electrical prowess either. Finally, when I couldn't stand it any longer, I said, "Despite your vast knowledge of all things electrical, why don't we just have Bob lower the light fixture while he's here to patch the hole? I'm sure your time could be better spent on tackling another problem."

My sarcasm flew over Rip's head like a misfired bullet. He had merely nodded, and replied, "You're probably right, dear. I've been wanting to clean the carburetor on the lawnmower and overhaul the motor."

"Swell. Good to know." It truly *was* good to know because,

while I was finding money in our tight budget for Bob to take care of the light fixture and drywall patch, I could search for some more to replace the lawnmower. After Rip screwed around with the motor and carburetor, he'd deem the lawnmower a piece of crap and declare it unfixable. And, thanks to Rip, by that time it *would* be.

Despite the irony, I did think it was cute Regina considered her father to be "handy". She'd always viewed her father through rose-colored glasses. And, to give credit where credit is due, Rip *was* handy to have around if you needed to have a beer bottle shot off a fence post from one hundred feet away and you only had three bullets to get the job done. He hadn't gotten the nickname of "dead eye Dick" during his career as a lawman for no reason. In this case, the "Dick" was slang for detective, a position he'd held for years, not for being a jerk. Rip was highly respected and well-liked by about everyone who knew him. He later retired as the sheriff of Aransas County, where Rockport was located and had been recognized for keeping the crime rate low during his tenure.

He was also handy if you needed someone to polish off an entire sack of pork rinds in thirty minutes or less while lounging in a recliner, washing those salty snacks down with beer, and reciting all the names of the players on the entire Dallas Cowboys football team.

Rip was even adept at naming and explaining the use of every one of his twenty-seven wrenches, four screwdrivers, and six pairs of pliers. However, if you expected him to be able to fix, build, or replace anything with those screwdrivers, pliers, and wrenches, you'd be pretty much shit out of luck. Rip loved collecting tools. Using them was a different matter altogether. As with the light fixture and lawnmower, after a commendable effort he usually ended up calling in an expert to do the work, or he just pitched the item he was trying to repair and bought a brand new one. To be fair, I collected patchwork patterns, and had yet to produce a single quilt.

"So, what do you think, Mom?" Regina asked. "Can you two come down?"

"We'd be happy to help out as much as we're able," I assured our daughter. "I'm certain your father will do what he can to help with repairs around the place. Just keep in mind, he's not certified to complete any major repairs: plumbing, roofing, drywall, electrical—especially electrical—or tasks of that nature."

"I know, Mom. To be honest, we mostly need him here to be a gopher for Milo."

"Did you say gopher?"

"Yeah. Gopher. You know, go for this, and go for that," Regina explained with a laugh. "But don't tell Daddy I said that. We need you both here for moral support more than anything."

"Well, we can definitely supply that."

"The problem is that nearly everyone in town is in the same shape as we are, or worse," Regina said. "There just aren't enough tradesmen and contractors to go around. It'll take months for people to settle their insurance claims, get SBA loans, or even get funds from FEMA to rebuild."

"Gosh! It sounds even grimmer than I imagined. Do you want us to head on down tomorrow?"

"No. Not yet. I'll let you know. We'll have to wait until some of our utility services are restored, which will no doubt take weeks. Right now we're staying at a motel, but we'll be purchasing a motorhome in the next few days. There's currently a curfew throughout Rockport, anyway. No one can be in town between seven p.m. and seven a.m. until further notice."

"Why on earth would—"

"Think about it," Regina cut in. "They are trying to limit the amount of looting going on. The police department is spread really thin as it is. Plus, there's no electricity, water, sewer, phone service, or internet services. There are few, if any, businesses open right now—no restaurants, grocery stores, gas stations, schools, or public offices, like city hall—and no one knows how long it will take until the situation improves."

"Oh, my! Have they given any estimates on how long restoring the electrical power to town will take?"

"They said it could be months, and longer for other services, most likely. However, the way these electrical linemen are going at it, I can see us getting power back much earlier than originally anticipated."

"That's good news. Where are you and Milo staying?" I asked.

"We were able to find a motel room in Marble Falls this morning, which is why I was able to get a signal to call you," Regina said. "It'll be a long commute back and forth to Rockport, but it's the closest place we could find with a vacancy."

"Good grief! Why that's something like five hours from Rockport." It was hard to imagine every hotel room between Rockport and the Texas hill country was booked. But considering how many residents had to evacuate before the storm and were unable to return to their homes, and how many reporters, contractors, and electrical linemen were congregating in the affected areas, it was definitely conceivable. "I'm so sorry. How are you holding up?"

"I'm all right. I've been helping out friends and neighbors as much as I can, which has kept me busy. I've had some crying spells, of course, but I haven't really had time to fall apart or grieve over all that's lost."

"That's probably a blessing." I tried to put a positive spin on the extremely negative situation.

"If you (bleeping) say so." As Regina had been conversing with me, I noticed she'd been using a lot of profanity, which I didn't normally let slide without commenting on. But I figured under the current circumstances, I could hardly blame her for being so upset. I kept mum about her four-letter words and listened as she continued. "While Milo's been busy dealing with the house and moving all of our belongings into storage, I've been taking photos of the damage and trying to put together the paperwork for our insurance claim with the Texas Windstorm Insurance Association, which promises to be a damned nightmare. I'm sure you're familiar with TWIA."

"Yes. We had coverage with TWIA on our old house." We'd had a couple of other policies, too, as we were also required to carry flood, fire, and personal property coverage. Insurance was not cheap when you lived on the coast. "Has there been any looting going on?"

"Oh, sure. There are always assholes who put the mighty dollar above all else and will take advantage of other people's misfortune."

"Oh, my! Looters are the lowest of the low. They rank somewhere below spoilt milk," I said. "I feel so bad for everyone there. I'm curious to hear how all our friends made out, and the ladies in my bunko club. At least three of them have homes on Key Allegro. Gracie Parker just lives one street down from you."

"Yeah, I drove by her house yesterday. It was heavily damaged, so I stopped in to check on her. I'm going back over this afternoon to help her box up photos, sentimental mementos, and important papers. I told her we'd keep them in our storage unit until she figured out what she was going to do. She may opt to raze the house, sell the lot, and move back to Illinois, where two of her children live."

"That's very kind of you, sweetheart. Thank you for helping Gracie."

"Any friend of yours is a friend of mine, Mom. I couldn't *not* offer to help. Our neighbor's house, four doors down, took a really big hit. Jo Jo Wallinski's top floor was completely obliterated, and the back half of the house has been reduced to rubble."

"I hate to hear that. Keep your chin up, as hard as that is to do. I'm sure Rockport will come back bigger and better than ever." I was trying to cheer up my only child, but the words sounded hollow even to me.

"I know, Mom. Everyone is saying the area will come back bigger and better than ever. But the amount of time they're predicting it's going to take is so damned long. I wonder if Rockport will ever be the same charming little town it's always been."

"Rockport came back following Celia. She'll do it again, I'm sure," I said. The last major hurricane to hit the area was Hurricane Celia in 1970, when my daughter was only a toddler. Her memories of that storm were naturally limited, and it hadn't been nearly as destructive, or deadly, as Harvey.

"It'll sure be a lot easier once you and Daddy can join us. I'll let you know as soon as we can get back on to our property. We'll have a new motorhome to stay in by then."

"You and Milo can save money by staying with us," I offered, hoping she'd turn me down, even if buying a new RV would take a big chunk of dough out of the Moores' bank account. Our travel trailer didn't have any of the modern slide outs, and space was cramped with just Rip and me living in it. Dolly, our chubby tabby, didn't help with the space restraints, either. Fortunately, she didn't mind sharing the couch with Rip when the two napped. To save living space, and divert the odor, Rip had cut a hole in the floor behind his recliner and installed a small ramp down to a storage compartment under the floor. Dolly had her own personal bathroom in that compartment, which she grudgingly shared with boxes of photo albums, Rip's toolbox, a couple of fishing poles we'd purchased the last time we were in Rockport, and other miscellaneous stuff we kept stored in that undercarriage compartment. "The trailer would be a little cramped, but we could make do somehow."

"No, we won't need to stay with you. And you know I'm allergic to cats," Regina said without preamble. She sounded even less enthused about my offer than I'd felt when I extended it. "But thanks for the offer. We'll buy a new motorhome. We've been wanting one and we certainly wouldn't want to intrude on you guys."

Thank God, I thought, as I uncrossed my fingers. The very idea of two more adults living in the Chartreuse Caboose made me want to slice my wrists with dental floss. I'd chosen that name after I'd painted the exterior of our trailer chartreuse, and then added bright yellow sunflowers for more color. Regina cringed every time she looked at it. I hate to admit this, but that was half the fun of turning our home into somewhat of an eyesore. "Eyesore" was Regina's description, by the way, not mine. I found our home joyful and vibrant, like a ray of sunshine. It definitely stood out in a crowded RV park. "Well, okay. But you would be welcome to stay with us, if buying a motorhome doesn't work out."

"All right. Thanks, Mom," she said.

"The offer stands if you change your mind. Are there any updates on your missing neighbor?"

"Unfortunately, no. Do you remember meeting Reilly Reynolds? You met her and her husband, Walker, at our holiday block party last winter."

"Yes, of course I remember them. They were the good-looking pair who wore the matching, and rather gaudy, Christmas sweaters, weren't they?"

"Yeah, but their sweaters weren't nearly as gaudy as the one you wore, Mom."

"That's debatable, dear. I recall Reilly had a flawless complexion and long hair so blond it was nearly white. She was the short, fragile-looking lady who was bubbly and outgoing. Am I right?" After Regina's "Yep!" I continued. "She and her tall, muscular husband were like polar opposites in both appearance and personality. He was a large man who pretty much kept to himself. He wasn't very talkative and made no effort to chat with us, while she treated us like long-lost friends. If I recall correctly, the couple were finding it difficult to keep their hands off one another that night. I was tempted to tell them to get a room."

"Ha! Ha! Yes, that's the couple. They'd just recently gotten married at the time of the block party, although they haven't seemed to be as affectionate to one another in recent months. I guess the honeymoon is over, as they say. Perhaps they realized their nonstop PDA's were making the rest of us uncomfortable." Regina chuckled. "PDA means public display of affection, by the way."

"I know. I read *People Magazine* on occasion, and——"

"When you find them laying around in an RV park laundry room?" Regina chuckled. Her laughter was usually contagious. Not so much today, however.

"My point is that I try hard to stay up-to-date."

"Of course." Regina's sarcastic tone quickly changed to melancholy. "What happened to Reilly is so (bleeping) sad."

"Yes, it is. *Very* upsetting. Do they know what happened to——"

"Look, Mom, I've got to go inside. I'm out by the hotel's pool and I have to pee like a sailor." Regina was so flustered, she'd screwed up the old adage.

I considered, but decided against telling her she actually had to pee like a racehorse. She'd already been cussing like a sailor. I was disappointed that Regina had cut me off in order to end the call before she could expound on the circumstances behind her next-door neighbor's disappearance. But when you've got to go, you've got to go. That old saying gets more true with every year older I get, it seems. I was sure I'd hear more about Reilly

Reynolds when we arrived in Rockport. By then, I assumed, either her death would be confirmed or she'd have been found alive and well and was back in the loving arms of her husband, Walker.

"Okay, dear. Be careful and take care of yourselves."

"We will. In fact, I'm going to take advantage of the free tetanus shots that they're offering today at the emergency care place by the Rockport post office. Don't fret. I didn't sustain any cuts or scrapes but thought I'd score a vaccination while they're free. I'll stop by Gracie's and see if she'd like to take advantage of the opportunity too. Stay put at the Alexandria Inn until you hear from me that they've dropped the curfew. Okay?"

"Okay, sweetheart. We'll wait for your call. We love you two."

"Love you guys more. Bye," Regina said before she and I hung up simultaneously.

I was pleased to hear a little bit of me had rubbed off on my daughter. "Score a vaccination while they're free" was not a remark I'd have ever expected to hear Regina say. I, on the other hand, had a tendency to *score* anything that was free, whether I had any use for it or not. It probably was more of a generational thing than a personality trait. Those of us who lived through some really lean times tended to be more prone to pinching a penny so tight that Lincoln's eyes bulged out of the copper.

We were still in Missouri, but no longer staying in the inn as Regina had indicated. We had moved our trailer into a nearby RV park so we wouldn't be underfoot and taking up a suite that Lexie Starr and Stone Van Patten could be renting out. They had insisted we stay on at the bed and breakfast establishment free of charge for as long as we wanted, as their personal guests. But Rip and I had felt that, like fish, we might begin smelling after a few days. We surely didn't want to overstay our welcome. Nor did we want to feel as though we were taking advantage of our dear friends' generosity.

We had given Stone an inspiration, he'd told us. "We'll be adding three or four full hookup RV sites on the premises in the near future. That'll allow us to be more accommodating to guests. One day people like you who own RVs will have a place to stay whenever they're in the area."

I looked forward to that day. A stay at the B&B visiting with Lexie and Stone was a joyful interlude I always enjoyed tremendously. I didn't look forward to heading down to Rockport, Texas, however. Seeing my beloved hometown in such a state of disarray would be heart-breaking. I prayed it wouldn't be as much in shambles as I was imagining.

Unfortunately, I discovered it was every bit as bad, if not worse than I'd visualized when we arrived in Rockport a few weeks later.

Even more disturbing, I'd soon discover that Regina and Milo's next-door neighbor, Reilly Reynolds, had still not been found. Her status remained "missing and presumed dead". Furthermore, there'd be circumstances behind the woman's mysterious disappearance that had me itching to do a little investigating. And that's rarely ever a good thing…

THREE

Despite all the images we'd seen on television and the Internet, Rip and I were still shocked at how overwhelming the destruction was when we drove through Rockport for the first time since Hurricane Harvey struck. Seeing the tent camps that had popped up around town brought tears to our eyes. People with nowhere else to go were now living in makeshift shelters, tents, and travel trailers supplied by FEMA, the Federal Emergency Management Agency. The early September heat was unrelenting and it had to be unbearable inside the small tents that, in some instances, held families of five or more people.

A philanthropic woman named Samantha McCary had set up such a camp on her property on highway FM3036. She'd allowed folks who'd lost their homes to set up tents, trailers, and various other forms of shelter on her land, and arranged for food and supplies to be brought in. She campaigned for donations of clothes, cash, and other necessities to help out those displaced individuals, and even helped find jobs for those seeking employment. It was the compassion and kind-heartedness of people like

Samantha McCary that was helping Rockport pull through the catastrophe and move forward again.

We made the nearly sixteen-hour drive down from northwestern Missouri, arriving at Regina's and Milo's without incident. We drove over the small, and now severely damaged, bridge onto Key Allegro Island three weeks to the day after Hurricane Harvey had made landfall. At the entrance to the island was a handmade sign stretched out in front of a pile of rubble that read, ROCKPORT STRONG. RIPPED APART, MENDING TOGETHER. We had passed other similar signs, a couple of which were less optimistic in nature. One was unrepeatable.

Upon seeing my daughter for the first time in months, I embraced her a bit harder and longer than usual. I was so relieved she'd been left unscathed by the hurricane, physically at least, even though her and Milo's home appeared a little worse for wear.

It didn't take long to get the Caboose set up and ensconced in Regina and Milo's driveway, directly behind their new thirty-five-foot motorhome. I can't be positive, but I got the impression Reggie tried to block the view of our travel trailer from their neighbors by stuffing our trailer behind their well-equipped motorhome, which was ironically named *Thor Hurricane*.

The 2017 motorhome Regina and Milo purchased had two electric slide-outs, one of them quite large, and slept about twenty-seven people. Twenty-seven might be a bit of an exaggeration, but it sure looked like it could hold that many. It was incredibly roomy compared to our travel trailer. The Thor Hurricane actually could sleep eight people, which was at least four more than I'd ever want "bunking" with us in the close confines of any recreational vehicle. I envied the theater seating and what seemed to be a garage-door sized television in their new RV. The unit even had an electric fireplace, which I felt bordered on grandstanding. I certainly hadn't raised Regina to be a showoff. Of course, that could just be the green-eyed monster coming out of me. In fact, I'm almost sure of it.

I'll admit I was more than a little jealous of the stacking washer and dryer units in the hall closest. Having to gather up all the dirty laundry and go to a laundromat once a week had become tiresome after our second week of life on the road. It had now been over seven years since Rip had retired and we'd become full-time RVers. In that time, we'd become more open-minded about what constituted dirty laundry, and more lenient about articles of clothing that could be worn another day or two without offending those nearest to us. Like anything, the RV life-style had its pros and cons.

"Once you guys get all set up," Regina began, "join us in the motorhome for some grilled cheese sandwiches I'm making for lunch. We've got potato chips and dill pickles, but if you want anything other than beer or water to drink, bring it with you."

Beer was always Rip's first choice, but was no longer a fixture in his diet. I fixed myself a tequila sunrise and his Crown and Coke to take with us. After eyeing some of the hurricane's aftermath, I was in desperate need of some alcohol. I also took along some homemade chocolate-chip cookies. I knew Regina had been born with a powerful sweet tooth, and I'd never known her father to turn down an after-dinner treat, either. Like beer, cookies weren't allowed in his diet, either, but I decided one or two wouldn't kill him. Seeing the destruction the hurricane had left behind must have had the same troubling effect on Rip's emotions as it had mine. I figured a couple of cookies might cheer him up a bit.

We were all hungry so there wasn't much conversation as we ate. Afterward, Regina and I cleaned off the table so the four of us could catch up with what had been going on since we'd last spoken. Milo looked exhausted, and with good reason. He'd been putting in fourteen hours a day helping a number of new customers clear away enough debris to enable them to begin the process of rebuilding. He'd had very little time to devote to his and Regina's home, which fortunately had sustained less damage than some of their neighbors whose homes were in shambles. Like the Moores, the Reynolds's house next door had been spared for the most part. It was by no means habitable, but with only broken glass, roof damage, and some miscellaneous exterior damage, it was still standing. A small travel trailer, perhaps twenty-feet long at best, was parked in their driveway.

"So, has Reilly been located?" I asked between bites of my sandwich.

"No." Regina shook her head slowly. "She's still missing. It's such an odd thing, too. Like many, Walker and Reilly ignored the mandatory evacuation order and stayed behind to ride out the storm. Walker said his wife followed Scrappy, their Maltipoo, outside—"

"Their what?" Rip asked.

"Maltipoo. It's a cross between a Maltese and a toy poodle," Regina explained.

"When did they stop referring to crossbreeds as mutts?"

Regina ignored her father's question and continued her story. "So anyway, when Scrappy got out and ran off during the height of the storm, Reilly raced after him. Apparently, the dog panicked and took off down their pier, according to Walker. Walker then got distracted by flying debris crashing through their living room window, and didn't see whether or not Reilly followed the dog down the pier. He assumes she did. By the time he went back to check on his wife and Scrappy, neither was anywhere to be seen. Like I told you, Scrappy turned up a few blocks away several days later, tired and filthy, but otherwise all right. A lady on Luau Lane found him curled up in her bushes and posted his photo on Facebook, which is how Scrappy found his way home."

"It's nice to hear that social media can be used as a beneficial tool now and then," Rip remarked. I was shocked he even knew what social media entailed. After fifty years of marriage, I still learned something new about my husband every day. I listened in amazement, as Rip continued. "More often, sites like Facebook, Instagram, and Twitter just seem to stir up trouble. They are occasionally employed as weapons, in cases like cyberbullying and shaming, or, worse yet, as a means to perpetrate a crime, such as pedophilia. Unfortunately, the anonymity of social media gives power to people to use it for reprehensible reasons."

"Uh-huh." Regina, who was constantly checking her Instagram and Facebook accounts, and tweeting out her thoughts and opinions, gave her father an odd look before continuing with her story. "So, anyway, Reilly has not been seen since. I feel so bad for Walker. He has been beside himself. One look at him, and you can tell he feels guilty he wasn't more attentive to her when she ran after their dog. He said he should have never let her go outside, or at least should have stood watch until she returned to the house."

"Poor guy," I replied. "Perhaps it'd have been wiser for Walker to go after the dog. Or, at the height of the storm, even let the little pooch fend for itself. Animals are pretty resourceful and resilient."

"I'm sure Walker would have gone after Scrappy," Milo said, "had he not been on crutches at the time. He'd just undergone knee surgery for a torn ligament a week prior to the storm. He's just now getting along all right without the crutches. With a bum leg and his wife missing, he's in no condition to do any manual labor. I offered to help him restore his and Reilly's house to a more livable condition, but he told me his best friend since high school had been hired to do it. I recall the two men playing high school football together. Anyway, he got an incredible deal on the project, and I'm relieved not to have one more job I feel obligated to tackle."

"No doubt," Rip said. "Regardless, it was certainly kind of you to offer your services, son. Not everyone would have been as thoughtful under the circumstances."

"I couldn't *not* offer to help, Rip, *because* of the circumstances," Milo said. "Walker's a really good guy who's not only recovering from knee surgery but also an emotional wreck right now."

"I'm sure. If what he suspects happened to his wife is correct, her body will be washing ashore soon or resurfacing somewhere. It's hard to believe several weeks have passed already without it being discovered."

"Yeah, I thought so, too." Milo nodded his head before standing up. "Sorry, folks. I need to get back to a job I'm working on over on Fulton Beach Road. Why don't you two get settled this afternoon? We'll regroup tomorrow morning to come up with a plan on where to start. I'll be able to help out here and there, but I won't be able to dedicate a lot of time to our place. I've got too many other jobs lined up, and more being added every day, it seems."

"We'll do all we can," Rip said. "I'm a little limited myself at the moment."

"Of course," Milo replied. "I don't want, or expect, either of you to do anything that's labor-intensive, Rip. More than anything, I need an extra hand picking up supplies. I don't have time to drive back and forth to Corpus every day, and that's the closest place I can obtain most of the materials I need right now. They'll load the materials into my truck for you. You won't have to handle it all yourself. Don't even try to do any heavy lifting."

"I won't. I'd be happy to run to Corpus anytime you need me to."

"'Run?' I'd rather you take my truck, Rip. Running might not be such a good idea with that new hip of yours." Milo chuckled at his own joke, then grew serious. "Thank you. That'll help me out more than you can imagine."

"It'd be my pleasure."

"You're going to have to learn to say 'no', honey," Regina said lovingly to her husband. "You are going to work yourself to a frazzle. You can't help every single person who asks."

Milo nodded with a warm smile. "I've noticed you haven't turned your back on any opportunity to help others."

"Yeah, I guess you're right." Regina smiled at her husband.

"It's always nice to lend a hand to others needing assistance," I said softly. "But neither of you will be of any help to anyone if you get ill."

"We know," Regina said. "It's just hard to turn down friends and acquaintances when we know what dire straits they're in."

Milo reached over to clasp Regina's hand. "But I'm going to have to draw the line somewhere. Like Regina said, I can't help every one of them. The extra money will come in handy, though, as I'm sure we won't be able to recuperate all we've lost from the insurance company. I wish Regina would slow down a bit though."

"I'll try, honey." Regina squeezed Milo's hand before standing up to clear the table.

Milo kissed Regina and grabbed a couple of cookies to take with him as he prepared to depart. Rip and Regina each helped themselves to several as well. I shook my head at Rip as he reached for a fourth.

As Regina was helping me wash the dishes, she said, "Take those cookies back to your trailer, Mom. They are delicious and I can't resist them. I'll never lose the ten pounds I've gained over the summer with temptations like those sitting around. You make the best cookies of anyone I know."

"Thanks, sweetheart, but we don't need the extra calories either." Regina looked thinner to me than she had when we'd last seen her. I'd chalked her weight loss up to stress following the hurricane and severely decreased dining options. However, she looked healthy and I didn't want to debate the subject. "Hey! Do you think Walker would eat them? He's probably not eating right with his wife missing."

"Great idea," Regina agreed. "I'm not sure 'eating right' includes gorging on cookies, but I'm sure they'd be very welcome. The poor guy looks as if he's lost twenty pounds since the storm. I doubt he's had any home cooking since Reilly disappeared. In fact, why don't you take over this extra sandwich and some chips, as well. There's no sense letting them go to waste if someone can benefit from them. In fact, let me have four of those cookies. I'll grill a couple more sandwiches and take them, the cookies, and a bag of Fritos from the pantry to an elderly couple up the street. I've been checking in on them daily and dropping off hot meals whenever I can."

"How thoughtful of you. I knew I raised you right." I kissed her cheek and asked, "How old are these elderly folks you're looking out for?"

"Probably mid-seventies."

"I see. Thanks for lunch, dear." I suddenly felt ancient, as if I had one foot in the urn and the other on an out-of-control skateboard.

I put the twelve leftover cookies back in the zip-lock bag I'd brought them over in and the sandwich and chips in two other quart-sized storage bags. I then thanked Regina for lunch again and told Rip I'd be in our trailer after I delivered the "comfort" food to the neighbor. I knew Regina didn't need us underfoot any more than necessary and I had to get the trailer back in order after being on the road for a couple of days. Everything needs to be stored away before bouncing down I-35, which seems to always be under construction. We wouldn't want Dolly, who rides in the trailer while we're traveling, to be beaned by a flying salt shaker after we'd dodged a strip of rubber that'd just unraveled from one of a semi's retreaded rear tires.

As I walked across the lawn with cookies in hand, I had no idea what kind of ripple effect my friendly gesture was going to initiate. Had I known, I might have hurried back to the trailer and washed down all the cookies with what was left of my afternoon highball of tequila, orange juice, and grenadine. The drink had the appearance of a sunrise. I called it my "Rockport Special" because beautiful sunrises and sunsets were two of the things the town was known for.

Naturally, I didn't snarf down the dozen cookies, but in hindsight, perhaps I should have. Even the bellyache that was apt to result, had I chosen that noshing option, might have been better than the undertaking I was about to immerse myself in.

FOUR

There was a red truck in the driveway next to a tan Ford Explorer with a "For Sale" sign in the windshield, so I figured Mr. Reynolds was home. I assumed the tan car belonged to his wife, Reilly, and he was trying to sell her vehicle since she was presumed to be dead. I was wrong on both counts.

I also expected to see a grieving husband in the entryway after I knocked on the door of the moderately damaged home. When I looked in through the busted-out window of the front door, my first thought was that I was not only wrong, I was dead wrong. Literally.

A very large man wearing blue jeans splattered with fresh concrete, a white wife-beater tank top, and concrete-caked work boots lay prostrate on the living room floor. The bald fellow was a very light-skinned Hispanic, most likely of mixed race. His arms were splayed out at his sides, his mouth gaped open, and a hammer lay ominously beside him. It appeared he'd been in the process of securing the threshold of the doorway into the kitchen when he'd been assaulted. Pardon my pun, but I quickly came to the conclusion he was deader than a doornail when I couldn't detect any rising or falling of his slightly protruding abdomen.

Was that hammer the weapon used to murder the man? I wondered. *Should I call the police? His skin still looks ruddy, so it might not be too late to save him. I need to at least make an attempt, don't I? But is it safe to go in and check for a pulse? His attacker may still be inside the house.*

These were just a few of the thoughts and questions whirling through my mind as I studied the lifeless body of whom I assumed was Walker Reynolds. I'd only had a few glimpses of Walker at a party months ago. I didn't recall the man being so bulky, but I'd been downing my Rockport Specials that evening like there was no tomorrow. The bald man on the floor resembled a bodybuilder. In fact, at first glance, he'd reminded me of Jessie Ventura. I couldn't see any obvious wounds, but my viewpoint was limited. To improve it, I slipped inside as silently as I could and tiptoed through the kitchen just far enough to listen for signs of intruders within the residence, but close enough to make a mad dash for the door should I hear anyone.

A frightening noise stopped me in my tracks. The hammering I heard was loud and ominous. I wasn't sure if it was an ax murderer in the living room or my own rapidly pounding heart. Fortunately, it was the latter, and I took a deep calming breath when I realized the thumping wasn't coming from a serial killer about to add me to his or her belt full of notches.

I stood quietly for several long moments, listening for other sounds that might indicate someone else's presence in the house. When I heard nothing but silence, I proceeded on toward the body. I crouched down and reached over to check for a pulse. When the lifeless body leaped to its feet like a star athlete who'd just been plowed over by a defensive tackle, I keeled over in a dead faint. Lucky for me I was already just inches from the Saltillo-tiled floor.

"Lady?" I heard a voice from afar. "Lady? Are you all right?"

I could make out the words, but I couldn't open my eyes or respond to the man's questions. Finally, when I realized I was lying face down on the floor, I said, "Yes. Please, help me up."

"Lady? Wake up. Are you all right?" When the man repeated himself, I realized I had not spoken the words out loud. Trying to open my eyes was akin to trying to speak after super-gluing my lips together, which had actually happened to me years ago, prompting a visit to the local urgent care clinic. My lips had refused to part then just as my eyelids were doing now.

When it became clear the man was utilizing his cell phone to dial 9-1-1, I found the strength to open my eyes and speak. "I'm okay. Please hang up. I'm sure the first responders have a lot more urgent situations to attend to right now."

"Oh, thank God," the man said with obvious relief. "I haven't been able to get a signal since before the hurricane. I was just hoping against hope I could get through to someone. Jeez, Louise. I thought you were dead, lady."

"Well, I'm not. I'm very much alive."

"I can see that. Why'd you come in here?" The man's hands were placed on his hips as if he was convinced I'd been up to no good when I trespassed into what I had believed to be his home. Having seen him up close, I realized he wasn't the owner of the house, after all.

"I came in to help you!" I tried to restrain the defensiveness in my voice.

"Why?"

"Because I thought *you* were dead!"

"Well, I'm not. I'm very much alive, too."

"Yeah, no shit!" Now my defensive tone had been replaced by one of annoyance. "When I looked through the glass pane of the front door, I saw you lying lifeless on the floor. Or at least you looked lifeless. After what's happened with Walker's wife, and all,

I…" I stopped speaking abruptly. I didn't know how best to approach the subject of the missing woman.

"Thanks for your concern, but Reilly was killed in the storm. I'm pretty sure there's not a serial killer on the loose." The man flashed a rueful smile.

"Don't be cheeky, young man. I never even gave that a thought". *Liar, liar, pants on fire.*

"Pardon my rudeness, ma'am. Give me your hand and I'll help you up." After he lifted me to my feet as though I were a child, he introduced himself. "I'm Jessie of Jessie Garza Construction."

"Jessie? No kidding?" I asked. "That's quite the coincidence. I'd actually thought you were Jessie Ventura at first glance. You look so much like him. He was that pro-wrestler turned governor of—"

"I know who he is," he said with a grin. "I've literally been told I look like him a million times."

"What are you doing here?" I asked, rather than explain to him what the word "literally" meant. I could've pretty much assured him he hadn't actually been told he looked like the former Minnesota governor a *million* times. For some irrational reason, the misuse of the word was a pet peeve of mine.

"I'm restoring Walker's home, with the help of a few subcontractors. But you're right. Poor Walker's entire world was ripped apart by Hurricane Harvey. I can understand why the sight of me lying on the floor frightened you. I've been working on the water lines all morning and was just catching some Z's on my lunch break."

"I'm sorry I startled you."

"That's all right. I was just caught off guard. I'm sorry I scared you so much you passed out." Jessie gazed longingly at the food in the plastic bags as I picked them up off the floor, having dropped them when I blacked out. He actually licked his lips before speaking again. "Was Walker supposed to meet you here or something?"

"No. We only met once and it was so brief, he probably doesn't even remember me."

"He told me he might pop in on his accountant today. He's been trying to get all the documents together he'll need for his insurance claim. I've been alone all day, but I'd be happy to tell him you stopped by."

"No, that's quite all right. I just came over to bring him some food. My daughter and son-in-law live next door. My name's Rapella Ripple," I said. "You can call me Rapella. Well, um, since Walker isn't here, and I just happen to have a sandwich, some chips, and a few cookies that need a home, they're yours for the taking."

I smiled as I held the food out in front of me. Jessie smiled even more broadly as he realized I was offering it to him. He took the Ziploc bags from my outstretched hands and thanked me. "This all looks delicious. I've been burning both ends of the candle and forgot to bring a lunch with me. As they say, my stomach thinks my throat's been cut. You are an absolute angel, Ms. Ripple."

"Rapella."

"Rapella is an unusual name."

"Thanks," I replied, although his comment hadn't really sounded like a compliment. "But just because it's unusual doesn't mean you can't use it."

"Yes, ma'am. I get it."

"No, I don't think you do. Please call me Rapella, not ma'am or Ms. Ripple."

"This food is very much appreciated, Rapella," he said with a wink. "I've been working hard this morning and I'm starving. I can't tell you how glad I am you thought I was dead and came into the house to save me."

I blushed the color of the cocktail I'd fortunately set up on the counter before passing out. I'd be wearing it now if I hadn't needed to free up my hand to check Jessie's neck for a pulse. Jessie laughed at my embarrassment. I clearly had overreacted out of a heightened sense of distress due to the overwhelming destruction surrounding us. The fact that the lady of the house had been lost in the storm didn't help matters any. A sense of foreboding filled the house like a natural gas leak. You couldn't see it, but you knew it was present.

Retrieving my drink from the counter, I turned to Jessie. "This truly is my first adult beverage of the day."

"Never had a doubt."

"And, speaking of which, do you need something to drink to wash down your lunch?"

"No, but thank you. I have a cooler full of water in the back of my truck."

"Is that Reilly's Explorer in the driveway next to your truck?" I asked.

"No. Walker sold her Lexus a week or so after the storm. The Explorer belongs to a friend of Walker's who lives way out in the country. He thought he'd have a better shot of selling it here than at his place, particularly after Walker was able to sell Reilly's car so quickly. A lot of people's vehicles were destroyed in the hurricane and they'll be looking for cheap transportation."

"I see. It sounds as if Walker is certain Reilly's gone."

It took Jessie a moment or two to respond. "Reilly's car had a big dent in the roof after a large palm tree fell on top of it during Harvey. I think Walker plans to buy her a brand new Lexus if and when she returns. But the chances of that are slim to none. I'm convinced she's gone forever."

"Don't you think her body will eventually be found?" I asked.

"I thought it might at one time, but I'm almost certain at this point it'll never be seen again." He looked pleased at the thought, which unnerved me.

"You're probably right. A lot of time *has* passed since her disappearance. Do you live here in Rockport, Jessie?" At his solemn nod, I added, "Was your home damaged, as well?"

"Yep. But, fortunately, it's still habitable, and nothing has to be fixed until I get the insurance check. The TWIA adjuster is coming this afternoon, in fact."

"That's good. I'm happy you were one of the lucky ones." We chatted a few more minutes and then I excused myself. I could sense he was anxious for me to leave so he could dig into the food I'd given him, obviously too polite to eat while we were conversing. Suddenly, he got more talkative.

"Thanks. I was a lot luckier than Walker, for sure."

"Sounds like he's lost hope that Reilly will show back up." The thought saddened me. I don't know that I could ever give up hope until I saw proof of my loved one's demise.

"I don't think he's totally given up hope," Jessie said. His next few remarks struck me as cold-hearted, but I didn't know Reilly as well as he likely did. "But he's had to be realistic about the situation and put it behind him. I know I would. Reilly was kind of a wrecking ball when it came to families. She'd lure a guy in, break his heart, and move on. This time, Walker's the one moving on."

"Moving on? His wife probably died a horrible death." I didn't appreciate Jessie's insensitivity. "Moving on" to me said he was already open to beginning a new relationship with another woman. "Is he already dating again?"

"I didn't say that. Although an attractive blonde about his age stopped by looking for him this morning. She was wearing shorts so short and tight you could see a freckle on her hip through the fabric. Said to give him that message over on the table when I see him." The man pointed to a yellow post-it note on the kitchen table. Considering the pile of papers, catalogs, envelopes, and fliers on the table, the blonde would be lucky her note didn't get lost in the shuffle before Walker had a chance to read it. Looked like the mail hadn't been sorted through since the hurricane. "If he is seeing the gal, I can't say I blame him. She was quite the looker. Built like a brick shit——"

The contractor stopped suddenly and began to apologize. I waved off his apology. "I get the picture. Just seems a little soon to jump back into the dating game. Reilly and Walker were still newlyweds. Seems he could at least wait for some kind of confirmation of his wife's death, if you ask me."

His expression clearly read "I didn't ask you". His actual words weren't much better. "I suppose. But hey! His wife, his life. Unfortunately, it's pretty much a foregone conclusion, even to Walker, that Reilly was washed away during the storm. He can't be expected to sit around and grieve for the rest of his life, you know. After all, it's been three weeks since she disappeared in the middle of the hurricane. She'd have surely shown up by now if she was still alive."

"Three whole weeks of grieving, huh?" *Poor bastard. How could anyone expect the widower to waste away in his house, no doubt crying his eyes out in angst, for an entire month?* I wanted to ask. *Especially when there's a blond bombshell, built like a brick shithouse, who's come sniffing around.*

I'd only asked Jessie about his comment because I thought maybe he'd heard something definitive regarding Reilly's fate. Now I wished I hadn't.

"Be a whole month 'fore long." Jessie evidently thought his remark was a justification for Walker to hook up with another woman already. I thought it was cold as a penguin's tail feathers.

"Are you married, Jessie?"

"No. Used to be, but for some reason it didn't last long," Jessie said. "Must of us thought she could do better."

"I see." I said, as I thought, *I can safely say she could've done better—much better—and I don't even know the woman.*

"Yeah. She was a piece of work. Expected me to come home after I'd put in a long day at work. Threw a hissy fit when I'd stop by the tavern and throw back a few beers with the guys instead."

"Imagine that. Have a good afternoon, Jessie." I shook my head and turned to leave once again. As I walked out the front door, which hung lopsided from one hinge that'd broken loose from the frame by the hurricane-force winds, I added, "Don't work too hard. This heat and humidity can be lethal, you know. Make certain to stay well hydrated. I don't want to find you *really* dead on the floor in here next time I stop by."

"The next time?" He asked. He then must have realized his question sounded rude, so he added, "Yes, Rapella. I'll be careful and drink plenty of water."

"See that you do." I'm sure I sounded bossy, but my concern was for the man's well-being, even though we'd only just met and he'd come across as a real jerk. Despite that innate trait of mine to worry incessantly about people—even jerks—and their sometimes questionable life choices, I walked away from Jessie Garza with that sense of foreboding I'd felt earlier coming back to me full force.

"Have a good day," Jessie said. "Thanks again for the vittles."

"You're welcome."

There was a lot going through my mind as I walked back to the trailer. *Could speaking of Reilly as if her death had been confirmed be more than just an assumption on Jessie's part? Could it be the man knows more about her disappearance than he admitted? And why did he infer Walker was already open to the idea of a new romantic relationship, with his missing spouse not out of the picture for even a full month yet? Why had the woman's body not resurfaced somewhere if she'd drowned? Could Reilly have left of her own accord and be hiding out, perhaps afraid of Walker's wrath should she be located? Was the grief Regina said he'd been displaying just a show to ward off suspicion? Is the fact Rip and I have been involved in a number of murder cases in the last couple of years clouding my judgment and making me see signs of guilt where none exists? Am I going berserk?*

These questions raced through my mind as I retraced my steps to the Chartreuse Caboose. After a moment's consideration, I decided to investigate the situation a bit further before I brought my apprehensive intuitions to Rip's, or anyone else's, attention. I had a good idea they'd be met with scornful disdain at this point. Even I knew I had nothing to base my suspicions on. It was merely a gut feeling, and my gut can occasionally be terribly unreliable—in more ways than one.

FIVE

I was met at the door of the trailer with the sound of a lumberjack sawing away on a mighty sequoia tree. Asleep in his recliner with Dolly, Rip was snoring loudly. Our seventeen-pound grey and white tabby was sprawled out across his chest and licking the orange residue of Cheetos off the fingers of his right hand. The venetian blinds on the window behind Rip's chair were chattering as if another hurricane had struck and was rocking the trailer.

I knew Rip was worn out from the long journey to Rockport and wasn't quite up to one-hundred-percent yet. When a person hits the seven-decade mark, healing from open-heart and hip-replacement surgeries takes longer to recover from than if they were younger. As luck would have it, folks rarely need those surgeries until they're much older. I tried to encourage Rip to walk the fine line between getting enough exercise to maintain good health without overexerting and pushing himself to the brink of exhaustion. For me, it was an exercise in patience sometimes to get him to exercise any at all. He was entirely too attached to his recliner, both emotionally and physically.

When I noticed a small Ziploc bag on the end table with a couple of leftover cookies remaining in it, an idea hit me. Curiosity was killing me. I was dying to know what the buxom blonde had written on the post-it note she'd left with Jessie to give Walker. I realized it was in no way any of my business and that finding a way to read it was a total invasion of privacy of both the woman who penned it and the man it was written to. However, this did nothing to quell the overwhelming desire inside of me to discover what it said. It irked me that Walker could even consider a romantic relationship with a new woman at this juncture. His wife had not even been officially declared dead yet.

An hour later, with Rip and Dolly still sound asleep, I quietly exited the trailer and softly closed the door behind me. I returned to the house next door, which was now under a noisy renovation. The Ford Explorer was missing, but two more trucks were parked in the driveway. One was an orange Chevy Avalanche with a magnetic sign on the door that read TNT Demolition. Painted across the back window of the cab was the slogan, "When we knock 'em down, they stay down."

The other vehicle was a beat-up white Ford F-350 with a caved-in tailgate. It looked like a number of tailgates we'd seen on trucks in RV parks over the years that had experienced the trauma of having the gooseneck of a fifth-wheel trailer coming unhitched and crashing down on them. The resulting dent was akin to a badge of shame for absentminded fifth-wheel owners who'd forgotten to put the jacks down on their trailer before pulling away from it.

I knew no one would hear me rapping on the skewed front door over the buzzing of saws, whirring of drills, and pounding of nails, so I let myself in as if I owned the place. For a moment I thought I was going to be able to snap a quick photo of the post-it note with my phone and depart undetected. But just as I glanced down at the note, Jessie walked into the kitchen. He looked at me oddly. I'm quite sure I blushed. The sensation was like being caught with my hand in the proverbial cookie jar.

"Um, hello again, Rapella," he said with a dubious expression. "Did you need something else?"

"Uh, oh, hello Jessie. Actually, I just came back to collect my Ziploc bags."

When the man just stared at me in disbelief, I began to ramble. "You see, when we retired a few years ago to become full-time RVers, we didn't have a huge retirement fund to fall back on. My husband retired as the Aransas County Sheriff, but I tended to have only short-lived careers in a variety of different fields, none of which offered 401K's or profit-sharing plans. I did everything from flipping flapjacks at Alice Fay's to volunteering my time at Castaways, the resale thrift shop in town, so I have little to contribute to our income now. But I've learned to become ultra-conservative to help make ends meet. And even though you might not think of Ziploc bags as being a major expense, when you use several of them every day at a cost of up to a quarter apiece, it begins to add up. Now, if you put leftover meatloaf in one, it makes perfect sense to dispose of the greasy bag afterward, but with a toasted cheese sandwich, for instance, you can easily shake the remaining crumbs out of the bag and it's practically good as new. Therefore, if you can reuse a majority of them, say seventy-five percent, you can save oodles of—"

"Listen, lady. I have some plumbing work I need to get done today." Clearly, Jessie didn't feel inclined to listen to me babble on about plastic storage bags all afternoon, which was understandable. Frankly, by that point, I was even boring myself. "If you want the bags, I think I tossed them in the big dumpster out front. I appreciate the food you gave me, but didn't realize I needed to preserve the plastic bags you'd brought it over in."

As he spoke, I realized how ridiculous I'd sounded. Not that I don't actually recycle Ziploc bags all the time; the activity just sounded more absurd coming from the burly construction fellow standing in front of me. Saying I was ultra-conservative with money had actually been an understatement. I was so tight you could bounce a quarter off me if you wanted to. Even so, admitting I reused plastic storage bags out loud was a bit humiliating.

"Oh, well, that's okay. No problem. We'll just let those three bags fall into the twenty-five percent that aren't recyclable." I couldn't make eye contact with him as I spoke. I was too embarrassed and just wanted to slink out of the house like a scolded puppy.

Just before I began to back toward the door, I couldn't resist casting another glance at the post-it note on the table. "**JJ's at 6 tonight. Bring the...**" it read. I couldn't make out the last word at all, but the next to last word looked like either "compact" or "compass", or maybe even "compost". I immediately dismissed the latter possibility. Why would Walker take decayed organic matter to JJ's with him? "Contract" would make more sense, even though I couldn't quite make an "r" out of any of the squiggly lines in the few seconds I had to study the memo. The lady's scribbling was so messy, the only two letters I was certain of were the first two.

JJ's Cafe was a popular local restaurant with great food and reasonable prices, and it had always been one of our go-to places when we wanted a quick bite to eat that wouldn't bust the budget. But Walker could easily take a contract concerning some form of agreement to the café or information about a contact his dinner date might need to get in touch with about some concern or another.

Maybe the meeting at the cafe wasn't a romantic date, but rather, strictly business-related. Perhaps Walker was signing a contract with the woman to have reconstruction work done on his and Reilly's house. It stood to reason he'd be making agreements with all kinds of service providers during the course of getting his house back into a habitable condition. The woman could represent a painting company, she could be a window covering designer, or even own a tile and granite store. For that matter, she could be in the process of buying the tan Explorer currently for sale in the driveway and wanted a proper bill of sale for the purchase. Maybe this woman was a loan officer at a local bank. That was hard to fathom, however. What loan officer would make a house call, let alone a house call while dressed in hot pants?

To think the get-together was anything but above-board at this stage was ludicrous. I had to stop myself from imagining there was something sleazy at play when this meeting was more than likely nothing but business. I had a tendency to envision scenarios that were above and beyond reason when I gave my imagination free rein.

Dang it! If I'd only had one more second to peruse the note, I might have made out the last word in the message. That one word would surely have explained a lot and kept my imagination from running as wild as a couple of unchaperoned twelve-year-old boys at a carnival. Thinking of another excuse to return to the house might look suspicious. Even as this thought crossed my mind, Jessie picked up the post-it note he'd observed me looking at and stuffed it in the front pocket of his blue jeans.

Still backing toward the door, I suddenly came up against what felt like a brick wall. When the brick wall inhaled sharply, because I'd stomped on its toes, I gasped and spun to face a deeply tanned man with dark brown hair and even darker eyes. His chest spanned the entire doorway between the kitchen and the living room, but his hips were slim and sexy. Like most of the other blue-collar workers in town, the man was Hispanic. When he smiled in reaction to my alarm, his pearly white teeth sparkled as if he were filming a Pepsodent commercial.

"*Mis disculpas*." I apologized in his native language to let him know I hadn't heard him walk up behind me. I'd picked up some of the most common Spanish phrases from living in such close proximity to the Mexican border most of my life, although not nearly as much as Rip had as a law enforcement officer for so many years. He was multi-lingual, speaking fluent Spanish and Italian, along with English. His mother had been born in Milan, Italy, and had taught him her native language. Rip inherited his olive-colored complexion and shorter than average stature from her. As for the Spanish, he'd picked it up over time. There was naturally a heavy Hispanic presence in the area. Although the majority of them were fluent, or near fluent, in English, not all were and I didn't want to appear rude by not offering an apology.

"*De nada, señora. Sólo camino en el fondo*——" He began in a captivating voice that was almost melodic in nature. I thought the Spanish language was music to the ears to begin with, but coming from this handsome hunk made it even more beautiful. To me, he looked more like a Chippendale dancer than a construction worker.

"*Quiero semillas de aves para el desayuno.*"

"*Perdóneme?*" There was an amused expression on the large man's face as he spoke. "*No entien-*"

"*Perdón, yo solo hablo un poco español.*"

After I cut in to inform the gorgeous fellow I only spoke a little Spanish, he nodded and responded in flawless English. "I kind of assumed that when you told me you wanted birdseed for breakfast."

I laughed along with him and Jessie before I apologized again for stepping on his foot.

"No worries, ma'am. Besides, I only walk on the bottoms of my feet, so you might as well walk on the tops of them." He smiled to let me know he was kidding, and I nodded with a grin that no doubt resembled a love-struck teenager who was being serenaded by Justin Bieber.

Jessie chuckled, and said, "Ms. Ripple, meet Anthony 'Bigfoot' Torres. And, Tony, this nice lady is Rapella Ripple. Her daughter and son-in-law, Milo Moore, live next door. I'm sure you're familiar with Milo."

"*Sí.* I've known Milo for years. Nice to meet you, Ms. Ripple. I go by Tony. My middle name is actually Noël, not 'Bigfoot', hence the TNT in TNT Demolition, the name of my company." Tony moved a pair of vise-grip pliers he was holding in his right hand to his left and shook my hand. His hand was warm, but rough as coarse sandpaper from hard work, no doubt. "I'm in charge of the demo detail here. I guess you could say I'm better at tearing stuff up than building it back."

"Call me Rapella, please," I said warmly. "It's nice to meet you as well, Tony. I'm pretty good at tearing stuff up myself. The difference is that I can do a remarkable job of it without even trying. Just ask my husband, Rip."

"Rip?" The expression on Tony's face was unreadable, but I instantly got the impression he and Rip had crossed paths before. "As in Rip Ripple, former Aransas County Sheriff?"

"That's the one. Have you two met?"

"You could say that," was his ambiguous response.

When Tony didn't appear inclined to elaborate, I stalled for an uncomfortable length of time before I said, "Well, I guess I best get out of you guys' way now. I know you're busy and don't need me standing around keeping you from doing your work."

Tony shrugged. "I'm in no rush. I'm getting paid by the hour. You must have made the cookies Jessie gave me. Thanks, ma'am. They were delicious."

Before I could respond, Jessie added, "I couldn't eat all twelve cookies by myself, so I shared half of them with Tony. Bruno, my drywall subcontractor, arrived at the same time as Tony, but, unfortunately, he's on an insulin pump and avoids sugar as much as possible."

"Oh, that's too bad. Well, I'm glad you gentlemen enjoyed the cookies. I'd be happy to drop some more off tomorrow if you'd like. I've got a few in the trailer that need to find a home before my willpower goes to hell in a handbasket. Better a moment on your lips than a lifetime on my hips, as they say."

Tony smiled in response to my remark, while Jessie glanced at my hips and nodded, as if in agreement, which was a bit disturbing.

"Any cookies you drop off over here will disappear quickly," Tony said. Jessie's expression seemed a little hesitant, but I tried not to read too much into it. Tony was more enthusiastic at the thought of another cookie delivery. He confirmed his delight when he said, "I can demolish snickerdoodles even faster than I demolish houses."

"What a coincidence. That's exactly the kind of cookies I have." Truthfully, I'd brought the men every cookie we'd had left over from lunch, and they'd been of the chocolate chip variety. But if the handsome demolition boss preferred snickerdoodles, I could always whip up a batch of those in the morning in no time at all. I was certain Rip wouldn't balk if a few of the cinnamon-flavored cookies found their way to our kitchen counter, as well. I'd make a double batch and bring the bulk of them over for the construction crew at the Reynolds's house. It'd give me another opportunity to nose around and ask intrusive questions—that were none of my concern—about the missing lady of the house. I can't explain why I had a gut feeling there was more to the woman's disappearance than having been blown off the pier while chasing after her dog during the extremely powerful storm. And you know what I said about my gut being totally untrustworthy. However, the fact her husband was more concerned about getting their house repaired than moving heaven and earth to find her was playing into my hunch.

Although I had no personal connection to Reilly Reynolds, other than the fact she lived next door to my daughter, I couldn't help but feel concerned about the situation. If she were merely missing, she needed to be found and reunited with her family. If a reunion with Walker wasn't in the cards, and indeed the reason behind her disappearance, she needed to be placed in a safe place where she could go on with her life in as normal a fashion as possible. If she was a tragic statistic of Hurricane Harvey, her body needed to be located so that her husband, friends, and family could have closure. And, if by some odd chance, she was the victim of a horrible crime, justice needed to be served on her behalf.

I would be busy helping Regina and Milo bring their home back to order, but I'd still have some spare time to donate to the cause—that of discovering where Reilly Reynolds was and what had happened to her to put her there.

SIX

"As much as I'd love to take you out for supper tonight, it's not going to happen." Rip looked at me as if I'd just requested he fly me to the moon and serve me escargot, pheasant under glass, and a glass of fine wine to wash it down while we were there.

"Why ever not?" I asked. I felt both hurt and defensive at his rejection. I served him a nice warm meal every night while rarely asking him to take me out for supper. "I'm a bit worn out from the trip, too, you know."

"I've no doubt you are, my dear. But short of driving to another town, and stand in an incredibly long line, no doubt, we're going to have to make do with filets and grilled veggies, which I'd be more than happy to prepare. We have a bell pepper and a couple of squash in the fridge, and I pulled the filets out of the freezer earlier."

"Oh, crap! That's right." I'd forgotten hardly any businesses in the area had reopened yet, and some probably never would. Eating anywhere but JJ's Cafe would serve no purpose. "I've actually been looking forward to those filets. I hope JJ's wasn't damaged too badly."

"According to Milo, the café was demolished. It will have to be torn down to its foundation."

"That saddens me. I feel bad for the family. Sorry I asked you to take me out tonight. I just haven't quite wrapped my head around the total devastation the storm left behind." I'd also forgotten that we'd stopped in Oklahoma to stock up on as many groceries as we could cram into the storage compartments of the travel trailer. As Regina had recommended, we'd even filled the back of the truck up with cases of water, beer, booze, toilet paper, and other necessities we didn't know if or when we'd be able to procure easily once we reached Rockport. A locking tonneau cover over the truck bed had protected the supplies on our trip down.

"It hasn't totally sunk in with me either, honey," Rip said as he grasped my hand in his. "Everywhere I look, I see a grim reminder of just how destructive Harvey was to our beloved hometown. Hopefully, we can help others begin to heal and recover, besides just Reggie and Milo. I'm up for sticking around for as long as we can be of use to anyone in need of a helping hand. How 'bout you?"

"Absolutely!" And I truly was. We had many friends and acquaintances in the area. All of them had been affected to some degree, and no doubt some of them had been irreparably impacted by the hurricane. Regina had been reaching out to anyone she could think of who might need assistance, and I was willing and able to do the same. "Tonight we rest. Tomorrow we roll our sleeves up and get to work. I'll slice up the pepper, zucchini, and yellow squash, and season the steaks so they'll be ready when you light the grill later. That actually sounds even better than eating out."

"I agree." Rip flashed a rueful smile. "We'll have to make the best of a bad situation for a while. But as soon as a local restaurant reopens, I will be more than happy to take you out on the town."

I flashed him a smile, trying not to look disappointed. I'd have to give the message on the post-it note more thought. If we were unable to go to JJ's for supper, so were Walker and his mysterious date.

While I quartered the zucchini and yellow squash, I mused about what the "JJ's" on the post-it note might stand for if not the local restaurant. Most likely, I reasoned, it was someone's initials, which probably narrowed it down substantially in a small town like Rockport. My original plan had been to show up at JJ's Cafe at around 6:10, scan the room for a well-built blonde and Walker, whose appearance I could only vaguely recall, and ask to be seated at the closest available table to them. I'd hope to be near enough to the pair to eavesdrop on their conversation. If no table close to them was available, their mannerisms alone would have spoken volumes.

I'd have been acting as nonchalant as possible, of course, even though I was at the cafe on a mission. Rip would have been none the wiser, and I'd keep it that way until I decided there was something more substantial, and hopefully more incriminating, to base my suspicions on. Only then would I consult with Rip about where to proceed with my suspicions. After all, a cheating spouse was always a suspect when their spouse went "missing". The motive was built right in when there's a romantic tryst such as that in the mix.

As the former sheriff of the county, Rip would know better than about anyone what to do with whatever evidence I'd managed to collect. But until I had some kind of proof that the neighbor's disappearance was due to foul play, I didn't want to speak up and look foolish. We'd been involved in a number of murder cases in the last eighteen months or so, and I knew Rip would think I was letting my imagination get the best of me. Frankly, it had crossed my mind, too, that I might actually be doing exactly that. Was I getting addicted to the excitement of solving murder mysteries? Maybe so. It did break up the monotony of our normal routine, which was a habitual pattern that rarely veered off course. I decided not to dwell on that thought and concentrate on a plan to delve deeper into Reilly's disappearance.

Now that plan A was out of the question, I'd have to think of a clever way to worm more information out of the construction crew next door. An idea was already percolating in my head. I nearly cut the tip of my index finger off due to being distracted by my scheming.

After I'd washed the blood off the zucchini spears, and cleaned and bandaged my finger, I tossed the vegetables in a plastic bag to be grilled later on for supper. I then prepared our evening cocktails, which had become a tradition following retirement. While we sipped on our drinks, we'd sit in our sling chairs under the awning, chatting about our day and reminiscing about times past. We'd discuss our dreams, thoughts, and opinions, and recall incidents that had made us laugh until we cried. I'd learned more about my husband during those seven years of evening exchanges than in all the years that proceeded them combined, which had only strengthened my devotion to him.

If the neighborhood hadn't resembled a war zone, and an atrocious mid-September heatwave wasn't warming my insides up like a microwave oven, it might have been an idyllic state of affairs. Instead, it was hot, muggy, sad, and strangely smelly. After about three minutes, I stood up and apologized to Rip. "Sorry, honey. It's too hot, and this is just too depressing for me right now. I think I'll go back inside."

"Can't say I blame you."

"Oh, yeah. Before I forget, do you remember a man named Anthony Torres?" I asked.

"Tony?"

"Yes. That's what he goes by. He owns TNT Demolition."

"I know. I saw his truck next door earlier. I don't know him well, but I do remember having to arrest him on a drunk and disorderly charge, and later on an assault and battery charge. Apparently, Tony doesn't hold his liquor well. Both incidents occurred at local taverns. That was years ago, however. Hopefully, he's grown up since then. You know what? I'm getting awfully hot now, too." Rip stood up and began to fold up his chair to store in one of the undercarriage compartments. A strong wind could easily pop up and blow the light canvas chairs into the bay.

I folded my own chair and handed it to him. "You are welcome to join me in my pity party inside."

"Not sure how I feel about that invitation," Rip replied, before placing both chairs in the storage compartment and enveloping me in a warm hug. He spoke softly. "Don't fret, honey. Everything's going to work out. It's going to take some time, but eventually Rockport will rebound and be the jewel of the Texas coast once more. Don't let this distressing situation get you down. We need to maintain a positive outlook for the kids' sake."

"I guess you're right. Pity party canceled."

"Good. I wasn't planning to attend it anyway." Rip laughed and added, "You go ahead. I'll be right in."

"Milo won't be home until late," Regina said. She had opened the trailer door and stuck her head inside. "He said not to wait on him for supper. He's helping his demo team gut the Strykers' home. Kathy Stryker's a good friend of mine. She and her husband, Bill, moved down here from Minnesota last year."

"Where do the Strykers live?"

"Holiday Beach. That area was especially hard hit. I spent two days helping her clean up and pack salvageable items, while Milo helped Bill tarp the roof and haul stuff to storage."

"That's too bad Kathy and Bill were hit so hard right after relocating down here but nice of you and Milo to help them out."

"That's what friends are for."

"Speaking of that, my friend, Adelaide, from my old Bunko club, lives out there too. I'll have to ring her up and see if there's anything I can do to lend a hand."

"That'd be nice of you, Mom. Just about everyone in the path of Harvey could use a helping hand right now. I'd be happy to tag along to supply some extra manpower—or womanpower in this case." Regina smiled warmly before switching topics. "What's for dinner? You said you and Daddy had something special you wanted to cook for all of us tonight."

"Yes, we do," I agreed. "We picked up four nice filets in Fredericksburg on the way down. Your dad's going to grill them along with some fresh veggies I sliced up earlier. Milo can just zap his already-cooked steak and vegetables in the microwave when he gets home. I'll throw together a salad to top off our meal."

"Sounds awesome," Regina said. "I'll bring the wine. I have some news about the neighbors I want to share with you."

"Oh?" My ears perked up like a bird dog who'd just heard a covey of quail flush. "Walker and Reilly Reynolds?"

"Yeah. Something's come up about Reilly's disappearance. Apparently, the assumption she was swept away by the storm is now in question."

"No kidding?" I tried to sound as if I was only being conversational, even though I was dying to grill my daughter in an entirely different way than her father was going to grill the filets. "What came up?"

"I'll tell you about it over supper. I need to run to Portland to pick up a few items for the Massons. I don't think they should be out driving right now."

I considered suggesting that rather than "running" to Portland, she should take her car, as Milo had jokingly suggested to Rip, but changed my mind. Instead, I asked, "Are the Massons the ancient couple up the street?"

"Okay, maybe elderly couple was not the best way to describe them earlier. But they definitely seem older than you and daddy do. Age is just a number, you know. You two make seventy look like the new fifty." Regina leaned over and gave me a quick peck on the cheek. "Am I forgiven?"

"Of course you are. I like that you think I act young for my age. Besides, my love for you is unconditional, and always will be. I'd advise you not to push your luck, however."

"Deal! Is there anything I can pick up for you 'kids' while I'm at the store?" Regina laughed at her own quip.

"Do you mind picking me up a few apples? I'll reimburse you when you get home."

"No problem. What kind?"

"Either Gala or Fuji." I cut one of the sweet apples up to share with Rip for breakfast daily, along with whole-wheat toast. I'd used our last one that morning. "And if you don't like low-carb, fat-free, gluten-free balsamic vinaigrette, you might pick up a salad dressing you like."

"Okie-dokie," Regina said. "Apples and ranch dressing it is then. Anything else?"

"Perhaps a two-liter bottle of Coke, as your dad's getting low."

"All right. Not that I haven't seen Daddy drink Crown Royal on the rocks."

"True. But without the cola to dilute his daily highball, he'll be short on Crown Royal in a couple of days. In fact, please pick up a fifth of Crown while you're out, too. If you don't mind, we could also use a bag of fresh kale. I'm almost out of that too."

"Daddy eats kale?" Regina's eyes opened wide in surprise.

"Yes, but he doesn't know he does. I sneak some into dishes whenever I can because of its health benefits. Let's keep that between us. Okay?"

"Of course," Regina agreed with a grin. "Is that all you need? Maybe I should make a list."

I nodded my head. "That's all we need. Thanks for helping me out. I was kind of in a crack. In fact, you can use the word 'crack' as an acronym to remember my list: Coke, ranch dressing, apples, Crown Royal, and kale."

"Crack. Got it." Regina laughed at my suggestion, and then added, "Good idea, Mom. That truly *might* help me remember the five things you've requested. I'll be back in time for supper, even if Milo isn't."

"Sounds good." I felt impatient but knew Regina had a lot on her plate. I'd just have to wait until she had the time to share her news about the neighbor. I looked at my watch to see it was three o'clock. We had planned to eat at six, but I didn't know if I could stand the curiosity that would eat away at me like a cancer for an entire three hours. "You know, honey. I'm famished for some reason. Since we won't be waiting around for Milo, anyway, why don't we plan on eating at five instead?"

"That's a little early for supper, but whatever," Regina replied. "I'm kind of hungry myself. I should be home from the store and ready by then."

I found Rip piling up some hurricane debris on the curb. Huge trucks were driving through neighborhoods picking up the piles in front of nearly every home in town and adding them to the mountain of rubbish in the median strip on the Highway 35 Bypass. The debris field was growing taller and longer with each passing day. The incinerators just couldn't keep up with the massive amount of trash the trucks were hauling in.

"Dinner's at five, dear. I don't know about you, but I could eat the south end of a northbound cow."

"Lucky for you, that's exactly the cut of beef I'm grilling up for you." Rip laughed and added, "I'll season the filets shortly and fire up the grill in about an hour and a half."

"Thanks, babe." I knew a five o'clock supper would pose no problem with Rip. It was never too early for him to eat. An early supper only meant his customary evening snack-fest would commence at seven rather than eight and last an extra hour.

I went inside to throw together a salad, complete with what little kale I had left in the fridge. I chopped it so finely, Rip wouldn't have a clue what he was eating. I then waited eagerly for the clock to do almost two full rotations. It was like watching cheese mold.

We had barely sat down at the table when I asked, "So, Regina, you were going to tell us about the news you heard today concerning the neighbors."

"Oh, yeah. Mind if I fill my plate first?"

"Of course not, dear. No rush," I replied nonchalantly.

"Pass the veggies, please."

I handed the dish to Regina and waited on pins and needles for her to dip out a spoonful of the bell peppers and squash and transfer it to her plate. *Has she always been this tediously slow?* I wondered. *I could have filled my plate, polished off all the food, licked the plate clean, and gone back for seconds in the time it's taking her to arrange the food on her plate.*

Finally, when I thought she was never going to speak, Regina said, "I spoke to a friend who works as a secretary at city hall, which is now operating out of the old Ace Hardware since their former building was destroyed in the storm. Her husband is a Rockport police officer. It seems as though an anonymous eyewitness has come forward who insists he saw Reilly get into a car during the lull."

"The lull?" I asked, trying not to sound overly anxious.

"Yes, there was a pause in the terrifically high winds when the eye of the hurricane was directly over Rockport. We actually thought the storm was over until it came back with unbelievable brute force. The whistling of the wind sounded like hundreds of alley cats screeching at the same time. It was so eerie-sounding. We quickly realized we were in for another round of hell on earth when the eye had passed over us and the back side of the hurricane unleashed its fury."

"Wow." I wondered again what had possessed two reasonably intelligent adults to stay in their home throughout a hurricane rather than follow a mandatory evacuation order when they had the opportunity. "So did the eyewitness say Reilly was forced into the vehicle or did she get into it of her own accord?"

"The tipster assumed she got in the car willingly, but he couldn't be certain. Apparently, the car pulled up alongside her, spoke to her out the driver side window and then waited as she walked around and climbed in on the passenger side."

"That doesn't mean the driver of the car wasn't up to no good."

Before my mouth even quit flapping, I knew I'd spoken too rashly. With a look of disbelief, Rip said, "Come on, Rapella. Don't let your imagination get ahead of you. Who abducts someone in the middle of a hurricane? Use some sense."

"You're probably right." I concurred with my husband to keep the peace. But that doesn't mean I didn't still have my doubts. Women willingly got into Ted Bundy's tan Volkswagen Bug, too. Lots of them, in fact. Finally, my compulsion to make a point overrode my desire to not stir up an argument. "So if the driver of the car didn't give her a lift for nefarious reasons, where is Reilly now?"

"That's a good point." Rip had to agree it was odd she hadn't been seen since. "I don't know. Hopefully the eyewitness gave the police a good enough description of the vehicle that they'll be able to track down the driver and question him."

"That's just it, Daddy," Regina cut in. "All he remembered was that it was a light-colored car, maybe an SUV. Obviously, the tip line caller was under extreme duress with a destructive hurricane in progress."

"That doesn't narrow it down very much, does it?" Rip asked.

"No. I passed more than twenty white SUV's this morning alone when I drove over to H-E-B's parking lot," Regina said. H-E-B was a chain of more than 350 grocery stores in Texas. It seemed as if there was one in every Texas town we passed through. "They were handing out cases of water, so I picked us up a few. Drinking water is a hot commodity right now. Thankfully, the Red Cross and so many other charitable organizations are stepping up to the plate to help out the hurricane victims in the area. They almost insisted I bring home a half dozen cases of MRE's, as well."

"Did you?" I asked.

"MRE is an acronym for Meal, Ready-to-Eat," Regina continued without responding to my question. She acted as if she was explaining the birds and the bees to a class full of eager-to-learn sixth graders.

I listened patiently so as not to burst her bubble. "How does it work?"

When Regina shrugged, Rip supplied the answer instead. "The package contains a flameless heater and is designed to actually heat up the food inside of it when water is added to a flexible pad containing magnesium dust, salt, and a little iron dust. A chemical reaction occurs that causes the playing-card sized pad to reach a boiling point, bubble, and steam. It takes about ten minutes to heat up the food inside the pouch. The U.S. Department of Defense hands out these MRE's during natural disasters such as Harvey, when organized food facilities are not available."

"Yes," Regina said. "As you know, H-E-B sustained roof damage, and it will take some time to get it back up and operating."

"Yes. Not too long, I hope. Hard to do without a local grocery store." I was glad I'd heeded Regina's advice to stock up on necessities before heading to Rockport. The five items she'd picked up for me in Portland that afternoon were handy, but hardly essential.

"Despite H-E-B's own loss, they are donating supplies for local citizens who've been impacted by the storm," Regina said.

Then Rip spoke up again. "I'm not surprised by H-E-B's generosity and kindness. It's very nice that businesses, relief organizations, and selfless volunteers hand out water and MRE's to storm victims. Years ago, when I was serving in Vietnam, we had to eat our C-rations cold, or light a little chunk of C4 explosive in a small can and——"

"C-rations?" Regina looked confused. I noticed her glance at her father's left ear to see if he was wearing his hearing aids. Naturally, he wasn't.

"MRE's are the modern version of what used to be referred to as C-rations. That's what your dad ate when he was serving in Vietnam," I explained.

"Except for when I had nothing but a bag of dry rice to sustain me for weeks on end." Rip spoke between bites of his filet. "They used to put a four-pack of cigarettes, like Lucky Strikes, and a can opener in the C-rations packs. The can opener, or P-38, which we called a 'John Wayne', was needed to open the tin cans. Some of the meals weren't too bad, like the beans and weenies, but I still have nightmares about a few of them."

"I remember your dad griping about the ham and lima bean meals in letters he sent home to me. He hasn't touched a lima bean since." I then repeated my earlier question. "Did you bring any of the MRE's home this morning? I'm curious to see what's included in one and how it tastes. And I'm sure your dad's interested to see how the meals have changed."

"Not really," Rip said around a mouth full of tender beef.

"No," Regina replied. "I only brought home water today. I finally assured him there were a lot of other people who needed the MRE's a lot worse than we did."

"Oh." Disappointment must have been evident in my voice because Regina was quick to reassure me.

"But we already had at least ten cases of MRE's in the house from a couple of weeks ago when the Red Cross was going house-to-house handing them out." She smiled before continuing. "We actually had to rely on the pre-packaged meals for a few days after our supplies ran out and no store in town was open where we could buy groceries. They aren't bad, Mom. Better than the dry rice Daddy had to eat at times, for sure. What do you say we have them for lunch tomorrow so you can see what they're like?"

"That would be nice." I was anxious to try one, but it was clear from Rip's expression he'd just as soon eat some of Dolly's Fancy Feast cat food. "If you'd prefer, dear, you can have whatever veggies we have left over."

"Gee, thanks." I could tell by his tone the idea of sharing Dolly's lunch with her was sounding better and better.

"That's right," Regina said. "No sense wasting whatever we can't eat tonight. You know what Mom always says. Waste not, want not."

"Suddenly an MRE sounds a lot better to me than it did a minute or so ago." Rip looked at both Regina and me with a comical expression. We all laughed in unison. It was so nice to spend time with our only child, even under not so nice conditions. "But, I promise you, Reggie, if my MRE has ham and lima beans in it, your name will be swiftly removed from our will." His warning was accompanied by a stern expression, followed by a teasing wink. Regina could be arrested for conjuring up a Ponzi scheme that took us for every dollar we had, and yet still be the executor and sole heir of our estate. The joke would be on her, however, as we'd have no money left to inherit.

After a satisfying supper, and a relaxing nightcap later on, Rip and I went to bed around ten. I tossed and turned half the night, thinking about what might have happened to Reilly Reynolds after she'd climbed into the unknown driver's car during the lull in the storm.

Had she been tricked into getting into the car? Or, alternatively, had she called someone and asked them to pick her up? Was it a man or woman driving the car she'd gotten into? Had she thought it was an opportune time to fake her death and escape an abusive husband? Or, perhaps, a cheating husband? Was it she who was being unfaithful? The blonde who'd left a note for him to meet her could have factored into a decision to leave him, I thought. *Did she have a mother, sister, or close friend in the area who might have been hiding her out the last three weeks? Was Reilly alive and well, and waiting for her moment to reappear? Or was she hoping to be passed off as dead so she could live out her life in peace, somewhere far away?*

It was just as likely she been murdered by an abductor I realized, but I didn't want to even think of that probability quite yet. I wanted to operate on the assumption she was still among the living, as remote a possibility as that was.

There were so many questions and possible scenarios filtering through my mind that I couldn't turn my brain off long enough to fall sleep. It was almost dawn before I finally drifted off into slumber, no doubt from sheer exhaustion.

SEVEN

I felt a little groggy and out of sorts the next morning, but the fog cleared after I'd indulged in several cups of strong coffee. I usually limited myself to two cups per day, except when visiting with Lexie Starr at the Alexandria Inn. For some reason, there the coffee flowed like lava from an erupting volcano and a piping hot cup, filled to the brim with a robust brew, was always sitting right at my fingertips. It was easy to over-indulge in caffeine when it was eternally present. For that reason, I'd experienced some of my most restless nights in Lexie and Stone's lodging facility. Of course, some of my restlessness might be attributed to the fact Lexie nearly always seemed to be knee-deep in a mysterious murder case when we were there.

As I was sipping on my third cup, Regina stuck her head inside the door of the trailer. "Mom? You up and at it?"

"Well, I'm up anyway."

"One out of two ain't bad." She laughed and stepped inside, closing the door behind her as she'd been taught always to do as a child. I'd imagine she'd heard the questions, "Were you born in a barn?" and "Are you trying to cool down the entire neighbor-hood?" too many times to count by the time she was a teenager.

"What's up?" I asked. I offered her a cup of coffee, which she declined.

"I wanted to see if you'd go to Corpus Christi with me this morning. Daddy's going to be tied up doing something else for Milo."

"Sure. What's in Corpus?"

"Milo has his daily list of things he needs at a hardware store there. Unfortunately, the ceiling caved in at the Lowe's in Aransas Pass, and it's closed indefinitely. A lot of work needs to be done to the building before it can reopen."

"That is unfortunate. Their merchandise is in great demand right now and Lowes is a lot more convenient to folks in Rock-port than the hardware stores in Corpus. What time would you like to leave?"

"The store opens at nine, so let's leave at eight-thirty."

"Okay. I'll be ready." It was seven o'clock and I wanted to bake several batches of cookies. I also wanted to make a small batch of sugar-free chocolate chip cookies from a recipe I'd found online. I'd feel bad not taking a batch for Bruno, the diabetic drywaller. I'm sure it was hard enough dealing with the terrible disease without having to watch your co-workers gobble down cookies all day. "Well, you run along now. I have a few chores to do before we leave."

Regina gave me a funny look and nodded her head before departing. "See you at eight-thirty then. I'm looking forward to spending as much time as I can with you and Daddy. Now that you're retired and traveling all the time, I don't get to see you as much as I used to."

"I miss spending time with you too, sweetheart. It's one of the drawbacks of being full-time RVers."

I was getting my first view of some of the storm damage as we drove through Rockport and Aransas Pass on our way to Corpus. The towns south of Aransas Pass, like Portland and Gregory, had not been as adversely affected by the hurricane, because the storm had headed north after ravaging Rockport. Like Rockport, Port Aransas, also known as Mustang Island, which is considered the northernmost stretch of Padre Island, had sustained severe damage. Corpus Christi, the largest city in south Texas, had been spared for the most part. Population-wise, it had truly been a blessing the hurricane had turned north in the final few hours before making landfall in the much smaller town of Rockport.

"This is so sad," I muttered at one point during the ride.

"Yeah, I know." Regina was driving Milo's work truck so we could haul our purchases in its large bed, and seemed to be deep in thought. I left her to reflect on whatever had her so distracted. Or at least until she had veered into the path of an oncoming sedan.

"Look out!" I shouted.

Regina yanked on the wheel and pulled the truck back into the proper lane just in time. I felt my stomach doing cartwheels as my chest pounded like a four-year-old with a new set of bongo drums. "Whoa! That was close. Sorry, Mom. I wasn't paying attention."

"Clearly," I replied. "Would you like me to drive?"

"No. I'm fine. We're almost there anyway."

"Thank goodness! My entire life just flashed before my eyes."

"That was a lot of flashing, wasn't it?" Regina asked playfully.

I laughed and smacked her on the shoulder. "Better straighten up or you'll be lucky to see your fifty-second birthday, much less your seventieth."

"At this point, I'm not sure if I want to see my next birthday." The playfulness was now gone from Regina's voice.

"Come on, honey. Keep your chin up. As they say, this too shall pass." It pained me to see her down in the dumps. I hoped getting their home back to normal would brighten her outlook.

After loading up the building materials and supplies at the hardware store, we headed back to Rockport. I'd been so interested in viewing the damage Harvey left in its path that I hadn't even brought up the subject of the missing neighbor lady. I didn't want to miss the opportunity to question Regina in case she had more information to divulge, so I broached the subject before we'd left the parking lot.

"Have you heard who the anonymous eyewitness was who saw Reilly get into a car in front of her home during the storm?"

"No. You do know what anonymous means don't you, Mom?"

"Of course I do. I just spoke without thinking." I swatted my daughter on the shoulder again. "Don't be so sassy. You are not too old for me to bend you over my knee."

"Yeah, I think I *am* too old for that. You never spanked me as a child, so I'm not too worried about you doing so now." Regina chuckled as she spoke. She grew more serious as she added, "I'm assuming the anonymous tipster was one of our neighbors who rode out the storm like we did."

"Last night you referred to the eyewitness as 'he' a couple of times. Does that mean you've heard it was a male?"

"No. I really have no idea. I just used that pronoun out of habit. My guess is that it was Suzanna Pandero. I don't know about my other neighbors, but I know she rode out the storm in their house next door to us. I heard her about-to-be ex-husband,

Percival, requested shelter from the storm in their house. Their separation has been anything but amicable, but it'd be tough to leave anyone outside to fend for himself in a situation like that."

"So she let Percival in?" I asked. I was thinking the husband must have arrived during the "lull" Regina had spoken about, for he could hardly have been out driving around with wind speeds approaching 140 miles per hour.

"Nope! Like I said, their separation is anything but amicable."

"Wow!" I shook my head. "That's pretty heartless, don't you think?"

"Yes. Even if I suspected Milo was having an affair, as Suzanna suspects Percival was doing, I couldn't be that merciless."

"What kind of car does Percival drive?"

"An ivory-colored Subaru Forrester."

"SUV?"

"Yeah. Why?"

"Just curious," I replied. "You told us the eyewitness said Reilly got into a light-colored car that was probably an SUV. Is it possible Percival picked her up after being denied entry by his estranged wife?"

"Yeah," Regina said. She thought silently for a moment before continuing. "Actually, it's very possible. Reilly is the woman Suzanna suspected Percival was cheating on her with. I hadn't really thought about that. She would definitely call in the tip if she suspected Percival was involved in Reilly's disappearance."

Now I was suddenly thinking less about her neighbor, Suzanna, being the possible eyewitness, and more about Suzanna's husband being the man who abducted Reilly. "It sounds highly likely then that Percival was the driver of the car the tipster said Reilly got in to."

"I don't really think——"

"It's something to consider though, isn't it?" I asked. It would be nice if I could get Regina, Milo, and Rip all interested in helping me look into what really happened to Reilly Reynolds. I was optimistic about this outcome until Regina's next remark.

"No. Not really. If Percival had picked Reilly up, she'd have contacted someone by now. He just isn't the type of guy to physically assault a woman. Any woman. He can be kind of loud and belligerent, but he's basically a harmless dude. And if Percival truly was interested in Reilly in a romantic way, why would he do anything to harm her? She'd have been heard from by now."

When I didn't respond, Regina went on to say, "Although I still think Suzanna might be the eyewitness, I highly doubt it was Percival who picked up Reilly. As hateful as their separation has been, she'd have recognized him and his vehicle and definitely reported him to the authorities as the abductor of the missing woman. She wouldn't call the hotline with a tip that might or might not lead them to Percival."

Regina had a point, I realized. But, on the other hand, there was no confirmation that her suspicion of Suzanna Pandero being the "eyewitness", that now being mentioned by the media, was correct. Granted, a high majority of the properties on Key Allegro were second homes and few were occupied by full-timers. Still, it had been reported that nearly forty percent of the full-time Rockport citizens rode out the storm in their homes. I'm pretty sure nearly one-hundred percent of that forty-percent would never ride out another one, as those I'd talked to that had admitted it was a terrifying experience they'd never want to go through again.

"There could easily have been another neighbor who witnessed Reilly get into a light-colored SUV-type vehicle," Regina reasoned.

"Yeah, I suppose. It's hard to imagine a couple who haven't

been married a full year both having affairs with other people," I said, again without thinking it through first.

"What are you talking about?" Regina asked. Her mouth had dropped open so far, I could have removed her tonsils with a pair of hedge clippers. "What makes you think Walker was having an affair?"

I swallowed so hard, the breath mint I'd just popped into my mouth got lodged in my throat. I began to hack harshly in an attempt to dislodge the disc. Concerned by the fact my face was turning purple, Regina pulled over to the shoulder and began to wallop me on the back. Even though I was on the verge of passing out from being unable to breathe, I was glad to have a momentary respite from trying to explain my comment. Finally, the mint flew out of my mouth and bounced off the glove compartment. I inhaled deeply, and said, "Thank you."

"Of course. Are you okay now?" Regina asked.

After I'd nodded, she pulled back onto the road and repeated her earlier question. "What makes you think Walker was having an affair?"

"Give me a moment," I said in a ragged whisper, trying to sound as if I was barely able to speak. I had deemed it best not to spread unsubstantiated rumors—rumors I had concocted myself, no less. When I couldn't delay my response any longer, I said, "I'm sorry. I must have misunderstood something you said earlier. I thought you said Walker was having an affair when you actually probably said he was having the house repaired."

Regina just laughed at my explanation. "Maybe you should start wearing Daddy's hearing aids."

"Somebody needs to," I replied. "Your father doesn't, and they cost almost as much as the Chartreuse Caboose."

"Do you really need to call it that?" Regina asked with a long, drawn-out groan. "Please don't refer to your travel trailer by name around my friends. Or anyone else, for that matter. Okay?"

"I suppose." I was a bit offended by Regina's request but willing to agree to almost anything as long as it kept the conversation from reverting back to why I'd inferred Reilly was not the only one in the Reynolds household who was having an affair. Not to mention, she *had* just saved my life.

As Regina negotiated the heavy Corpus Christi traffic on South Padre Island Drive, or SPID, as it was called, I thought about how I might determine the true identity of the eyewitness the media had mentioned. I had to find a way to canvass the residents at the end of the cul-de-sac on Flamingo Road. The Moores' home was the third one from the end. The huge orange house on the end had once been owned by the Eastman-Kodak Company, and I knew it was not occupied full-time. But there were three or four, maybe five, other possible homes where the eyewitness could reside.

I was considering possible ways to accomplish that feat when I glanced out the window and saw a business on Cantwell Lane named JJ's Insulation.

As nonchalantly as I could manage, I pointed toward the building and asked my daughter, "Is that one of the subcontractors Milo uses?"

"No."

"How about Walker next door?"

"I don't think so. Why do you ask?" I swear Regina's voice sounded suspicious, but I tried to convince myself it was just my imagination.

"Oh, I was just curious." I shrugged and attempted to sound as if I were being sentimental. It was too early to bring up the post-it note I had seen on her neighbor's kitchen table. I surely didn't want to come across as being nosy and having infringed on her neighbor's privacy, even though I was guilty of both charges. "It made me think about JJ's Cafe in town. I noticed their building was flattened, and I feel so bad for them. Your dad and I always loved that place."

"Yeah, me too. The folks who own it are extremely good people, too. Not sure what they'll do now, but I certainly hope they rebuild."

I agreed and became more interested when Regina said, "When I see the name JJ, I think about a gal I went to high school with. She used to work at Bealls and part-time at Quang Lé Bait Shack, her uncle's bait stand down by Fulton Marina. Like so many others, she lost both jobs when both businesses were forced to close until they can be rebuilt."

"That's too bad. Is JJ Vietnamese, like most of the bait stand owners?"

"No, but her uncle is. He's her uncle by name only. Quang Lê is her dad's best friend. Jenavieve Jacobowitz is her name. She was a grade ahead of me."

"I can certainly understand why she prefers to go by her initials. Her real name is a mouthful." I was just making conversation at this point because I didn't see how I could connect this old schoolmate of Regina's with Walker Reynolds.

That changed quickly, however. In fact, I nearly wet my pants when Regina replied, "Yeah. No kidding! I noticed her ex-fiancé is doing the drywall work next door."

"You mean Bruno?" I asked breathlessly, realizing too late I'd spoken before giving my words any thought. Again!

Regina almost drove off the road when she turned to me and asked, "How in the (bleep) do you know about Bruno Watts?"

"Watch your language, young lady!" I reprimanded in order to stall for time. Finally, to appease Regina, I gave her a rudimentary version of my visit next door. I basically told her the head contractor in charge of rebuilding the Reynolds's home had mentioned his drywall guy named Bruno was a diabetic when I dropped off the cookies. When my explanation seemed to appease her, I asked, "Are you still in contact with JJ?"

"No. Haven't seen or talked to her in several years. Another friend told me JJ recently married a guy out of Austin and is working as an Uber driver up there." Regina ceased talking so she could concentrate on driving, as we were now in extremely heavy traffic on the Crosstown Expressway.

As she studied the road ahead, I thought it must be a different JJ who'd left the note for Walker. I thought about asking Regina if she knew of any other woman in the area who went by the initials JJ. Regina wasn't the best driver under normal circumstances, though, so I didn't want to distract her. I spent the rest of the return trip to Rockport gazing out the passenger-side window at uprooted live oak trees and destroyed buildings. Every once in a while we'd pass a structure that looked totally unaffected by the hurricane. It was as if God had placed a protective shield around that particular building while the storm roared through the area. It seemed hurricanes were indiscriminate, in the same nature as tornadoes.

I remained silent as Regina sang along with the radio in a key about three octaves too high. My ears were beginning to hurt after about four songs. The poor girl had inherited her mother's inability to carry a tune in a dump truck, much less a bucket. Holding my hands over my ears might be considered a touch offensive, so instead, I tried to block out her singing by mulling over what I'd just learned.

Now I had even more to think about. As they say: the plot was thickening. Was Regina's friend named JJ back in town and the same blonde who left Walker a note about meeting her? The odds of another young lady being nicknamed JJ in a town the size of Rockport were not infinitesimal, but they were low, I'd guess. Or was the note left by a contractor who wanted Walker to meet him at the insulation store in Corpus? More likely, did the note on Walker's kitchen table have no significance whatsoever in his wife's disappearance? It was quite possible I was trying to create a mountain out of a molehill where not even a molehill existed. I had a tendency to create a lot of pointless mountains out of imaginary molehills.

I wasn't sure if I was getting closer to determining who or what was behind Reilly's disappearance or further away, but I did know I now had a drywall guy I wanted to talk with. Even as this thought crossed my mind, I wondered, *by going to the trouble to make the man sugar-free cookies, am I pandering to a killer?*

EIGHT

As we reached the Rockport city limits, Regina received a text on her cell phone. After glancing at it, she set the phone back down in the truck's console. "Milo said to tell you Daddy is helping him with a little project this morning."

This was welcome news. I wouldn't have to explain why I was taking snacks over to the workers next door—again!

Regina and I parted ways as soon as we arrived back at the Moores' house; she to work on her insurance claim, and me to gather up my Ziploc bags full of cookies. On each bag was a name. I'd used a permanent marker to write "Jessie" and "Tony" on the snickerdoodle bags and "Bruno" on the bag of sugar-free chocolate chip cookies.

While everyone was busy elsewhere, I slipped next door to deliver the promised treats. I was met at the door by a man of very short stature and slight frame who looked more like a librarian than a construction worker. I was pretty sure I could easily turn him horizontal and bench press him a dozen times.

"Hello," I said in greeting. I figured this man was the accountant Jessie had mentioned was helping Walker with his own insurance claim. "I'm sorry. I was looking for Jessie, Tony, or Bruno. Are any of them here today?"

"I'm Bruno. Whaddya want?" His impatient tone was anything but welcoming. I hadn't met him before, but he looked nothing like I'd expected a man named Bruno to look. He looked more like a Francis or an Ira. To be truthful, without the well-trimmed mustache he sported, he'd have looked more like a Frances or an Irene. He was extremely effeminate in both looks and manner. His baritone voice had been totally unexpected.

"You're the drywall contractor?" I know I sounded surprised but hoped I hadn't also sounded skeptical.

When he stood silently, glaring at me, I handed him the bag of cookies with his name on it. "It's nice to meet you, Bruno. I'm Rapella Ripple, the mother of Regina Moore from next door. Jessie and Tony asked me to bake them some snickerdoodles, which I was more than happy to do. Jessie told me you were diabetic, so I made you a batch of sugar-free cookies. I hope you like chocolate chip."

"I don't like anything that's sugar-free. Something in the synthetic sugar gives me the shits." Bruno quickly apologized for his offensive language. "Pardon my French. I meant to say it gives me the runs."

"I'm not sure which sounds best, but I understand completely. Sorbitol, maltitol, and other sweeteners have the tendency to give me either gas or diarrhea, too." I was a little embarrassed by my confession and was surprised when the grey-eyed man's glare turned into an amused grin, exposing a beautiful mouthful of straight, white teeth. The diminutive fellow was quite attractive when he smiled. "Perhaps, there's something else I can make for you that you *can* tolerate."

"Thanks," he replied. "But I'm good. I don't want you to go to any trouble for me. Jessie and Tony are out back removing the forms from around the concrete patio that was poured a couple of days ago. While Walker's having all this other reconstruction done, Jessie convinced Walker to have the rear patio enlarged too."

"I see. And what are you working on?" I was trying to engage Mr. Watts in conversation without appearing to be prying into his business. I was relieved he seemed genuinely happy to discuss his work with me. In fact, I must have given him the impression I was much more interested in the art of drywalling than I really was.

"Come in here," he replied. He led me into the living room, where the overwhelming stench of mildew was even stronger than it had been in the foyer. I was about to comment on the odor when Bruno pointed to a surprisingly thick wall separating the living room from a smaller nook. "As you can see, I've already put up all of the sheetrock. Currently, I am finishing taping the final wall in here, and then I will begin sealing the joints with a drywall compound of what's primarily gypsum dust mixed with water to form a mud-like consistency. Then, I will use aluminum stilts to——"

"Oh, my! There is so much more to the art of drywalling than I'd imagined." I'd cut him off because I couldn't afford to stand around all day listening to the ins and outs of Bruno's trade. Not to mention, it was stifling hot inside the house. Pointing to the far corner of the room, I asked, "What's with the thick wall and little open area behind it?"

"Oh, that," Bruno began. "Well, you see, the lady who lived here——"

"You mean Reilly Reynolds? The lady who's missing and presumed dead?"

"Well, um, yeah. That's the one. Walker told me that Reilly had always wanted to have a library in her home and he'd repeatedly pooh-poohed the idea. As you can imagine, he's holding out hope she'll return home safely and, of course, soon.

When and if she does, he'll be able to give her the library she's always wanted, even if it does make the living room a bit smaller. Creating the new walled-off area was kind of my idea, actually."

Bruno was obviously pleased with himself for coming up with the inspiration of surprising Reilly with her very own library. But it seemed to me to be putting the water skier in front of the boat. So far, there was nothing to indicate the woman would ever return to her house on Flamingo Road. By originally referring to her in the past tense, Bruno made me think he didn't hold out much hope Reilly would turn up alive and well.

"That's nice, but I thought everyone initially assumed she was blown off the pier during the hurricane and her body had washed out to sea. Does Walker truly think there's a chance Reilly's still alive?" I asked.

"Yeah, I think so. I guess it's hard to give up hope when it's someone you love. But there's really no explanation other than the one you just mentioned."

"Maybe, maybe not. I heard on the news that an anonymous eyewitness reported seeing her get into a car out front during the time the eye of the hurricane was directly over the island."

"I don't know anything about that, but it sounds like hogwash to me. It was probably that half-witted goofball, Barlow Barnaby up the street, who called in the bogus tip. It was nice to meet you, Rachel."

Bruno turned as if the conversation was over. I didn't bother to correct him on my name. He either hadn't been interested enough to pay attention when I introduced myself just a couple of minutes prior, or he was like Rip, who occasionally had trouble remembering names. He picked up a roll of drywall tape and walked toward the unfinished section he'd probably been working on when I'd knocked on the front door.

"Hmm," I mumbled. I had so many more questions to ask Bruno. I hadn't even gotten to the point of somehow bringing

Jenavieve Jacobowitz into the conversation. In the form of a question, I said, "I assume the thick wall is intended to serve as a sound barrier since libraries are notorious for being quiet places? It's probably well-insulated too."

"Uh, yeah. Sure." Bruno stuck a large flat carpenter's pencil in his mouth and turned away again. He walked over to the wall, measured a large void with a tape measure he'd yanked off his belt, and wrote the measurement down on a piece of sheetrock.

"So how's JJ doing?" I asked. I know this was a bold move, but I couldn't think of any better idea about how to broach the subject of his former fiancée.

"Say what?" If Bruno hadn't removed the bulky pencil just before I asked the question, he would've swallowed it whole. He spun around so fast, I saw spittle fly out of the corner of his mouth. "What'd you say?"

"I was just curious how JJ's doing. I know her uncle, Quang Lê, and he'd told me a while back that you two had once been engaged. We used to buy our fishing bait at Quang's little bait shop all the—"

"I haven't seen JJ in months. We broke up. She told me she found someone else. No big deal, though, because I have, too."

"Oh, well. I'm glad to hear you found a new girlfriend." I began to formulate another question in my mind when Bruno waved me off. This was probably a good thing as I was about to ask if he'd heard JJ had married a guy out of Austin, and I had no idea how he'd take that kind of crushing news if he still carried a torch for his former fiancée. Chances were, his new girl-friend was just a rebound fling to prove to his ex he could move on just as easily as she had.

"Sorry, lady, but—"

"It's Rapella."

"Whatever," he said, rather rudely. "I should get back to work. As you can see, I need to get the rest of this room taped.

Thanks anyway for going to the trouble to make the sugar-free cookies for me. Sorry I won't be eating any of them."

"You're welcome. No problem on the cookies. My husband will see to it they don't go to waste. I'll let you get back to work now and go hand off these other bags to Jessie and Tony." I wasn't finished questioning him, so decided I might as well roll the dice and break the news to him. If nothing else, it might prolong our conversation to the point I was able to dig more info out of him. "Just, F.Y.I., I heard from a fairly reliable source that JJ recently married that new guy she left you for and moved to Austin. She's driving for Uber now and—"

"Sorry, lady, but I've really got to get back to work." The steely look he gave me made it clear he had no interest in continuing our little chat-fest.

I walked out of the room, realizing I'd learned very little new information from the drywall contractor. I can't be positive, and I was afraid to retrace my steps to check it out, but it sounded as if Bruno had slammed his fist through a sheet of sheetrock just about the time I turned the knob on the door to the back deck.

My final remarks about his former flame must have really hit a raw nerve.

NINE

"Good afternoon, Ms. Ripple," the handsome demolition man greeted me on the back porch of the Reynolds's home a minute or so later, after I'd left the drywall man to return to his work. As he spoke, Tony tossed a long two-by-four into a pile next to the patio.

"Please call me Rapella, Tony," I said politely. "How are you today?"

"Just fine, thank you." After noticing the bags of cookies I was holding, he added, "I can't believe you actually brought me some home-baked snickerdoodles."

"I told you I would, didn't I?" I returned playfully. "I would never promise cookies and not deliver."

"Well, thank you again." Tony gallantly raised my right hand to his lips and kissed the back of it. "But, please, don't bring me any more after this. I'm already doing a ton of crunches and sit-ups every morning to keep my body mass index at an acceptable level."

His BMI looked to be ideal to me. I admired his perfect physique for a moment and nodded. I didn't want to sound like a flirt, but I felt compelled to compliment his build. "You don't appear to have a single molecule out of place, and I agree it should stay that way."

Jessie walked around the corner before Tony could finish blushing and respond. The general contractor had a broad smile on his face. "Ahhh…It's the cookie lady. I heard what Tony said. I want you to know that I have officially let myself go and no longer care about how buff I look. Feel free to drop off as many cookies as you'd like, and I'll personally see to it that they don't go to waste."

Jessie appeared much more relaxed than the last time I'd seen him. I wasn't certain if he was teasing or serious so I chuckled in response. I might need to bring over cookies in the future just as an excuse to question someone working inside the Reynolds's home, so I wanted to keep that option available if at all possible. I handed him the bag of snickerdoodles with his name on it.

As Jessie scrutinized the contents of the bag, he said, "I see you fulfilled Tony's request for snickerdoodles."

"You dislike snickerdoodles?" I asked. I'm sure I sounded disappointed.

"Oh, heavens no! I love any kind of cookie. Look at me for goodness sakes!" Jessie opened up his arms to bring attention to his slight stomach paunch that had his stained sleeveless t-shirt stretched as tight as a banjo string. "I just can't figure out why every woman from eight to eighty seems so eager to do Tony's bidding."

"It must be his pleasant personality," I replied. Jessie's comment had been made in jest, but I hoped he didn't think I was eighty. I might feel that old sometimes; however, I didn't think I even looked seventy, much less a decade older.

"His pleasant personality? Yeah, right," Jessie said while rolling his eyes. "It pains me to say this, but Tony actually is as nice as he is good-looking. A little rough around the edges when you get him schnockered, but an all-right guy, nonetheless."

"I've heard as much." I winked at Tony as I replied, which was a little brazen of someone old enough to be the handsome stud's grandmother. I wanted to ask him if it was his face I'd seen on a romance novel while waiting in line at Wal-Mart. While I had the two men in good spirits, I decided to see if I could withdraw any useful information from either of them. Although I had no way of knowing what kind of guy Walker Reynolds was, I said, "Speaking of being a nice guy, how is Walker doing?"

"He's hanging in there," Jessie said. Tony remained noncommittal.

My question had yielded no worthwhile information, so I switched course. "Did you hear an eyewitness reported having seen Reilly getting into a car in front of the house here during the lull of the storm?"

"Hadn't heard," Tony stated.

"Yeah," Jessie replied. His response was at least a trifle more revealing. Jessie sounded almost as if he was pissed off when he continued. "I also heard that over eleven hundred tips have come in through the tip hotline and none of them have led to any useful discovery. Tipsters can be so unreliable. I sometimes think they call in with vague information in hopes of getting lucky and cashing in on the reward money. I even heard a psychic called in and said she sees Reilly's body in a large body of water. Well, duh. I could have predicted that, and I don't claim to have any kind of sixth sense or psychic abilities. I'll believe Reilly's still alive when I see her with my own eyes."

"So you're totally convinced she was blown off the pier while trying to chase down the couple's dog and was washed out to sea?"

"Yep!" Jessie said with a definitive nod. "As is Walker."

"That's funny," I said. "Bruno seemed to think Walker still believes his wife might be alive."

"Nah," Jessie replied, with a shake of his head while Tony remained quiet. "I'm pretty sure Walker's convinced she's gone for good. He saw Scrappy run out the back door with Reilly right behind the pooch. He hasn't laid eyes on his wife since. Do the math."

"I agree with Jessie. By the way, Scrappy is a something-poo, Walker said," Tony clarified.

"Maltipoo," I supplied for him. "A cross between a toy poodle and a Maltese. Where is Scrappy now?"

Before Tony could respond, Jessie began to explain. "Walker couldn't care for him here, in a house with broken-out windows and all, so Reilly's older sister, who lives down in the valley near Mission, Texas, came and picked him up. Scrappy will live with her until the house is rebuilt. He's an older dog, like thirteen or fourteen, and if he were to get sick there are veterinarian clinics he can go to down in the valley. Not so here in Rockport right now. Walker knew Reilly would want her sister to care for Scrappy under the current circumstances, so he didn't hesitate to let the pooch stay with her."

"I see." I was curious why Jessie and Tony both seemed so determined to convince me that the presumed fate of Reilly Reynolds was the correct one: she had accidentally drowned during the hurricane, eventually her body would wash ashore, and life would go on for Walker, and Reilly's other survivors, including her elderly pet. "It's a shame her body hasn't been discovered so her loved ones can have closure."

"Yeah. Closure. Sure." Tony's tone and expression clearly indicated he thought the notion of a person finding "closure" following the death of a loved one was a joke. Overrated, at the very least. I had to admit, I had a tendency to agree. Closure had never made me feel any better, or cry any less when the cause of a loved one's death was determined. Closure did not lessen my grief to any extent. It certainly didn't bring my lost loved one back to life. And it didn't make it any easier for me to go on living without them.

My pa's body was found in a field behind the old farmhouse I grew up in when I was in my early twenties. It was several days before the medical examiner determined his death had been caused by the inhalation of toxic ammonia nitrate dust that had been spewed by a faulty fertilizer sprayer he was using earlier in the day. His respiratory tract became inflamed and gradually swelled up to the point it suffocated him. Knowing what happened to him did *not* bring me closure. It brought more heartache because I knew his senseless death could have been prevented if he'd only had the sprayer inspected before using it.

"I understand," I replied simply, with sadness in my heart from the memory of my father's death. "Nonetheless, if she truly did drown, I hope her body is found soon so Walker can go about making peace with her loss and get back to the business of living."

"Me too," Tony said, as Jessie merely nodded. "Although I think he's handling her loss very well, so far. He seems pretty pragmatic about it."

Maybe too pragmatic, I thought. *It almost sounds to me as if Walker is being lackadaisical about his wife's disappearance. Is he glad she's gone? Is he, in fact, the reason she's missing? It sounds as if this JJ woman might have Walker in her sights and is trying to hook up with him, if she isn't already doing so. Could she have something to do with Reilly's death?*

When it seemed clear the two men were becoming impatient to resume the job they'd been doing when I interrupted them, I wished them a good afternoon.

"Thanks again for the snickerdoodles, Rapella," Tony said.

Jessie thanked me again, as well. "Don't worry about your Ziploc bags, ma'am. I'll make sure they don't get thrown away."

I'm sure my face flushed at his remark, but I couldn't take another tack on the tight-fisted issue at this stage. I'd used it as an excuse to make a return visit to the neighbor's house before, and I'd probably need to use it again. "I appreciate it, Jessie. Waste not, want not, you know."

After repeating the words Regina had used the previous day, I made my way back to the trailer. It was still early in the afternoon. While I fed Dolly, I thought about a reason to canvass the folks at the end of Flamingo Road. I wanted to question those folks who had a view of the street in front of the Reynolds's house. I was determined to unmask the anonymous eyewitness.

Why is the tipster requesting to remain anonymous in the first place? Is she or he afraid of the perpetrator exacting revenge in the event he's identified? Or, as Jessie suggested, is the "eyewitness" guilty of calling in a prefabricated tip for some reason? And, if so, does the reason have anything to do with covering up the tipster's own involvement in the woman's disappearance? Once again, my mind was full of unanswered questions.

TEN

When I stepped into the Moores' motorhome a few minutes later, Regina was standing in front of the refrigerator. She grabbed a couple of bottles of water and handed one of them to me. "We need to drink a lot of water in this intense heat. You about ready for lunch?"

"Sure." I twisted off the lid and took a long swig. It was two o'clock, but lunch had been delayed due to the project Milo and Rip had tackled that morning. "Thanks for the water, honey. I needed that. As my pa used to say, I was so dry I was pooping dust."

"Thanks for the visual," Regina said with a mock grimace. "Grandpa died the day after my fifth birthday. I still remember his bear hugs and that I loved the smell of his pipe tobacco. I wish he'd lived long enough for me to get to know him better."

"Me too, sweetheart. You would've adored him. As a little girl, you were the apple of his eye." I gave Regina a quick hug. The conversation was making my eyes grow misty, so I changed the subject. "What's for lunch?"

"You have a choice between vegetable lasagna, beef ravioli,

or chili mac. Or, you can have what Daddy chose: penne with vegetable and sausage crumbles."

"I'll just have what your father's having. There's no sense in making more than one dish."

"They're the MRE's, Mom," Regina said gently as if dealing with a parent suffering from dementia. "Everyone can choose their own meal."

"Oh. Of course. I'd forgotten about our conversation last night. Not that I have memory issues. I've just had a lot on my mind." I paused when I noticed Regina's eyebrows were cocked. "I'll take the chili mac."

"Okay, good. Then your lunch is ready as soon as you activate the heating element inside and cook it." Regina smiled after she'd reached into a box, withdrew a plastic-covered package, and handed it to me with a metal fork. "We're using real utensils. Daddy said he'd be here in a couple of minutes."

"All right. Thank you, sweetheart. As your dad said yesterday, it sure is nice that all of these relief organizations team up to help out folks who've been affected by Harvey."

It was then that I realized I had the perfect reason to canvass Regina and Milo's closest neighbors, or at least those within eyeshot of the street in front of the Reynolds's house.

"Good afternoon, ma'am. My name's Rapella Ripple." The tall, willowy auburn-haired woman in front of me was a classic beauty. In my hand was a clipboard with a pen clipped to it, and in my stomach was some chili mac playing rugby with the pop tart that had been included in the MRE package. The pop tart had been cold and crumbly, but I'd been determined to polish off the entire meal so I could give it an honest evaluation. In retrospect, I wished I'd pitched the pop tart when I'd noticed it's condition.

The meal had tasted fine—although it was probably not something I'd eat again if I had my druthers—but it just didn't seem to be agreeing with me. Then again, it could have been the four or five sugar-free cookies I'd snarfed down after lunch from the batch I'd made for Bruno Watts. Like Bruno, sugar substitutes had a way of upsetting my naturally strong constitution. Either way, my stomach was roiling like a vat of boiling brew. I'd suppressed a belch just as the Panderos' front door opened. I studied the pretty woman in front of me for a second, and said, "I'm serving as a volunteer with one of the hurricane relief teams. May I have your name please?"

"I'm Suzanna Pandero. It's nice to meet you, Rapella." Suzanna's voice was so high-pitched, it sounded almost like a squeaky dog toy. As she watched me write her name down on the sheet of paper on the clipboard, she corrected me. "That's Suzanna with a 'z'. S-u-z-a-n-n-a. Last name is Pandero, P-a-n-d-e-r-o."

"Thank you, Suzanna with a 'z'," I said good-naturedly. "It's so much easier when folks spell their names for me. I have to keep a record so we don't hit the same homes time after time while overlooking others who might be in great need."

"Of course." Suzanna seemed just as nice as she could be. I found myself seething at the idea her husband, Percival, could have been sniffing after their newlywed neighbor. She opened her front door wide to allow me to enter. "Please come inside. It's brutal out there."

I thanked her and followed her into the house. "It must have been unbearable with the power being out for two or three weeks."

"I went and stayed at my mom's house in Horizon City. With no water, sewer, electric, Internet, phone, and all, it was impossible to stay here. Had I known how bad it was going to be, I'd have gone to her house *before* the storm. I've never been so scared in my entire life. I truly thought I was going to die. The outer walls were actually moving in and out as if the house was breathing. It was surreal."

"At least you probably had your husband with you, for both moral and physical support." I was hoping my fishing expedition would net some valuable information and was pleased when it did.

"What makes you think I have a husband?" Her expression was one of skepticism.

"Oh, well. It was merely a supposition on my part. So you're single?" I knew I was pushing my luck asking such personal questions, but Suzanna seemed willing to oblige me with information.

"No, but I will be soon. My husband is a cheat and a scoundrel. I'd just kicked him out and refused to let him stay here during the storm. I haven't seen or heard from him since." Suzanna brushed her hands together as if ridding them of potato chip crumbs. I knew it was to illustrate how she'd washed her hands of her dastardly spouse.

"Good for you!" I raised my hand as if to instigate a high-five. I lowered my arm awkwardly when she didn't respond. "Where do you think he stayed during Harvey?"

"Don't know, don't care. Probably with that slutty girlfriend of his." Suzanna's voice was now so high-pitched, it would've made a bloodhound howl if she'd had one.

"Oh, doesn't that just piss you off to no end?" I asked, trying to match her indignation to get her to engage in an open discussion as if we were BFF's from way back. She shrugged without replying to my probing inquiry. I waited for her to reveal more pertinent information about her husband's mistress, but after a while the silence became uncomfortable. I decided to turn toward a less invasive topic. "It must have been terrifying to be here alone during that fierce storm."

"Yes, it was. I'm lucky this house fared so well, but I will never again ride out a hurricane."

"I wouldn't think so," I said. "In fact, I think you'd have to be half-crazy to have done so this last go-round. My daughter and her husband rode it out too."

"Um, well." Rather than form a complete response, she merely glared at me if I'd just told her that her newborn baby looked like Don Rickles. I hadn't meant my remark to come across as insulting, but I was convinced it had when Suzanna said, "Then I guess I'm crazy."

"Half-crazy," I said. "But in a good way, of course."

"Can a person be crazy in a good way?" She asked, still burning holes through my head with her eyes.

"Half-crazy," I corrected her again. Just then I saw what looked like a cross between a roof rat and a baby bunny slither out from underneath a marble-topped table. I stifled a gasp and shook my head, convinced the creature was a figment of my overworked imagination. Reeling from the hallucination, I'm sure my expression lent credence to my next comment. "And, yes, half-crazy is a compliment. I'm full-blown bat-crap crazy myself. In fact, I'm beginning to see things I'm certain don't actually exist. The way I see it, sane folks don't have nearly as much fun."

"If you say so."

I realized I needed to change the subject again, and fast, lest I be shown out the door as quickly as I'd just been welcomed in. "But that's neither here nor there. The reason I stopped by was to make sure you have enough food on hand. I'm going door to door checking on folks to see if there are any supplies they desperately need. I'm sorry I ran out of cases of water, but I still have a case or two of MRE's to hand out to anyone who needs them."

I suppose Mrs. Pandero was wondering where I was going to get the boxes of MRE's should she need them because I had walked over from the Moores' home. A case of the ready-to-eat meals was too heavy to lug around. However, I knew if she said she could use a case or two of them, I could snatch a couple of cases out of the kids' house without them ever knowing and wheel them next door with Milo's dolly. Fortunately, Suzanna said she had more than enough of them and would be happy to donate six or seven cases to the cause. "I'll be content never to depend on one of those for sustenance again in my lifetime. In fact, from the last three, I ate only the Tootsie Rolls and threw the rest away. I suppose that's being wasteful if another family can use the entire meals."

"I suppose so, even though I have to agree with you. The Tootsie Roll was the best part of the MRE I had for lunch."

Suzanna chuckled along with me. Her next remark made it clear she hadn't picked up on the fact I was afoot. "I have them stacked in the garage if you want to load them up now."

"No. I'm just canvassing the area right now. I'll stop by later with the vehicle and pick them up when I'm out making deliveries. It's very thoughtful of you to donate yours to others in need." That was the last thing I wanted to do, but didn't see any way to avoid it. I wasn't ready to leave, having yet to broach the real reason behind my visit. If I didn't ask now, I'd have to do it later when I picked up the cases of packaged meals. "Say, did you hear about your neighbor's disappearance during the storm?"

"Of course I have. I was just questioned yesterday for the second time by the local police department. For some reason, they aren't completely convinced Mrs. Reynolds was blown off her dock by the high winds. I thought they'd already declared her dead."

"Presumed dead, more likely. However, I heard an eyewitness had reported seeing her get in a light-colored SUV-type vehicle during the lull in the storm. That's probably what prompted the police's new interest in her whereabouts." I sounded like a gossipy old lady who was talking to the patron next to her as she was getting her hair rolled in a beauty salon. "Had you heard that?"

"Yeah. It was probably the old whack job in the yellow house down the street who called it in. Not only has Mr. Barnaby spent numerous stints in the mental ward at Christus Spohn Hospital, he's also a notorious drunk. And a nasty one, at that. Barlow Barnaby keeps the tip hotline number on speed dial, because every time he gets liquored up he 'sees things' and calls them in."

Suzanna had used air quotes to highlight 'see things', making it apparent Mr. Barnaby was in the habit of having hallucinations when intoxicated. That answered one question. Suzanna was clearly not the anonymous eyewitness. I had no desire to tell her my daughter suspected her, not the "old whack job down the street". I thought it heartless of Suzanna to refer to the man in such a derogatory way.

Mental illness was a disabling disease, not something to be ridiculed, and growing older was something none of us could prevent as long as we were still breathing. Suzanna included. But it brought up a second question. If the alcoholic neighbor was prone to having imaginary figments and calling in dubious sightings, how credible was Mr. Barnaby's observation that his neighbor had gotten into someone's car that night if indeed he was the anonymous caller? It was beginning to look probable, as Barnaby had been Bruno's presumption, too.

Suzanna's statement had me once again doubting the likelihood that something nefarious had happened to Reilly Reynolds. It made more sense that the missing woman had been blown off her dock while chasing after her Maltipoo, and her body had yet to wash ashore somewhere.

Maybe, I thought, I should stop by and see if Mr. Barnaby

needed any MRE's to sustain himself until food was more readily available. If he was as elderly as Suzanna Pandero implied, he might've been unable to travel to one of the locations handing out supplies. With any luck, he'd be able to use a few cases. Because, after all, I'd need to do something with the six or seven cases I'd be picking up from Suzanna's house. I could hardly show up at my daughter's house with them. Regina had made it clear she didn't want any more MRE's, and there was nowhere in the Chartreuse Caboose to store more than a couple of boxes.

I could dump the rest, even though I hated to be so wasteful. There were mountains of rubbish and debris in front of nearly every home in town, and the piles were growing larger by the day.

I was certain the cases of MRE's would go unnoticed if I pitched them on a neighbor's pile. An added bonus to this option would be that I wouldn't have to explain to Rip or Regina how I'd ended up with them in the first place. And, with this thought in mind, my conservative nature was beaten out by my desire to keep my investigation to myself until I had something substantial to share.

I really wasn't actually pursuing an investigation at this stage. It would be more accurately described as an inquiry. I was merely analyzing the situation to determine if I thought something was amiss. The way I saw it, the victim deserved justice if her life was taken by anyone other than God himself.

ELEVEN

No one was home at the other houses within view of a vehicle that might have parked in front of the Reynolds's home during the hurricane. The houses on Key Allegro Island were primarily vacation homes, rentals, and weekend retreats. Currently, Rockport, Texas was not on anyone's list of appealing vacation spots, other than from curiosity about the storm's aftermath.

Very few of the homes were even habitable. What was once a beautiful two-story home, two or three doors up from the Reynolds, was in the process of being dozed down. It'd likely be replaced by a brand new dwelling that met the now-mandatory building codes designed to withstand category 5 hurricanes. The entire top floor had been ripped apart as if a bomb had exploded in the hall closet. I vaguely remembered Regina mentioning this home to me during a phone call and said a little prayer for its owners, praying they had good insurance to cover the cost to rebuild. Many, I knew, did not!

Saddened yet again by the devastation all around me, I was

thankful my daughter's home was still standing. I walked back to the trailer to use the restroom and drink a bottle of water to keep hydrated. It was hotter than smoldering coal, and I was sweating like a cow moose in labor.

When I noticed Regina's car was gone, I sent her a text. **Where R U?**

On my way to Beeville to get my oil changed and my tires rotated, she replied. **Both are way overdue so I thought I better get it done today.**

Don't blame you. You aren't driving right now, are you? I asked.

Of course not. I pulled over to read your text.

Good. It pays to be safe. Beeville's a long way to drive to get your vehicle serviced, I typed.

I know, but Jiffy Lube in Rockport is closed indefinitely. Corpus Christi is nearly as far away as Beeville and has more traffic to contend with, Regina's text read.

Okra. Drive safari. Just then I realized I needed to borrow Milo's dolly. **Did you lick your garage door?**

SMH. Whatever. And, no, the garage is open. Why do you ask? There was a laughing face emoji at the beginning of Regina's text. I didn't know at the time that SMH in texting lingo meant "shaking my head", but I knew using "whatever" as a single-word response was usually a way to dismiss something or someone. It wasn't until I reread my last text and saw what the auto-correct feature had done to my response that I understood the reason behind Regina's emoji. I sent one more text that began with an emoji of a laughing cat's face.

I meant to say okay, drive safely. And I wondered if your garage was locked because I need to borrow Milo's dolly to haul a box of crap from our storage compartment to the curb.

I'll be careful, was her immediate reply. A second one quickly followed. **Our garage door is open. And just so you know, I rarely ever lick it.**

I laughed at Regina's wisecrack and stuffed the cell phone into my back jeans pocket. I knew her appointment would keep her away from home for two to three hours, at least, and Rip and Milo were out helping a friend of Milo's on a time-sensitive project. Now would be a great time to collect Suzanna Pandero's unwanted cases of MRE's and then try to foist them off on the elderly fellow up the street. I chugged a full bottle of water before grabbing my keys off the kitchen counter.

"Well, that was quick!" Suzanna said when she opened her front door. Her squeaky voice reminded me of an animated character in one of the cartoons Regina watched as a child.

"Yes. I decided to begin my scheduled deliveries and resume canvassing the area later on. Picking up your cases of MRE's was the most sensible place to start."

"Can you back up to my garage? The cases are heavy."

"I already did. You told me earlier where they were stored." I smiled and turned toward the garage as she closed the door behind her. The garage was located on the ground floor of her stilt home. Along with a flight of stairs, she had an outdoor elevator that went up to the main living area on the second floor. The Moores' home had an elevator too, but I always took the stairs when given a choice.

There turned out to be nine cases of MRE's she wanted "out of her hair", as she put it. It was clear Suzanna's thoughtful donation was based more on the notion of a free trash pickup than a charitable contribution. We loaded seven of the boxes——or to be more exact, I loaded five and she loaded two.

She then led me to a rudimentary bathroom in the rear of the garage. She unlocked the lockbox on the door of the john with a digital code, which I thought was security overkill. When we stepped inside, she pointed to the last two cases, which were resting on top of a large chest freezer set into a niche in the wall. "That's the last of them."

As I began to hoist one off the lid of the freezer, Suzanna stopped me. "You know what? Maybe I should keep a couple of them. Just in case."

"Of course." My voice sounded dubious, even inside my own head. She'd appeared so anxious to be rid of them and had mentioned never wanting to eat one of the meals again. Surely she didn't want the Tootsie Rolls in them that desperately. You could buy an entire bag for a few bucks at nearly any store.

"Plus, it helps keep the lid closed on the freezer. It's an older model, probably twenty-five years old or better, so the lid doesn't seal as tightly as it used to. I wouldn't want the contents to thaw out."

"Of course not," I said. "You probably lost a lot of meat and other frozen food items already when you were without power for so many days."

"No. I have a small generator, and I hooked it up to the freezer."

"And the fridge no doubt."

"Well, no, there wasn't——"

"And a fan along with a few lights?" My remark was said in the form of a question, to which Suzanna shook her head. "Did the generator supply enough power to keep the A/C running?"

"It's just a small generator," she replied. She sounded defensive, but I'd only been trying to make polite small talk. "I didn't need any of that stuff. Like I told you before, I went to stay with my mother in Horizon City until the power, sewer, and water were restored. Percival insisted I keep the freezer running so the contents wouldn't rot."

"Makes sense. Meat is expensive these days." As I replied, Suzanna covered the two boxes on her chest freezer with an old, grease-stained bedspread that'd been wadded up and stuffed into the corner of an old tub that clearly hadn't been bathed in for years. "Looks like that spread has seen better days."

"Yep. Percival used it when working on his car."

"Looks like he needs a new one, and maybe a toolbox for Christmas," I joked as I studied the bathtub. The old tub was basically a cast iron storage box. It was full of miscellaneous household maintenance stuff like a nail gun, a ball-peen hammer, several different kinds of hand saws, a bag of rags, a bottle of Clorox bleach, and a rusty iron skillet that looked as if it'd be more useful for knocking out intruders or cheating spouses than frying up bacon. There were also a few quarts of synthetic oil and an opened, but empty, orange box that had once contained a Fram oil filter. The grimy bedspread Suzanna had draped over the freezer looked as if her estranged husband, Percival, had laid it under his vehicle when he'd changed the oil.

When I gazed at her curiously, she stumbled over an explanation. "Well, um. Percival, um, he's my ex—well, he's my soon-to-be-ex. I booted his worthless, lying butt out. All he'll be getting from me for Christmas are divorce papers."

"Oh." I wasn't sure how to respond. Suzanna appeared nervous and was repeating things she'd already told me. Her comments had nothing to do with putting the stained spread on the freezer. She clearly felt uncomfortable, as she continued. "This old rag was his, and now I want it off my garage floor and—"

"On top of your chest freezer?" I supplied when she paused.

"Well, just for now." She led me outside as if in a hurry for me to leave. Her anxious demeanor made me ache to see what was really inside her chest freezer. She did have a bone to pick with her missing neighbor, after all, if the rumors were correct about her husband having an affair with the woman. "I've been meaning to get that freezer defrosted and cleaned out. Some of the stuff in there is old and probably freezer burnt. I'll probably get on that in the next day or two."

"Oh, no!" I exclaimed, bending over at the waist in the middle of her driveway. I had experienced a slight rumbling in my belly—the kind that is often a preview of upcoming attractions of an unpleasant nature—and decided to use it to my advantage before I had to rush home to camp out in the trailer's little bathroom. I was dying to see what she was so anxious to dispose of inside that freezer. "I ate something for lunch that didn't agree with me. I think I'm going to throw up. Could I possibly use this restroom?"

"Very well," Suzanna consented, after a lengthy spell of consideration. "But I'm not certain the toilet still flushes."

"Hmm." *That's not good*, I thought. I pointed toward the stool. "There's a small plastic trashcan next to the toilet I could use. If I soil it, I will replace it with a new one."

"No need. I don't want it anyway. We'll just throw it on the pile of debris on the curb."

"Thank you," I said, before an unexpected belch erupted from somewhere down around my naval. "Pardon me, dear."

For a moment, I thought she was going to stay in the bathroom with me. Luckily, she stepped outside and closed the door before I had to ask for some privacy. Was she now going to press her ear to it while I was inside supposedly tossing my cookies?

Just in case my suspicion was correct, I tried to make some believable gagging noises as I gently lifted the bedspread off the freezer and sat it and the two cases of MRE's down on the floor as quietly as I could. I lifted up the freezer door and was shocked to find nothing but a large plastic garbage bag inside. The black bag was covered in frost as if the old freezer had not been defrosted in over two decades.

I gasped out loud in alarm. I'm not sure if it's from watching too many episodes of *Criminal Minds* on television or what, but my first instinct was that I'd just discovered the body of Reilly Reynolds. My second thought, though, was, *How can that be when the frost on top of the bag looks as if it hasn't been disturbed in years, and Reilly disappeared less than a month ago? Had the contents thawed out and then refroze once she'd hooked the generator up to the freezer? One thing's for sure. This freezer definitely needed to be defrosted and cleaned out.*

"You okay in there?" I heard from outside the door. Not wanting her to know I'd possibly uncovered the truth behind her missing neighbor, I let out a feigned puking sound. Her voice sounded genuinely concerned when she asked, "Should I come in? Maybe get you a wet rag or something?"

"No. I'm all right. I'm about done. I think it was the heat of the day that has gotten to me. Either that or that damned dried-up pop tart I ate from the MRE I had for lunch."

"Well, all right. I'm right here if you need me."

"Okay, thanks!" *Gag, belch, upchuck* noises. "I'll be out in a moment."

There was no way I could chip the ice off the frozen trash bag to get an idea of what was inside. I hadn't noticed an ice pick in the conglomeration of items in the bathtub. I took a photo of the ice-covered bag with my phone before gently closing the lid of the freezer and hoisting the cases of pre-packaged meals back on top of it. I then arranged the bedspread as best I could remember it looking before I'd taken everything off the freezer to scrutinize its contents.

Before leaving, I tried to flush the toilet. Nothing happened. There was very little water in the bottom of the toilet and when I lifted the lid off the back, I saw there was none at all in the tank.

"I didn't think it would flush." Suzanna said as she opened the bathroom door and walked inside.

"Uh." I was at a loss for words, so I merely stared at her like a deer caught in the headlights of an oncoming freight train.

"I don't know how many times I asked that no-good bast—" Her chattering came to an abrupt stop when she looked down into the toilet and saw nothing but a cup or two of water. She then glanced into the still unsoiled plastic trash can.

I shrugged and forced a smile. To explain the lack of vomit in the toilet despite all the gagging and gross noises I'd faked, I said, "Dry heaves. Don't you just hate when that happens?"

Suzanna looked at me as if I'd just told her I'd hacked up a pipe wrench and placed it in the bathtub with all the other random tools.

When she didn't reply to my dry-heaves remark, I added, "But that's not apt to last, so I'd better get going. Thank you again for the use of your facilities. You never know when a dry heave might take a bad turn, and the next thing you know you're spewing like a geyser in Yellowstone."

I walked straight through the garage without making further eye contact with the homeowner, who probably was ready to spew like a geyser herself. I don't know about other folks, but just the sound or mention of someone upchucking makes my stomach queasy as well, and it's all I can do not to join them. That might have explained the sudden green tint in Suzanna's cheeks. I know I was now feeling sick enough to my stomach to actually throw up.

Somehow, by the time I'd returned to the truck and started it, my stomach had managed to settle down a bit, and I no longer felt on the verge of an actual bathroom emergency. I decided while Rip, Regina, and Milo were away from home, I'd pay a visit to Barlow Barnaby. If he called in the tip about Reilly getting into a vehicle during the lull of the storm, I might be able to drag more information out of him. I could be pretty persuasive when I wanted to.

I'm also a pretty good judge of character. I expected to determine if the man's observation was a true sighting or merely a vision brought on by self-inflicted insanity—the kind caused by too much alcohol—if indeed he was the anonymous eyewitness. What I didn't expect was to see the body of a butt naked man when I peered through the small window in his front door. Thanks to Harvey, the ceiling had caved in, exposing a row of two-by-fours bisected by a cross beam. Tied to that wooden cross beam was a rope from which Barlow Barnaby hung by the neck.

At least this time there was no mistaking the man's condition. Unlike Jessie Garza, the contractor in charge of rebuilding the Reynolds's home, this man really was deader than a doornail. His neck was bent at an unnatural angle, his tongue lolled out of his open mouth, and his skin was a pale blue from his forehead to his toes. I tried not to look at the rest of him, lest my respite from nausea be short-lived. *Who undresses down to their birthday suit before offing themselves?* I wondered. *Even dead, I don't want anyone gawking at my nude body. If I'm ever discovered dangling from a rope, you can be certain I'll be decked out in layers. If I'm nude, call the homicide detectives, because clearly my suicide was not self-inflicted.*

I tried the front doorknob, which was locked. But I could see through the window that the sliding glass door at the rear of the kitchen was wide open. I raced around the house and ran inside. I sprinted through the kitchen and into the living room, thinking I might be able to save the man. Barlow was definitely beyond help when I examined his condition closer. He also had the gnarliest toenails I'd ever seen on a person. Good grief, had the man never heard of podiatrists or, at the very least, toenail clippers?

I ran back to the kitchen to close the back door, but it'd already been secured. I'd had difficulty with it a few moments earlier, but it must have slid shut on its own somehow. I didn't want the man to be hit with a higher electric bill than necessary, which I later realized was an illogical thought given the home-owner would never again be responsible for paying any bills.

I quickly dialed 9-1-1. I knew I had to report the man's death to the authorities. I couldn't just walk away and leave the poor guy hanging. And, while I waited for them to arrive on the scene, I had to come up with a reasonable excuse as to why I'd been peering inside his house to begin with. Rip and Regina were not going to buy some convoluted story about how and why I was trying to find someone who could use Suzanna Pandero's seven unwanted cases of MRE's. Nor would the detectives who were undoubtedly already en-route to Mr. Barnaby's home.

In the few minutes I had to think before they arrived, I also had to decide if I wanted to bring the frozen trash bag in the Panderos' chest freezer to the officer's attention. If I chose to do so, how would they react to the knowledge I'd taken it upon myself to nose around in the case of the missing Rockport citizen? Worse yet, how would Rip, a career lawman, and my husband of half-a-century, react? I wasn't sure I was up to having to explain my actions, so I decided to play it by ear. In my experience, that was not always a stellar idea.

I returned to the living room and unlocked the front door for the police officers to enter through when they showed up. I took a quick glance at Barlow's body, swinging from the ceiling like a *piñata* at a kid's birthday party. Before I could even react to the realization that my nausea had returned full force, I spewed chili mac all over the living room floor right beneath the homeowner's swinging corpse.

It probably goes without saying that it was not a pretty sight when three detectives, who had worked for my husband when he served as the county sheriff, arrived on the scene.

"Rapella?" Joe Peabody, the current sheriff of Aransas

County, asked in surprise after he walked in behind the detectives and locked eyes with me. "What are you doing here?"

I don't know if it was the heat, the nausea, or shock due to the situation I'd found myself in, but I collapsed to the floor like the ceiling had three weeks earlier.

TWELVE

W hen I opened my eyes, I was staring into the light brown peepers of my husband's. When he spoke, it sounded as if his voice was echoing from the bottom of a deep well. "Honey, are you okay? What in the world-world-world were you doing-doing-doing-doing in here-here-here-here?"

I shook my head, still too dazed to respond.

"You passed out, honey. Out of pure shock, no doubt. But you're going to be okay. Just sit here for a moment while I go get you a glass of water." After Rip got up to walk to Barlow's kitchen, I looked around and noticed the room had swelled with people, mostly first responders, and wondered how long I'd been out. It had only seemed like seconds but must have been longer.

After Rip returned with a bottle of water he'd found in the man's refrigerator, he waited for me to take several sips. The coolness of the water seemed to work. I instantly felt more refreshed and alert. But when Rip repeated his earlier question about why I was in the deceased man's home to begin with, I considered closing my eyes and pretending I'd slipped back into unconsciousness. I knew I'd just be delaying the inevitable so I gave him some half-baked version of the truth. I didn't really think he'd be interested in all the unnecessary details.

"The lady next door to Regina and Milo told me she had some cases of MRE's she thought Mr. Barnaby might need. I volunteered to haul them up here, never expecting to find the man dangling from his ceiling. The shock of finding Barlow——"

"——Barlow? You were on a first-name basis with him?"

"No, of course not. Suzanna told me his name."

"Suzanna?"

"Yes. Suzanna Pandero is Regina's next-door neighbor. She's the lady who had the extra cases of MRE's she didn't want."

Rip shook his head. "You seem to be getting awfully familiar with the neighborhood."

"Well, dear, you may not remember them, but we met most of the neighbors at Regina and Milo's Christmas block party last year." Neither the Panderos nor Barlow Barnaby had attended the party, but that was beside the point. My statement was the perfect truth, without actually saying specifically which neighbors we'd met at the get-together.

"Oh. Sure. Now I remember them." He didn't remember them. I knew it and he knew it. At the moment, however, I was content to let him believe I believed him. His desire not to look as if he was losing his memory, or worse, his mind, was going to get me off the hook.

Or so I thought.

Sheriff Peabody quickly moved everyone but the coroner and a couple of detectives outside of Barlow's house. Rip had me sit on a bench in the front yard because I still felt a bit unstable. We watched as Barlow's body was brought outside to be transported to the morgue. Before you could strike a match to a bag of doggie doo-doo on someone's porch and skedaddle, a crowd began to gather. There was something about the county coroner pulling up to the curb and hauling a body, draped in a white sheet, out of the house on a gurney that made the entire neighborhood come out of the woodwork. I know it did me when we actually lived in a neighborhood. Now we were most often camped in a crowded RV park full of retired folks, where you don't give the coroner's van a second thought. *Another one bites the dust*, being your first thought, of course.

"Is that you, Ms. Ripple?" A deep voice asked from over my shoulder. Another male voice chimed in with, "Are you all right?"

"Yes, Tony, it's me. And, yeah, I'm okay, Bruno. Just a bit dazed at the moment from the shock of discovering Mr. Barnaby's body."

"I'll bet!" Tony said before they both moved on to mingle with others in the growing group.

"Tony Torres?" Rip asked. "Bruno? Were they at the holiday block party too? How much whiskey did I drink that night?"

"Um, no, dear. Remember I asked you about knowing Tony? Well, Tony and Bruno Watts are a couple of the subcontractors working on the Reynolds's home. And, if memory serves me right, you nearly killed off a fifth of Jack Daniels that evening."

"Oh. How is Mr. Reynolds? Any news on his missing wife?"

"No, not yet. I'm beginning to think there's something suspicious behind her disappearance."

"Well, of course you do." While Rip said this with absolutely no inflection in his voice, I knew there was a heavy dose of sarcasm cleverly embedded in his five-word response.

"You would too if you'd heard the things I have in the last two days."

"How have you—" Rip began to question me but was interrupted by a woman who'd just walked up behind us.

"I saw the ambulance and decided I'd better come down and

check it out, knowing you might be here." I groaned when I recognized Suzanna's shrill voice. Once again, I considered faking another fainting spell. I was afraid she'd say something I'd have to scramble to find a way to explain. I hadn't underestimated her, either. She crouched down to speak to me face to face, and asked, "That hurricane relief organization you work for is never going to believe this, are they?"

"What is she talking about?" Rip stared at me, ignoring Suzanna.

"Don't be silly, dear. We'll discuss it later. Why don't you go say hello to Sheriff Peabody?" I pointed toward his friend, Joe. "I'm sure he'd love to see you."

Rip gave me a look that could melt glaciers in Antarctica. After he reluctantly walked away, I turned toward Suzanna. "You are right. This is just unbelievable. I certainly never expected something like this would happen when I volunteered to help storm victims. Why in the world would your neighbor go and kill himself like this after surviving the hurricane?"

Suzanna sat down, Indian-style, on the grass. "I'm no detective, but I guarantee you Barlow didn't kill himself. He was as crazy as a besotted loon, no doubt. But he never came across to me as being suicidal. My guess is that the same person who abducted Reilly Reynolds murdered Barlow. Probably heard Barlow called in to the tip hotline and was afraid he'd call in again with more incriminating information."

"Wow. You think so?" After Suzanna nodded, I asked another, more pointed question. "Why are you so convinced it was Mr. Barnaby who called in the anonymous tip?"

"Actually, I only suspected it." A rueful smile was on Suzanna's face as I studied her. It quickly morphed into one of self-satisfaction when she continued. "Now I'd bet the ranch on it."

"You own a ranch?"

"No. I just meant——"

"Oh, I get it. Figure of speech. Sorry. I'm still a little light-headed. I agree with you. This suicide looks more like a set-up to me. If so, who do you think did it?" I asked, hoping to catch her off guard. No such luck, however.

"I have my suspicions, but I'd never say them out loud," she said.

"You don't think Percival could be involved, do you?"

"No. Definitely not in Barlow's case. He might have picked up Reilly and ran off with her," Suzanna began as she looked solemnly up at the coroner's van, which was slowly pulling away from the curb with Barlow's body inside, "but he'd never do something like this."

"Why would you never voice your suspicions?" I asked.

At my puzzled expression, she replied, using air quotes once again, "I have no desire to be the next 'suicide' victim on the block."

———

I had no option but to discuss everything I'd discovered about Reilly's disappearance with Rip later that afternoon. I hoped my sensitive state would encourage him to listen to me and want to help me look into the situation. I told him I didn't really want to get Regina and Milo involved in my investigation, at this stage anyway, but would welcome his assistance. I wholeheartedly expected his response to be a big, fat, juicy, "Hell, no!"

Imagine my surprise when instead he replied, "It does sound awfully suspicious. I wonder why Joe hasn't opened up a more active investigation into her disappearance?"

"Could it be that he has a lot more on his plate right now than one missing citizen? Granted, that's a major concern, but so is putting the lives of all of Rockport's residents back on an even keel. He's probably being pulled in all directions."

"Yeah," Rip agreed. "He told me as much today when I chatted with him. Said his life is a chaotic mess right now with his own house in shambles and his kids having to be driven to Portland to attend school. Unfortunately, all of Rockport's kids are having to be absorbed by other schools in the area until their own schools can be repaired. Joe never mentioned Reilly Reynolds or the possibility her disappearance could be tied to the death of Barlow. But then, I hadn't really expected him to."

"I imagine Joe's got a lot on his mind other than just Reilly's fate. Regina's next-door neighbor, Suzanna Pandero, suspects her husband was having an affair with Reilly. She's convinced Barlow Barnaby was the anonymous tipster, but that the police didn't take it seriously because he had a habit of 'seeing things' after imbibing a little too much and then calling it in to the police." Now I was using air quotes. "She also indicated he suffered from a mental illness, but that might've been spitefulness on her part."

"Oh!" Rip exclaimed. He'd plainly had an epiphany. "*That* Barlow Barnaby. Now I know why I recognized his name. He's been calling in questionable eyewitness accounts for years. Most were pure nonsense, but on a couple of occasions, his tips led us to an arrest. One case netted Mr. Barnaby five thousand dollars in reward money. So, although we were tempted to put no effort whatsoever into following up on his tips, we were obligated to, just in case he truly did witness something and was phoning in a credible tip. As you can imagine, after he was awarded the five grand, the volume of tips he phoned in increased significantly."

"Oh, yes. I can imagine," I said. "Suzanna is convinced the same person who abducted Reilly also murdered Mr. Barnaby. She doesn't believe it was an actual suicide."

"It might not have been," Rip said. "Just between you and me, Sheriff Peabody and I discussed the preliminary findings of the medical examiner, Chuck Beatty, who was at the scene today. He seems to think there's a chance Barlow was a victim of murder. He's keeping this on the down-low for now while they do a little more investigating, so don't mention this to anyone. All right?"

"Well, okay," I said reluctantly.

"Not to the ladies in your Bunko club, or the random stranger in front of you at the grocery store."

I had to suppress a smile. Rip was always confounded by my propensity for engaging in conversation with whoever was in the checkout line behind or in front of me. "You don't even know them," he'd say. He couldn't seem to understand that every friend we had we'd spoken to for the first time somewhere, whether it was at another friend's party or the checkout line at Ace Hardware.

He went on, "Not even to Regina, Milo, Tony, or the other subcontractors next door. Got it?"

"Yes, dear. My lips are sealed. I promise." I ran an imaginary zipper across my lips, which made Rip shake his head. Rather than react to his cynicism, I asked, "What made Dr. Beatty suspect it might have been murder rather than suicide?"

"Chuck mentioned something about the direction of the fibers on the rope, suspicious ligature marks on the victim's neck, and a hematoma on his chin."

"Hematoma?"

"Bruising, as if he might have been hit in the jaw. But it could have been an injury he sustained prior to committing suicide and not related to his death. Apparently, Barlow was prone to taking bad falls. Six months ago, he broke his collar bone tripping over a loose carpet thread."

"A loose carpet thread? Good grief. And I thought I was a klutz," I said. "It doesn't sound like much to base a murder on. How about the fact he was naked?"

"Granted, that seems a little disturbing. However, Chuck wouldn't consider something non-scientific as significant proof pointing either to suicide or homicide. He's arranging to have a tox screen done to determine if the man might have been drugged before being strung up from the ceiling. Barlow was an average-sized guy, but that's a lot of weight for most people to handle, even if the victim was comatose at the time. Chuck will also perform a full autopsy."

"I'm glad they're looking into the cause of death." I nodded as I sipped on my drink. It was too steamy to sit outside in our lawn chairs, so Rip and I sat at the kitchen table in the Chartreuse Caboose enjoying the one daily highball we allowed ourselves. Our primary physician had diagnosed Rip as a borderline diabetic and warned us about the medical hazards of overindulging in alcohol. Dr. Herron had not been specific about the size of that one allotted drink each day, so my tequila sunrise and Rip's Jack and Coke were served in quart-sized Ball canning jars. I didn't want to make Rip wish he was dead by trying to help him live longer. However, I did try to cut out all other sugar from his diet and limit his carb intake. "Did Sheriff Peabody happen to mention it was Barnaby who'd called in the anonymous tip about his missing neighbor?"

"No. He is bound by confidentiality laws to not reveal the identity of an anonymous tipster. Besides, how would I have known to ask Joe about that to begin with?" Rip replied with a look I recognized. It was the look of someone who has been left out in the cold during an important discussion. I just smiled at him lovingly. I currently had him on my side of the fence. I didn't want him to crawl back over to the opposite side by scolding him for not paying attention to what was discussed at the dinner table. At the time of the discussion with Regina, Rip had been totally engrossed in his savory filet. Even though he'd participated in the conversation, he clearly hadn't taken it all in. I was surprised when he asked, "Would you like me to stop by the police department tomorrow and speak with Joe about it?"

"I don't think so. Not yet, anyway. I don't want him to think we're meddling in a police matter. At least not until we have more evidence. Maybe we should do a little more snooping on our own before we bring the sheriff into it."

"Yeah. You're probably right. We'll discuss our strategy in the morning. I invited Reggie and Milo over for a drink, and I'd rather not bring them into it yet either."

Once again, I was so shocked at Rip's response, I almost choked on my cocktail. I sputtered like a fountain running out of water for nearly five minutes. I'd assured Rip my lips were sealed about the medical examiner's conclusion that the apparent suicide was not so apparent after all. I'd soon make it clear they weren't sealed tightly enough. I could already feel the imaginary zipper giving way. I'd have had to super-glue my lips together again in order to keep *that* promise.

THIRTEEN

"Joe Peabody wants to see you in his office this morning as soon as you get around." The sound of Rip's voice the following morning brought me from a dead sleep to full consciousness in a split second. His statement was more effective at being an instantaneous eye-opener than a phone call at two-thirty in the morning when you just know bad news is on the other end of the line.

Why would the county sheriff want to see me? I wondered. *To tell me to keep my nose out of police business? To ask me if I had an alibi for the time Barlow Barnaby died? To arrest me for impersonating a hurricane relief volunteer?*

"Say what? Why ever for?" I asked with a distinct catch in my voice. I'd convinced myself I didn't really want to hear the answer. I'd never expected to be delighted by Rip's response.

"He wants to question you further about what you witnessed at the neighbor's house yesterday. Due to your frazzled state at the time, they didn't want to traumatize you any more than you already appeared to be. Joe thinks you might have information that can help them nail down the identity of the perp."

"The perp?"

"Perp stands for perpetrator. As you're probably aware, a perpetrator is——"

"I know what perp means!" I exclaimed. "This isn't my first murder investigation, you know. I meant I was surprised they're investigating his death as a murder now."

"Joe wants to speak to you about your involvement in the investigation into Reilly's disappearance, as well."

"Oh. He does, does he?" *Crap! I knew it was too good to be true.* "How does he even know about my interest in the case?"

"I told him."

"Oh. Of course." *Dang it! I knew I should've kept my fly trap shut.* I should have waited until I had more evidence to share with Rip that pointed toward a crime, as opposed to an accident. Now I was in a position of having to justify my obsession with finding out what really happened to the missing lady, and if Barlow's death had anything to do with it. I never liked having to justify anything, particularly my actions.

"And, to be clear, they're investigating Barlow's death as a possible homicide even though they've made no final determination on his COD yet. COD stands for——"

I held my hand up to stop him. "I know what COD stands for too, Rip. Cause of death. Now, when does the sheriff want to speak to me?"

"As soon as you get up and around."

As I got dressed, I thought back to the first time I'd met Reilly at the Moores' block party. She'd been just as warm and friendly as could be. I recalled her complimenting the six-bean salad I'd contributed to the buffet table and asking me to email her the recipe. She'd also told me she loved my "ugly Christmas sweater" and said red was definitely my color because I just glowed that evening. I didn't have the heart to tell her I had worn the sweater because I thought the sewn-on bells, sequins, and lights were delightful and made for a beautiful holiday ensemble along with my green suede slacks. Come to think of it, the fact I was glowing that night might have had something to do with the string of LED lights outlining the sleigh on my sweater and lighting up Rudolph's nose. When I'd mentioned Reilly's caustic remark to Regina after the guests had all departed, my daughter had replied, "Of course it's an ugly sweater. That's what's so cool about it."

Despite being offended by both Regina and Reilly's ugly sweater remarks, I'd felt an instant fondness for Regina's neighbor. A backhanded compliment was still a compliment, which was better than an outright insult any day of the week. Now I wanted justice for Reilly—if justice was warranted, that is.

When Rip first said the sheriff wanted to question me, I'd hoped to use the opportunity to wheedle as much information about Reilly's disappearance out of the sheriff as I could. I hoped to ask questions like: had they considered the missing woman might not be a casualty of the hurricane; had they questioned her husband, Walker; and did they happen to know a buxomly blond woman in town who went by the initials JJ? Instead, it now looked like I was going to be told to back off, butt out, and get back to baking cookies and dusting cobwebs off the ceiling.

Cobweb dusting and cookie baking were actually tasks I planned to do as soon as possible. The cobwebs had been beckoning for weeks and I'd successfully managed to ignore them until Regina referred to them as disgustingly creepy and said she was beginning to feel like Wednesday Addams, Gomez and Morticia's daughter. I had replied jokingly that I was decorating early for Halloween.

More urgently, I wanted to bake more cookies as an excuse to speak with Tony and Bruno again, even if I wouldn't be taking any snacks over for Bruno. I'd have to think of a different excuse to strike up another conversation with him since sugar-free cookies were no longer an option. Perhaps I could take him some of the beef jerky or paper-shell pecans Rip had picked up at a roadside market in the Texas hill country on the trip down to Rockport. I wanted to determine what prompted the sheetrock specialist and the demolition expert to walk up to the Barnaby house the previous afternoon.

Granted, when the county coroner pulls up in front of a neighbor's house, such as an elderly lady who shook her broom at the kids across the street every time they played in their own yard and turned her porch light on every single night of the year except Halloween, you might be tempted to walk over and investigate the situation. Your interest might be piqued out of morbid curiosity, if nothing else. But if you are a subcontractor who has had no interaction with anyone else in the neighborhood, would you really walk into the home of the recently deceased, or in this case, inject yourself into the crime scene? I didn't think so.

"You about ready?" Rip hollered from the living room.

"As soon as I grab a bite for breakfast, you can take me down to the sheriff's department. To be perfectly honest with you, I don't know if I will be of any help to their investigation. I don't know any more about what happened to Mr. Barnaby than they do."

"You might have observed more than you think. One small little detail you noticed that barely registered with you at the time could turn out to be the clue that blows the case wide open."

"I truly don't believe I witnessed anything of significance. I was too overwhelmed by the sight of the man hanging by a rope in his own living room."

"Don't worry, honey. It'll be okay." Rip had no trouble picking up the apprehension in my voice. "I'll be with you."

"Oh, that's a big relief. I was afraid I'd—"

"Well, other than when they're questioning you in the interrogation room."

Interrogation room? The next thing I remember, Rip was patting my cheek and looking into my eyes with concern. "Rapella, dear, it's not like you to pass out the way you've done the last two days. I want you to make an appointment with a cardiologist in Corpus so you can get a complete cardio assessment. I wish Dr. Murillo lived in south Texas instead of Seattle."

Rip had recently undergone a triple bypass immediately following an Alaskan cruise we'd taken to celebrate our golden wedding anniversary. The procedure had been done in a cardiac care center in Seattle. I didn't really believe there was anything amiss with my heart, but rather anxiety was causing my fainting spells. But I didn't want to argue with Rip about my health. When he put his foot down about my well-being, there was no swaying him.

Thinking about the grilling I might experience in the sheriff department's interrogation room did nothing to quell my anxiety. I almost preferred to spend the morning hooked up to an electro-cardiogram machine.

"Good morning, Mrs. Ripple. I'm Detective Chad Morris, and I'll be asking you some questions this morning. Let's start with where you were between two and three yesterday morning."

"Asleep, next to my husband."

"Can anyone verify that?"

"Duh." *What a stupid question, rookie!* I wanted to shout. "My husband, Rip, can confirm my whereabouts. You may also know him as Sheriff Peabody's predecessor. Ask him, if you don't believe me." I was trying to hide my irritation, but not succeeding very well.

"That won't be necessary. Where were you at twelve-fifteen yesterday afternoon?" The young detective leaned forward in his chair and stared into my eyes from mere inches away. It was an attempt to intimidate me, I'm certain.

"You know exactly where I was. I was at the home of Barlow Barnaby." I squirmed in my chair. The interrogation room was even scarier than I'd imagined, as I knew multiple individuals were observing my every move and hanging on my every word from the other side of the one-way mirror.

"Were you alone?"

"Of course, I was. Other than the dead homeowner, that is."

"Can you explain why you were at Mr. Barnaby's house?" The detective with heavily freckled cheeks looked as if he were a sophomore in high school. I wanted to wash his mouth out with turpentine for using such a disrespectful tone.

"I explained to Sheriff Peabody why I was there." I was indignant and couldn't help feeling as though I was being treated like a suspect.

"Mrs. Ripple, it'd be a lot easier for you if you just answered the questions without responding in such a defensive manner," Detective Morris said.

"How could I not react defensively? I feel like I'm being accused of killing the man when nothing could be further from the truth. I was actually there to be of assistance to him if he was short on food supplies. Am I being badgered into confessing to a crime I didn't commit? Do I need to have a lawyer present?"

"I don't know. Do you?"

Smart-ass kid! I almost spat out but stopped myself just in time. Instead, I refused to respond.

"Do you?" he repeated. "It appears you are intentionally evading my questions. Why is that, ma'am? Do you have something to hide?"

At his last rude question, I stood up and faced the one-way mirror. "Rip? Sheriff Peabody? Whoever's on the other side of this mirror needs to know I'm not saying another word until I've retained an attorney."

I'd barely gotten the last word out when the door opened. Sheriff Peabody chastised Detective Morris for his antagonizing tone. He then put a hand on each of my shoulders. "Relax, Rapella. No one's accusing you of anything. We know damn well you had nothing to do with that man's death."

He glared at the detective for a moment before continuing. "We're just trying to get all of the facts on record. We thought you might have seen something odd, or something no one else noticed. We're just looking for something to help us determine who might have committed this crime, if indeed a crime was committed. Whether or not Mr. Barnaby's death was actually a suicide remains undetermined at this time. An autopsy is being performed by the medical examiner as we speak. If it turns out Chuck's findings indicate it wasn't a suicide, we want to be on top of the case."

"I understand that, but——"

"I'll take over from here, Detective Morris." After sending the rookie detective away, Sheriff Peabody turned back to me. "You seem to have a knack at this kind of thing, you know. No one has forgotten how helpful you were in finding the truth behind Cooper Claypool's death last year. I'm sure you, as much as anyone, want to see Mr. Barnaby's killer brought to justice if his death turns out to be a homicide. We're just hoping you'll join us in seeing this case get solved."

"Really?" I'm sure my expression was akin to that of the proverbial cat who swallowed the canary—whole and with great gusto—and I tried to contain the smugness that was enveloping me like a cloud of Saharan dust. "You want my help?"

"Well, um, yeah. Sort of," the sheriff muttered. He appeared to be having second thoughts. "Maybe not officially, but anything you can remember would sure be helpful."

I wanted to hawk up the aforementioned canary and spit it in his face. I felt my smugness vanish like the Statue of Liberty at one of David Copperfield's magic shows. The sheriff didn't actually want me to assist in the investigation. He just wanted me to calm down, tell them everything I could remember and then step back and let them use the information I'd provided to solve the case and then take all the credit. Even though I knew that's the way the case should proceed, the idea of being patronized by the lawman was aggravating, much like a piece of gravel stuck in my craw. I decided then and there I'd limit the information I provided them. I was about to develop an acute case of temporary and self-induced amnesia.

Once I was back home, I was determined to spend the day going over and over every little detail I could recall—from the moment I first spoke to Suzanna Pandero about the victim until the first responders arrived on the scene. Perhaps I really would happen upon some minute detail that could break the case wide open. And then I'd use it to try and solve the case myself. How *dare* they patronize me! I'd show them, by gosh!

"I have to say, dear, you didn't recall very much about what happened yesterday. I think Joe was a little disappointed you didn't have more information to offer," Rip said as he drove us back to the island.

"Yeah, I sensed as much. I'm sorry I didn't have more to share with Joe and that rude rookie. Perhaps there really is something wrong with my heart, and I wasn't getting enough oxygen to my brain yesterday while I was at, um…well, you know, the victim's house. I can't seem to recall his name at the moment." I decided to take a page out of Rip's book about not remembering names. Maybe it'd support my claim of oxygen deprivation.

Rip glanced at me with an odd expression. I couldn't tell if it was one of disbelief or exasperation. "His name was Barney Barbeque."

"Barney Barbeque? That's preposterous."

"Oh, yeah. My mistake. I'm hungry and we just passed Mac's Pit Barbeque. I meant Barlow." I was greatly impressed for a moment, until Rip continued. "Barney Barlow."

He'd gotten the Barlow part right, even though it wasn't actually the man's surname. I just shook my head, totally disgusted. Rip looked over at me and started to chuckle.

"I was just joshing you, Rapella. I know the deceased man's name is Barlow Barnaby. It's just that you seem so uptight, I thought a little levity might help you relax a little. One way or another, I'm certain they'll get to the bottom of both Barlow's and Reilly Reynolds's deaths. I don't want to see you drive yourself nuts trying to solve these cases yourself. It's not your responsibility to do so."

"It'd be a short drive." Even as I'd replied in jest, I thought back to the discussion I'd had with Suzanna where I'd described myself as being full-blown bat-crap crazy. I was starting to wonder if perhaps the description was more accurate than I'd thought.

FOURTEEN

I woke up in a cold sweat in the wee hours of the morning. After I used the restroom, because that's what older people habitually do in the middle of the night, I tiptoed out of the bedroom so as not to wake my husband. The tiptoeing was probably unnecessary, as it would've been difficult to hear a heavy metal band jamming in the living room over his snoring.

The thought that had awakened me from a dead sleep was the memory of something odd I'd seen when I'd peered through the window on Mr. Barnaby's front porch. Obviously, the first thing I'd noticed was the man's body hanging from a rope wrapped around the ceiling joist. Immediately I'd tried the front door, only to find it locked. I'd peered through the window again to make sure my mind wasn't playing tricks on me, and discovered it wasn't. I noticed then that the sliding glass door in the kitchen was wide open, as if someone had left the house in a hurry. Curtains, sucked outside by a slight breeze, were flapping. I'd rushed around the back of the house to enter the premises.

I now realized, if there was an intruder—besides me, of course—he or she couldn't have left long before I'd arrived. It'd been quite hot in the mid-afternoon sun—close to ninety degrees, I'd say—and terribly humid. Although it hadn't occurred to me at the time, I remember feeling relief from the coolness inside when I'd stepped into the living room. Had the door been open for very long, the temperature in the room would have been noticeably warmer, and the air conditioning unit would have been running, which it wasn't.

The only reason I remember the a/c unit wasn't running was that I could distinctly hear a cuckoo clock marking the hour in the kitchen as I stood outside on the back deck, which would have been difficult had the a/c unit next to the deck been running. I stepped inside and briefly tried to get the sliding glass door to close. When the heavy glass door didn't slide easily, I told myself I'd force it closed later after I checked to see if Mr. Barnaby still had a pulse. As it turned out, I couldn't reach him to check for one and thought he appeared beyond reviving. Anyhow, I'd ended up calling 9-1-1, and the rest is history.

Did I tell the police about the back door? I wondered. *Did I mention it was open when I got there, but closed by someone other than myself by the time the first responders arrived? I don't think so.*

When Joe Peabody had asked me in the interrogation room how I'd entered the victim's home, I'd simply replied that I went through the door, which was unlocked. No lie there. Evasive, perhaps, but the absolute truth. I *had* gone through the unlocked door. Just not the *front* door. The sheriff probably assumed the front door was already unlocked when I arrived on the scene when in reality it was I who unlocked it after calling 9-1-1.

The important factor about my recollection is that before the first responders had arrived, I'd gone back into the kitchen to close the sliding door only to find it already closed. Now that I was thinking more clearer, I realized there was no way it could have shut on its own. The salty air had no doubt caused the door track to rust, making the door difficult to slide. Living on the coast for many years had taught me that even I would begin to rust if I didn't keep moving.

The door having been closed by the time the detectives arrived told me one thing: Mr. Barnaby had been killed shortly before I arrived and the killer had probably still been inside the victim's home when I'd entered through the back door. After I walked into the living room to check on Mr. Barnaby's condition, the perpetrator had apparently exited through the back door and closed it out of habit. I also recalled the pantry door had been ajar when I'd first entered the home and closed when I'd returned to the kitchen. It seemed likely the killer had hidden in the pantry until he could exit the house unobserved.

The mere notion the killer was in the house at the same time I was, possibly only a few feet away at some point, nearly made me pass out again. The hair on the back of my neck stood on end when I realized he might have ended my life right then and there, to eliminate the possibility I'd seen his face through the front window and would later be able to identify him.

In that scenario, I'd have been a raving lunatic to have seen the hanging corpse and then the murderer and still been stupid enough to enter the house. But the killer was certainly in a frazzled state of mind, as well, having just murdered someone and staged his body to look like a suicide victim. He surely wouldn't have been thinking clearly at that stage in the game. In the end, he'd apparently decided his best course of action was to flee the scene and hope I never had any clue I wasn't alone in the house the entire time. Not including Barlow Barnaby, naturally, who wasn't going to be telling any tales out of school any time soon.

I don't know why I felt so strongly that Barnaby was a victim of homicide rather than a suicide, but the fact he was naked had something to do with it. An elderly man in his eighties, who looked as if his pale white skin needed to be ironed, was not your typical exhibitionist, especially when about to hang himself in the middle of his living room. Also, the chances of two unexpected deaths on the same small street in one month didn't sit well with me. I wasn't one to believe in coincidences.

I knew I'd never get back to sleep, so I curled up on the couch with my Kindle and engrossed myself in *Double Threat in Ripley Grove*. It was a page-turner kind of mystery by a new author named Shirley Worley, and it kept me absorbed until Rip got up several hours later.

As I placed a bowl of steel-cut oatmeal in front of him, I casually remarked, "I've been trying to remember exactly what I witnessed yesterday and am coming up with very little so far. I do kind of recall the medical examiner sticking a thermometer into Barnaby's abdomen. In fact, that might have been what caused me to pass out."

"No. Chuck checked the temperature of Barnaby's liver quite a while after you regained consciousness. That's how they determine the approximate time of death."

"Oh, really?" Once again Rip was explaining things to me I already knew, but I let him think he was teaching me something new. I was hoping to use my feigned ignorance of the process to my advantage. "How does the liver temperature relate to the time of a person's death?"

"Well, it's not actually the temperature of the liver, *per se*. The liver can give you the most accurate core temperature of a body, however. It's more accurate, and in my opinion, less…well, icky, than taking a rectal temperature, which is an alternative method."

"That *is* icky. I recall the vet having to take Dolly's temperature that way a few years ago. Dolly wasn't too excited about it either, if I remember right."

"Who would be? Yikes!" Rip gave me a look of feigned horror, stroked Dolly in a belated show of sympathy and continued with his explanation. "Assuming the deceased's body temperature was about 98.6 before he died, they can figure how long he'd been dead by how cool the body temp is at the time it's checked. Chuck Beatty once told me the body temperature drops something like 1.5 degrees Celsius per hour, until it reaches ambient temperature."

"Ambient temperature? What's that?"

"It's equal to the temperature of the environment around the body. Rigor mortis is also an effective measuring stick, although not as accurate, because it generally doesn't begin to occur for roughly two hours after death and can last from twenty to thirty hours." Rip had a fairly extensive knowledge of things like this from his lifelong career in law enforcement, yet he had rarely brought his work home with him.

"So, am I correct in assuming rigor mortis had not begun to set in yet when Chuck was at the crime scene yesterday?" I was fishing for an answer to act as a confirmation of my earlier supposition that Barnaby had been murdered just moments before I'd arrived, and the killer had departed through the back door soon after I'd entered through the same door. My husband would not be pleased to know I'd inadvertently placed myself in such a perilous position. I wasn't in the mood for a lecture about how I was getting as bad as our friend, Lexie Starr, when it came to reckless behavior, so I wanted to keep the information to myself. Lexie had a bad habit of nearly getting herself killed every time she dabbled in a murder case, and I'd experienced some close calls myself. In fact, we'd almost been killed together in a swimming pool in Wyoming a little over a year prior along with her daughter, Wendy.

"What makes you think rigor mortis hadn't set in yet when Chuck examined the body?" Rip looked puzzled as he responded to my question with one of his own.

"Well, it's just that it didn't look as if Mr. Barnaby had been dead long. That's all. Not that I had time—or the desire—to scrutinize his naked corpse before calling 9-1-1 and unlocking the front door for the EMT's to enter the house. It's just that I recall him looking as if he had taken his final breath only moments earlier."

"When Jim called me this morning, he said Barlow had been dead for nearly ten hours. Chuck estimated Barlow was killed between two and three yesterday morning."

"Really?" I was surprised by Rip's remark, but it explained why the brash young detective has asked about my whereabouts during the same time frame. "Barlow's body looked pretty fresh, considering how long he'd been dead. Is that method of measuring time-of-death a pretty accurate science?"

"Yes. Within an hour, I'd guess."

"Oh." I tried not to look as if the news I'd just heard had blown my earlier notion plumb out of the water. The idea the killer was in the house when I arrived now seemed implausible.

Or was it? I asked myself. *Could the perpetrator have returned to the scene of the crime hours after murdering his victim? That's not an uncommon practice among killers, I've heard. Either way,* someone *was in the house with me at the same time I was in the living room checking on Barlow's condition.*

FIFTEEN

I recognized Jessie Garza when I rounded the back corner of the Reynolds's house. He and an extremely tall man I didn't recognize were standing side-by-side on the back patio, which consisted of recently cured concrete and a wood-and-rope railing around its perimeter. A portable concrete mixer stood nearby. The two men stood rigidly with their hands on their hips as they stared at the long pier extending out into Little Bay. The small bay, referred to as the "ski basin," was just off the much larger Aransas Bay.

The guys appeared to have been having a tense, if not contentious, discussion when I called out a greeting. Although I hadn't been able to make out their words, their voices had been loud and had a harsh tenor to them. They spun around at the sound of my voice and their angry expressions quickly changed into ones of polite indifference at the sight of me approaching them.

Without speaking, I held out a bag with Jessie's name written on the plastic in permanent marker.

"Oatmeal raisin?" Jessie asked, studying the contents of the bag. His friendliness seemed forced when he added, "My absolute favorite."

"Good to know. I also brought a bag of snickerdoodles for Tony. Bruno declined the sugar-free cookies I made for him before because they had a tendency to get his colon rolling, if you know what I mean. I brought him a bag of beef jerky we picked up at a roadside market in Burnet instead." I then turned toward the other man and apologized. "I'm sorry. I didn't know there'd be another worker here or I'd have brought another bag of cookies or jerky. Perhaps, Jessie will share his with you."

Jessie looked at me as if I'd just asked him to donate one of his kidneys to the guy. "Share? Did you say *share?*"

"Well, um...I guess I could go bake another batch of—"

"I'm just yanking your chain, ma'am. Of course, I'll share my cookies with Walker." Jessie opened the bag and let Walker reach in and select his own cookie. The second man studied the contents of the bag for several long moments before choosing a cookie, as if skeptical of my motives. I almost felt obligated to assure him I hadn't added any glass shards to the batter.

If nothing else, I now knew the second man was Walker Reynolds, owner of the property we stood on. I hadn't recognized him because his appearance had changed so much in the nine months or thereabouts since I'd last seen him at the block party in December. His hair was now much longer and somewhat unkempt, and like my wavy mop of hair, contained more gray than brown. His eyes appeared rheumy and a bit sunken in their sockets, and his entire frame had lost much of its cushion. Walker looked as if he'd lost at least twenty pounds since the holidays. A naturally slender man, he hadn't had an extra twenty to lose. And although it was late summer, his skin was pale, not deeply tanned as it'd been the previous December. Rather than standing straight, with proper posture, like Jessie, Walker's shoulders were hunched over as if the weight of the world rested on them. The forty-something-year-old guy now appeared to be decades older than he actually was.

Stress, no doubt, I thought. *I hate to think what I'd look like if Rip had gone missing nearly a month ago. But could a guy, no matter what degree of grief he'd been suffering, change so drastically in less than a month? Maybe he's been under a great deal of pressure for some time, well before the hurricane struck in late August.*

Had I butted in as the two men were discussing the disappearance of Walker's wife? Or perhaps the status of his home rebuilding project? Walker hadn't seemed happy about something when I'd first walked onto his property and found him arguing with Jessie behind his house.

Perhaps he was letting his impatience over the time the rebuilding was taking get to him because of his concern for his wife. Supply and demand were adversely affecting every reconstruction job in the area, and I was sure this one was no exception. Jessie had obviously hand-mixed a great deal of concrete to pour the back patio himself because of a shortage of flatwork contractors and/or open and operating concrete plants. That situation would only get worse as more rebuilding began to take place. The vast majority of rebuilding projects hadn't even commenced, due to lack of funds and slow responses from insurance companies. Fortunately, many of the houses on Key Allegro were second homes, and the rebuilding of them was not as urgent.

I felt for the man as I studied the signs of strain on his face: black circles under his eyes, crinkles around his mouth that seemed to be created by a permanent frown, and an overall pastiness to his complexion. Anyone would be rattled if their spouse had suddenly vanished, and they had no idea if he or she was dead or alive. Knowing a number of his friends and neighbors might secretly question his involvement in his wife's disappearance would trouble him, as well. After all, the spouse was always the number-one suspect in the event of a mysterious homicide or disappearance.

I glanced down the wooden walkway the men were standing by, which extended out into the bay. The last time Walker had claimed to see Reilly was when she'd chased their little Maltipoo down toward this very pier during the storm. Just looking at it now would've traumatized me had it been the last view I'd had of my beloved spouse, as was supposedly the case with Walker. He, however, seemed unmoved by the view.

"You're Walker Reynolds?" I asked rhetorically. "I'm sorry I didn't recognize you. I am Rapella Ripple, Regina Moore's mother."

"Oh, I'm sorry," Jessie said. "I assumed you two were already acquainted or I'd have introduced you."

"We met at the holiday block party at my daughter's house last winter, but I doubt Walker remembers me from that, just like I didn't recognize him. We barely crossed paths that night, with so many people there and so much activity going on."

"Yeah, and I guess I did have a little too much to drink that evening," Walker said. His face actually flushed as he spoke. "I do remember your husband, though. He and I talked about the gang problem beginning to show its ugly head in parts of Aransas County."

"Sadly that's true of many counties in the country. I didn't mean to infer you were intoxicated that night. I think most every-body was," I explained. "It's just that I spent more time speaking with Reilly than you at the party. Speaking of which, I am so sorry to hear about your lovely wife. I sure hope she shows up safe and sound soon."

"Yeah, me too," he agreed. His somber expression remained unchanged. "But I'm beginning to think that's highly unlikely. I don't know how she could still be alive. If she was, she'd have come back home, or at least contacted someone by this time. The only possible explanation is that after she was blown off the pier while trying to retrieve our dog, she drowned and was washed out to sea."

"Wouldn't her body have resurfaced and washed ashore somewhere by now?" I asked gently. I didn't want to further upset him. I noticed as we conversed, Jessie remained silent, his eyes shifting back and forth between Walker and me as if he were watching a tennis match.

"You'd have thought so," he replied. "But maybe it got wedged up under something, maybe even debris from the storm. There's an unbelievable amount of debris in the bays and canals right now. My friend tried to get his boat out of the water to be repaired, and as he was motoring up the canal, he hit a Trane."

"How in the world did he hit a train in the water?" I asked, flabbergasted at the man's remark.

"Not a locomotive train. It's T-r-a-n-e. A Trane air conditioning unit that blew off the roof of one of the Key Allegro condos. It gouged a hole in his hull and then the condenser coils broke loose and got tangled up in his stainless steel prop. It really jacked up his Blue Wave boat."

"I can only imagine. How badly traumatized was Scrappy when he came back home? Is he doing okay now?"

"Seems to be fine. He's staying with Reilly's sister down in the valley."

"Mission, Texas, isn't it?" I asked.

"Yes. How did you know?" I'd like to say Walker's expression was one of surprise, but it was actually more a look of distrust. With his general contractor glaring at me intensely, clearly on tenterhooks as he awaited my response, I knew I couldn't tell Walker it was Jessie with whom I'd discussed Walker's personal life. I decided a white lie was in order.

"My daughter told me. Naturally, she and Milo are very upset about Reilly's disappearance, as they've always been very fond of you both."

"Oh." Walker still appeared dubious, while Jessie looked relieved. Maybe Walker and his wife had never been as close to the Moores as I'd thought. Pardon me if this sounds a bit biased, but Regina was as friendly as a gal could be, whereas Milo could rub someone the wrong way on occasion. He'd rubbed both Rip and me the wrong way several times, but we'd let it slide so as not to upset our daughter. She considered Milo her soul mate, and who were we to argue the point?

When, at eighteen years old, I'd told my pappy I'd met the love of my life and was going to marry him, he had snickered and replied, "No, you aren't. Keep looking. No way I'm going let my little girl marry that good-for-nothing punk." When I'd then told him I was pregnant with that good-for-nothing punk's baby, he could not have gotten us legally hitched fast enough. It was what they used to refer to as a "shotgun wedding". To no one's surprise, when Pappy died, he loved Rip as if he'd given birth to him himself. His first granddaughter, Regina, was the apple of his eye from the day she entered the world.

After a prolonged silence I'd spent mentally reminiscing about my father, I told Walker, "Rip and I are here to help Milo and Regina out as much as we can. Rockport is our hometown, you see, but my husband and I became full-time RVers after he retired from his position as Aransas County Sheriff. We just happened to be visiting at the time of last year's holiday party."

"That's nice."

When the silence grew more uncomfortable this time, I decided I'd learned all I was going to learn from Mr. Reynolds. At that point in time, anyway. I bade farewell to the two men and asked, "Mind if I give this bag of cookies to Tony?"

"I can give Tony his bag when he gets here," Jessie offered politely. "He's due here in about half an hour, most likely. At least someone's showing up to work today. Bruno sent me a text saying he won't be around for a few days."

Would it seem odd if I asked why? I wondered. *Yes, it definitely would.* But I asked anyway. Being considered odd had never stopped me before, and it didn't on that day either.

"He requested some 'personal time'," was Jessie's ambiguous response to my nosy query. He'd also used air quotes, making it clear he was irked about the subcontractor's request and dubious about why Bruno needed to take time off work. Even though it was his house that was being rebuilt, Walker appeared less angry about Bruno's absence than Jessie.

I knew asking Walker's general contractor to elaborate would seem more than merely odd. It'd seem as if I was probing. I didn't want to scare away one of my main sources of information. "Sorry your sheetrock guy isn't showing up today, guys, but I do feel bad for Bruno, being diabetic and all. Don't work too hard. See you later."

"Okie-dokie," was Jessie's reply.

"Not if I see you first," was Walker's. I knew it was a common response to the phrase "I'll see you later", but I wasn't entirely certain he'd been teasing. His tone had been unreadable, and a person's tone of voice was something I'm usually pretty adept at reading. Nevertheless, I gave an amicable wave as I walked away. I was glad to have finally met Reilly's husband, but disappointed I hadn't been able to dredge any beneficial information out of him or Mr. Garza.

I'd have to speak with Milo, and Regina, too, I supposed, to see if I could determine why Walker Reynolds's physical appearance had changed so much in such a short amount of time. If he'd been having an affair with the woman named JJ, had the anxiety of sneaking around behind his new wife's back caused his hair to change color and his weight to decline? Could he have been suffering from some kind of medical issue, or instead, experiencing money problems? Could a cash shortage, rather than concrete or contractor shortage, be why Jessie had hand-mixed and single-handedly poured and finished the approximate fifteen-by-twenty-foot back patio? Under any circumstances, that was an extremely large project for one man to tackle alone, and one that had been undertaken purely on a whim. It had been Jessie's idea and Walker had agreed to his suggestion, according to Bruno.

And, speaking of Bruno, what was up with him? What kind of personal matters could he be dealing with today that weren't present yesterday when he and Tony had shown up at the crime scene within minutes of the three detectives who were the first to arrive following my 9-1-1 call? What had suddenly occurred since then that was so pressing Bruno was unable to come to work? I sincerely hoped the personal time he deemed necessary had nothing to do with the conversation I'd had with him about his former fiancé getting hitched to the guy who stole her from him. There was next to nothing positive that might result from a jealous, jilted lover trying to even a score.

It seemed as if my cookie delivery had created more questions than it'd answered. I was growing more intrigued with each passing moment, and more determined than ever to get to the truth behind the missing neighbor's disappearance. Perhaps I needed to concoct another reason to visit Suzanna Pandero.

Hmm…I wonder if she's heard her belief that Barlow's death was a homicide has been declared by the medical examiner to be a distinct possibility? I know I promised Rip I wouldn't mention it to anyone, but since Suzanna already believes murder to be the case, what difference would it make if I let her know her suspicions had been verified? The gruesome discovery of Barlow Barnaby hanging, sans clothing, from a cross beam in his own living room is just the kind of gossip most women want to chitchat about.

"Hello again, Suzanna!" I said cheerfully as she opened her front door just enough to peer out through the gap. I got the sense she was already trying to conjure up an excuse why she couldn't visit with me: a doctor's appointment in Corpus; bacon frying on the stove; food poisoning from a bad mussel that had her on the john every couple of minutes; or even not wanting to miss *Final Jeopardy*, which was about to air any second. Before she could spit her chosen excuse out, I said, "Did you hear they've determined your neighbor's death might actually have been a homicide?"

"Oh, my God!" It's probably a good thing Suzanna *didn't* have food poisoning or she'd likely have soiled her panties right then. The look on her face was one of pure shock. She grabbed my arm and nearly yanked me into her home before slamming the door shut. "Are you fricking serious?"

"Yes. Very."

"You're telling me the body's been found?"

I was surprised by how alarmed the woman appeared that her last question didn't register with me. Instead of replying to it, I began to ramble. "I was present when the medical examiner, Dr. Beatty, did the preliminary examination of the body. Actually, my husband told me what he said because I was being examined by one of the EMT's who'd just arrived on the scene. As you know, I was the one who discovered the body and ended up passing out, and you can just imagine——"

"What did he say?" Suzanna asked impatiently.

"Who?"

"The medical examiner!" She spat out, almost angrily.

"Oh, well," I began, now a little perturbed myself, "he said he found several indications that the death was a homicide and not suicide, as first suspected."

"Huh?" Suzanna appeared stunned. "Suicide? What are you talking about?"

"Well, naturally, that was the most obvious cause of death at first sight. Why on earth would they suspect anything else when the body was hanging from a rope?"

"Hanging from a rope?" Suzanna plunked herself down in a recliner as if her legs would no longer support her. I followed suit, setting down in the matching recliner across from her. I watched as she took a deep sigh of relief; the kind you take when you realize the furry blob your cat walked into the kitchen with was a cat toy rather than a real rat. I listened as Suzanna repeated herself. "Hanging from a rope? You're talking about Barlow, right?"

"Oh, dear!" I exclaimed. "I can see why you were confused. You thought I was talking about Reilly."

Suzanna nodded and then flashed me the most inappropriate smile I'd ever seen. I'd have thought my distressing news deserved a look of sadness, or an expression of alarm, not a delighted grin as though she'd just won a thousand bucks on a scratch-off ticket she'd purchased at the local gas station. When she was finally able to stop smiling and feign concern for her late neighbor, she asked, "I spent most of yesterday in Corpus. I hadn't heard what the coroner determined. Sorry, I was alarmed when I thought you meant they'd found Reilly's body."

No shit? I wanted to reply. *I think that pretty much goes without saying. I'm surprised your eyeballs didn't pop out of their sockets and land in the potpourri basket on your coffee table.* Instead I stayed silent and waited for Suzanna to speak again, which she did after an extremely long and awkward silence.

"Do they have any idea who might have killed him?"

"No. But I heard they're pretty certain it's the same individual who abducted Reilly." I'd heard no such thing, except in my own mind, but wanted to see what Suzanna's reaction would be to my remark. "Which is exactly what you thought was most likely the case."

"Yes, it was." Her expression at that point was more contemplative than apprehensive. "However, now I'm not so certain."

"Who do you think would want to harm both Barlow and Reilly?" I hoped my question would prompt her to explain her sudden skepticism. "Any ideas?"

"I have my suspicions, but I'd rather keep them to myself," she replied. "But I'd bet you anything Barlow was a victim of his own stupidity."

"What do you mean by that?"

"He shouldn't have called the tip hotline. In this day and age, people would just as soon shoot you as look at you if you upset them in any way. You don't dare get involved in road-rage incidents anymore, for example. Nowadays, when someone cuts you off, you just wave friendly-like and shout, 'have a good day', and get the hell out of Dodge. Whoever abducted Reilly was probably afraid Barlow would suddenly remember part of the license tag number or the year, color, and model of the car he saw picking Reilly up. You know, an eyewitness report that could provide a clue that turns the entire case around. Or, on the other hand, the killer might have just been ticked off that the guy would stick his nose in where it didn't belong."

"Yeah, I know what you mean, although I think it's everyone's civic duty as human beings to look out for each other and report crime, or the possibility of wrong-doing, when we witness it." I was dying to know who Suzanna suspected was behind both deaths, as you can well imagine. I tried a tactic that turned out to be very effective. "Do you really believe that two-timing, no-good scoundrel of a husband of yours could do something so atrocious to another human being?"

Without taking a moment to think about her response, she exclaimed, "You're damned right I think he could! He never laid a hand on me, but emotional and verbal abuse is just as hurtful, if not more so. I believe if provoked, he could get angry enough to beat up a person, maybe even kill 'em. Especially a woman. He almost killed a man in a bar one night. He told me he actually *was* trying to kill the guy but failed to get the job done."

When it occurred to her what she'd revealed about her estranged husband, she stopped talking abruptly. I shook my head slowly as I waved my hand back and forth. Before I could speak, Suzanna spoke again. "No, forget I said that. Please don't repeat that to anyone."

"Don't worry, dear. I would never say anything to anyone. I'm on your side, and I think you may be right. Any man who'd try to kill another person is a horse's behind, in my opinion. But it's not my place to accuse anyone of anything or to repeat anything you've said out of anger." I couldn't really tell if Suzanna was afraid of causing the police to pay attention to her husband because she still cared for him, or because she was afraid of the repercussions to herself if she pointed an accusatory finger at Percival. She was hurt, obviously, and with hurt came resentment, but that didn't mean she wasn't afraid of retribution from the man who'd broken her heart. Suzanna had no real evidence that Percival would try to kill someone, such as Barlow, so her say-so would hardly serve as proof of wrongdoing on his part.

I wanted to keep her in my confidence for now. "Speaking of not repeating anything, please keep what I just told you about Barlow's murder to yourself. The news hasn't been made public yet, and I swore to my husband I wouldn't tell anyone. I just thought you should know."

"Thank you. I promise not to say anything to anyone. To be clear, though, I really don't think Percival would physically harm anyone, male or female," Suzanna said, her head hanging in remorse for having even voiced something so damning about her husband. This statement completely contradicted the story she'd just told me about his bar fight. "If Percival's involved in Reilly's disappearance, I hope he gets what he has coming to him."

I noticed Suzanna had just spoken of Reilly in the past tense but didn't think it was a sign she knew the woman to be deceased. Reilly being dead seemed to be the opinion of everyone who knew her. If she were still alive, she would have returned home or contacted someone by now.

I noticed a tear escape from Suzanna's right eye and reached over and clasped my hands in hers as a sign of solidarity. The lone tear left a black streak of watery mascara down her cheek. I felt bad I'd upset her, but glad I'd been able to drag her suspicions out of her. Percival Pandero was now my number-one suspect, and I wanted to dig into his past and his whereabouts as much as I could.

"Where do you think the dirtbag is now?" I asked.

"I have no idea, and I don't care," she replied. "As long as he stays at least a hundred feet away from me, as written in the restraining order I filed."

"You do know those aren't always iron-clad, don't you?" I didn't want Suzanna to feel as if she were totally safe based solely on a restraining order. A false sense of security was often worse than no sense of security at all. "When my husband served as the sheriff here, I read a report that said restraining orders are violated forty percent of the time and lead to something worse occurring over twenty percent of the time. A restraining order often makes the individual you filed the order against even angrier. A lot of people, particularly abusive ones with anger issues, don't give a rat's behind about restraining orders. Some treat them as a dare."

"Yeah. I know. And Percival is exactly the kind of man to disregard a court order. It's not that I'm afraid he'll hurt me. I just don't want to deal with him right now. That's why I leave all the doors locked and chained, even when I'm in the house. I had a state-of-the-art security system installed right before the hurricane and was really nervous during the several weeks it took to get the electricity and wifi back up and operating."

"I can imagine. Don't take any chances. If you ever feel uncomfortable, or your ex shows up in your driveway, call this number, and Rip and Milo will come right over." As I spoke, I wrote our phone number on the back of a Dollar General receipt.

"Milo? As in Milo next door?"

"Um, yes." I'd forgotten I'd intentionally not told her my daughter was her next-door neighbor. To Suzanna, I was just a volunteer helping distribute emergency supplies. "I'm sorry. Did I fail to mention I was Regina Moore's mother? That's why I began my door-to-door canvassing in this cul-de-sac. We will be staying here with them for a few weeks, or even months, if necessary."

"So does that exotic-looking travel trailer in their driveway belong to you?" I'd always thought of "exotic" as being a complimentary description, but the expression on the woman's face as she spoke said otherwise. Before I recalled the promise I'd made to Regina, I said, "Yes. The Chartreuse Caboose is our full-time home now."

"You call your travel trailer the Chartreuse Caboose? How funny." Suzanna's eyebrows arched as she replied to my remark. "Well, thank you, Rapella. It makes me feel so much better to know that you and the former sheriff are right next door."

"Tack that number up by your telephone so it's handy if or when you need it."

"My iPhone is always in my pocket, so I'll put your number in my contacts under Sheriff Ripple, so I can auto-dial it quickly if necessary."

"Perfect. Sometimes my age shows when I forget people don't all have black telephones with rotary dials on their kitchen counters like everyone used to. In fact, very few folks have landlines these days, I reckon." I laughed when she nodded with a comical look on her face. Our age difference left me feeling like a tittering tyrannosaurus rex. "You take care, dear. If you get lonely, dial that number and I'll come over for a cup of coffee or glass of wine, and we'll have a tête-à-tête about the weather, the town's progress on the hurricane recovery, or even the couple up the street who stand in their front yard and hurl insults at each other."

"Can you believe those two?" Suzanna asked with a chuckle. I hadn't actually witnessed the couple arguing, but Regina had told me about some of their public disagreements. "Last week I saw Mrs. Willming yank a small lantana bush out of their flower bed and throw it at her husband. As soon as he roared off in his muscle car, she was out there replanting it."

"I guess she showed him a thing or two!"

We both laughed at my remark and then she asked if I had the time to join her in a glass of Cranberry Curlew. I felt sorry for her when she said, "I could actually use the company today, as I'm a little down now, having just heard about Barlow. The Cranberry Curlew and Calypso Bianco are my two favorites from Winery on the Bay. I'm glad I'd bought several cases of each a week before the hurricane hit. Now it could be a while before the winery reopens. I heard they'll be moving to East North Street, about a block from their old location, because their former building was heavily damaged by the storm."

"That's too bad," I replied. "We noticed the entire downtown area took a major hit. Thank goodness most Texans are resilient."

"That's true."

As we sipped on our long-stemmed glasses of red wine, we talked about everything from the fact there weren't nearly as many shore and wading birds, or even the smaller songbirds, around as there had been before the hurricane to the best way to get a wine stain out of a white blouse. The latter subject came up after Suzanna accidentally sloshed some wine on her shirt as she laughed at one of my stories about Dolly licking ice cream off Rip's chin as he napped in his recliner. I suggested hydrogen peroxide to remove the stain.

By the time I left, I'd formed a friendly bond with Suzanna. We even made plans to go shopping in Portland together the following day. Portland was one of the closest places to buy groceries now that so many businesses were closed due to hurricane damage. I hoped to get more details about Percival's personality, his relationship with Reilly, and why Suzanna suspected he was involved in the woman's disappearance. I was interested in learning where the man might be living at the present, and if he had viable motives to harm two of his former neighbors.

It was possible Reilly had willingly gotten into the car the eyewitness saw picking her up during the lull in the storm. It was even plausible she was currently hiding out with the vehicle's owner somewhere. Suzanna had not seen her ex in three weeks. Percival and Reilly could have established a new life together, under assumed identities, in Satan's Kingdom, Massachusetts, for all anyone knew. Satan's Kingdom is not only an actual town, albeit an unincorporated community, it's the most fitting name for a place for two such unscrupulous individuals to live if they'd truly run off together. Reilly might not be a victim, I realized. She might actually be a co-conspirator. Perhaps she was hoping to disappear without a trace in anticipation of being presumed dead, a victim of Hurricane Harvey. If that was her scheme, so far it had gone off without a hitch, and, if so, I hoped to be the "hitch" that threw a monkey wrench in her plans.

The general presumption was that Reilly had died after being swept away during Hurricane Harvey, but my gut was telling me otherwise. I couldn't help but think there was more to the situation than everyone knew. Her fate had been based entirely on the assumption she'd been killed in the storm, but there'd been no proof to verify that assumption. It troubled me there were no signs of anyone actively looking for her: no posters with her image on them posted around town, no candlelight vigils, no organized search parties. Without a body to confirm her death, I felt Reilly's fate was still up in the air. It was a mystery of sorts, and it appeared that no one other than me desperately wanted to see it solved.

Everyone, from the victim's spouse to the county sheriff, seemed content to set aside the matter of the missing woman so they could concentrate on rebuilding their homes, their businesses, and their lives. It was true that everyone in Rockport had a lot on their plates after the destructive hurricane, but not one person appeared to be overly concerned about finding Reilly. Life marched on as though she'd never existed.

Personally, if she'd been someone I'd known and loved, I wouldn't have rested until I had proof of her death. I'd barely met the woman yet felt as though I was more distressed about her disappearance than her own husband. Rather than rebuilding their house, Walker's number one priority should've been to bring his wife home one way or another—dead or alive!

I chewed over the situation that evening as Rip and I sat staring at the boob tube like we were in hypnotic trances. I was looking forward to talking with Suzanna the next day. I don't think I'd ever been so excited about buying milk and bread in my entire life.

SIXTEEN

"What in the Sam Hill?" I gasped in the middle of the Portland H-E-B's produce department. Suzanna had grabbed my arm and yanked me so hard, I nearly lost my balance. Unfortunately for the mound of oranges I was pawing through, they tumbled from the bin and rolled across the floor in all directions. One nearly made it to the meat counter before coming to a halt. My shopping companion swiftly dragged me around a display of Christmas decorations and into the cereal aisle. I don't know what surprised me the most: getting man-handled in the grocery store by Suzanna, or seeing holiday merchandise on display in September.

"He's here!"

I knew who "he" was without even asking.

"Did you notice the muscle-bound dude in the white tank top who was putting russet potatoes in a plastic bag?"

"Who could miss him? He looks as if he could power lift that large crate of watermelons next to him. I assume that's Percival. What do you reckon he's doing here?"

Suzanna splayed her hands out in a manner that clearly

meant "duh". "Buying food. What did you think he'd be doing in a grocery store?"

"I realize that." I rolled my eyes at her. "What I meant is, this means he's still living in the area."

Suzanna repeated her "duh" gesture. Suddenly I didn't like her as much as I had when we'd initially entered the store. I went on to explain why the thought of him living nearby should greatly concern her. "Well, that's good to know because it means you better stay on your toes. Remember to keep that phone number I gave you handy. He's alone, so that may also indicate he's not shacking up with Reilly."

Suzanna's head turned sideways like a startled great horned owl. "Shush. I don't want him to hear us. And why would that indicate he's not shacking up with Reilly? If he is, she's probably hiding out, wanting people to believe she's dead. Besides, it doesn't take two people to buy food to cook for supper. He never came to the store with me when I went grocery shopping."

"All right," I whispered in return. "Why did you seem so shocked when I mentioned your ex shacking up with Reilly?"

"Because I don't really think there's any fricking way that's happening." Suzanna appeared to be trying to convince herself more than me. She tended to waffle back and forth on the subject. Her next remark took me by surprise. "I'd rather believe he killed her before the eye of the storm even cleared the island."

"You'd rather believe he *killed* her? For your sake, I presume? It can't be for his or Reilly's. Where'd you get such an idea?" I asked softly. This was exactly the kind of information I'd hoped to get out of Suzanna. I just hadn't expected to be cowered down next to a box of Cocoa Puffs when I got it. "Yesterday you told me you didn't think he'd ever harm anyone, male or female. But then, that was right after you told me he tried to kill a guy in a bar, but failed."

"I lied. I don't want it to get back to him that I was spreading rumors he was probably the reason she was missing. You see, I found a text on his phone the day before Harvey. Percival was upset with her because she'd told him she had plans to break it off with her new husband, but no plans to dive right back into another serious relationship with Percival or any other man. Not sure if you knew this, but Reilly and Walker were still newly-weds." Suzanna continued after I nodded my head. "She was just looking for a good time, apparently, not a committed relationship."

"She's clearly not a big fan of monogamy. It sounds like Walker is better off without her."

"Yeah. I agree. Percival was better off without her too, the way I see it. As far as Reilly is concerned, good riddance is all I can say."

That came across as a little harsh, but I could understand her hateful regard for the home wrecker across the street. Not that I didn't think Suzanna wasn't equally better off without her slime-ball husband. Seemed to me as if Reilly and Percival deserved each other. Naturally, I kept that thought to myself.

"Can I help you?" Just then a booming voice behind us startled me. I lurched forward and knocked at least a dozen boxes of cereal off the shelf. Sprawled out in the aisle with a box of Lucky Charms between my legs, I knew I was a sight to behold. So much for lucky or charming. The boxes lay scattered all around me as I stared up at a rotund employee wearing an H-E-B badge and an apron. "Hey! Aren't you the lady who scattered the oranges all over the produce department?"

"Well, yes," I mumbled. In my defense, I added, "But not intentionally."

"Yet you just rushed off rather than notifying someone to clean up your mess. You seem to be leaving quite a wave of destruction in your wake. Your name's not Harvey by any chance, is it?"

I knew the man was trying to be funny, but I didn't see any humor in his comment. "I'm sorry, sir. I'll put these cereal boxes back on the shelf just the way they were before you startled me and made me lose my balance."

With his hands on his hips, the employee, a man hired to stock shelves, was putting on airs as if he was Howard Edward Butt himself, of which all the H-E-B stores in Texas were named for. It's easy to see why Howard's mother, Florence, chose her son's initials rather than his surname when she founded the grocery chain. "Butt Foods" just doesn't have the same ring to it. The snotty shelf-stocker glared at me, as he asked, "Did you drop something *else*? Why were you crouched down like that, anyway?"

"I have a medical condition." The man instantly looked contrite for putting such an emphasis on the word "else" in his last question. I felt vindicated even though, other than a mild case of osteoporosis, the only real medical condition I suffered from was an underactive thyroid. And, according to Rip, an overactive imagination. I wasn't lying by saying I had a medical condition, even though it hadn't exactly earned me a handicapped plaque to hang from my rearview mirror. The rude store clerk didn't need to know my Hashimoto's Thyroiditis had nothing to do with the "wave of destruction" I was leaving behind me.

"Oh. I apologize, ma'am. Do you need assistance in getting up? I'm so sorry. I didn't mean to scare you like that." He looked as if he'd just been made aware he'd accidentally run over a ninety-year-old with a forklift while restocking the shelves. I'd have felt guilty if he hadn't been so discourteous earlier.

"I'll be fine. Just give me a second." The man turned away and spoke into his two-way radio. I turned to see what Suzanna was doing, only to realize she was nowhere to be found. I'd soon discover she'd fled the store and was waiting in her car for me when a text came over my phone from her.

Whether she needed to pick up groceries or not, we were desperately low on a number of staples, and I wasn't about to waste this opportunity. I hurried up and down the aisles and then loitered around a rack of magazines within eyesight of the check-out counters.

"Clean up on aisle seven!" A voice called out over the store's intercom system. I continued to feign interest in a *Farm and Ranch* periodical until I saw Percival approach with a couple of steaks and two baking potatoes in one hand, and a bottle of white wine in the other. I quickly fell into line behind him.

As I've mentioned before, I often exchange polite small talk with people in front of or behind me in check-out lines. Today I actually had a reason to start up a conversation with a perfect stranger. Maybe "complete stranger" would be a more appropriate term. There didn't seem to be anything "perfect" about Percival other than perhaps his eyesight. Well into his forties, the man didn't seem to need eyeglasses to read the text that had just come over his phone. Looking over his shoulder I read his return text, which was **DINNER AT 7:00**.

"Oh, sorry. Can you believe how long these lines are?" I casually asked Percival after he turned around and caught me eyeing his phone. I had accidentally tapped his behind with the front of my grocery cart when I leaned forward to sneak a peek at what he'd typed into his phone.

"You should see the lines at Home Depot in Corpus," he replied good-naturedly. I hadn't expected him to be so friendly. "But, then, we shouldn't complain. We're lucky these stores weren't destroyed by Harvey."

"You're absolutely right! How did your home fare?"

"Not bad, considering. And yours?"

"Although Rockport is our home base, my husband and I are full-time RVers now. We came back to help my daughter and her husband get their lives back on track. Like you, their home was damaged, but not to the point it'll need to be razed. One house a few doors down lost its entire top floor, so I guess Regina and Milo were very fortu—"

"Regina and Milo?" He cut in, staring at me as if I'd just morphed into a rainbow-colored unicorn, like the one on the front of the cereal boxes I'd knocked off the shelf. I instinctively reached up to run my hand across my forehead to make sure I wasn't sporting a new horn. "As in the Moores who live on Flamingo Road?"

"Yes. Those are the ones." I'd forgotten he was their former next-door neighbor and would instantly recognize their names. At that juncture, I wasn't sure if my slip of the tongue would turn out to be a beneficial thing or a silly screw-up. "You know them, I take it?"

"Yes. I live next door to them. Or at least I used to. They're good folks."

"I agree. But then, I might be a bit biased." I smiled because I wanted to keep the conversation casual. On the other hand, I didn't want to miss an opportunity to learn anything I could about my current number-one suspect. Even as we chatted, I found it hard to believe the man in front of me could abduct Reilly or kill two people in cold blood. "Oh, so you've moved?"

"Only temporarily, I hope. My wife and I are currently separated. My bad. I was a total jerk. I'd do anything to win her back, even attend anger-management classes if I have to." I noticed Percival referred to Suzanna as his wife, even though she referred to him as her ex when she wasn't referring to him as something much less complimentary. He looked forlorn as he spoke of her, while she'd appeared mad as a rabid fox when she'd mentioned his name. I actually felt a tiny bit sorry for the guy, despite the fact I'd been told he was prone to inflicting verbal and emotional abuse, as well as being a two-timing scumbag. To his credit, he'd admitted the separation was all his fault and attributed it to his anger issues. He looked down at his feet, as he added, "I had a short fling with another woman, but it didn't mean anything. I feel terrible about it, too."

"As you should. If I were your wife, it'd be a cold day in you-know-where before I'd take you back. But that's just me." My remark was blunt but truthful. The look on Percival's face indicated he didn't appreciate brutal honesty. Either that or the idea of being married to a seventy-year-old woman made him sick to his stomach. It was probably a good thing I didn't ask him if he killed the woman he'd had the short fling with while making it look like she was a victim of the recent hurricane.

"I said I felt terrible about it. I swore I'd never do it again after seeing how badly I hurt Suzanna. I'm not above getting down on my hands and knees and begging her to take me back."

"First you need to give her a reason to want you back, as well as proof she can trust you this time around." I was wishing I'd turned my phone's voice recorder on before I'd approached Percival. I'd have loved to be able to play my conversation with him back for Suzanna on our ride home so she could hear the earnest quality of his tone. Reiterating to her what he'd said, explaining he'd appeared genuinely remorseful and held himself totally responsible for their issues just wouldn't have the powerful effect as hearing the words out of his own mouth. I'd just have to do the best I could to get the sincerity of his remarks across to her. *Perhaps there's still hope for the couple,* I thought.

"If your wife fears you'll abuse her again in the future or cheat on her, she'll leave you sitting out on the curb like a bag of garbage, which is a perfect description for anyone who'd intentionally hurt his spouse, even if it's not physically. She needs to feel loved, as if you appreciate her. She needs confirmation of your commitment to change your ways. She needs to feel as though your loyalty to her is unquestionable. She needs to feel protected. Above all, she needs to feel safe in her own home.

Maybe you should sign up for those anger-management classes right away so she can see you're serious about winning her back and willing to do whatever it takes to make things right." Suddenly I was acting as if I'd spent my entire life working as a marriage counselor rather than earning a living as a secretary, shoe salesman, ice cream store clerk, bartender, and a dozen other short-lived occupations. But, to my profound surprise, Percival was taking in every word I said. "You need to enroll in those classes today, or tomorrow at the latest, to have any hope of ever winning the love of your life back."

"That's not a bad idea," he said. "Thanks."

I should have stopped while I was ahead, but I was feeling full of myself at the moment, so I added, "She's not going to wait around forever, you know. She may already be looking for your replacement."

The glare he leveled on me after my rash comment could have made my head explode like a cherry bomb had I not felt my skull heating up and glanced away. Looking down at my hands, I said, "I'm sorry if I upset——"

"All I can say is, she'd better not be looking for another man."

"You just told me you cheated on her."

"That's different."

"Not really." Just then the line moved up and I realized Percival would be the next customer to check out. He turned around as if officially ending our exchange. I felt as though I'd learned nothing of any real value in my personal investigation into his neighbor's disappearance. I tapped him on the shoulder. "Say, Percival, have you——"

His headed twist around so abruptly I feared he'd need to get a chiropractic adjustment before he returned to his "temporary" home with his groceries. In an accusatory tone, he asked, "How'd you know my name?"

"Silly goose. You just told me you lived next door to my

155

daughter. Don't you think Regina and I have discussed the folks who live in the same cul-de-sac as she and her husband? She had nothing bad to say about anyone in the neighborhood, by the way."

"Oh, yeah." Percival had the decency to look embarrassed. I was just glad I hadn't used his name before he'd given me an excuse to already know it. "Oh, yeah. I'd forgotten about that."

"No problem. I've already forgotten what store I'm shopping in. Happens to the best of us." I chuckled amicably before getting down to brass tacks. "So, have you heard any new updates about the lady on the other side of Regina and Milo? You know, Reilly Reynolds, the one who disappeared during the storm?"

"No. Have you?" He appeared extremely interested in my answer, leaning toward me as if to ensure he didn't miss a single word of my response.

"I heard an anonymous tipster called in to report he'd witnessed her getting into a car in front of her home during the more tranquil period when the eye of the storm was directly over Rockport."

"Really?" It was clear this was the first he'd heard of the anonymous tip. He appeared neither alarmed nor surprised. He merely looked intrigued. "I hope that bit of information leads the authorities to her whereabouts."

He hadn't said "lead the authorities to her body", but rather used a phrase that might indicate he thought she might still be among the living. This told me he might be as perplexed as the rest of us about what had happened to Reilly. It could also indicate he knew she was still alive, but not admitting it. A Freudian slip like that could be very telling. I just wish I knew *what* it was telling me.

"I'm guessing Barlow was the anonymous tipster," he said with a rueful smile. "He called the police on me one evening when I walked up the street to put a piece of misdelivered mail inside the rightful recipient's screen door. To the 9-1-1 dispatcher he referred to me as a 'peeping Tom'. Irritating at the time, but kind of amusing thinking back about it."

"He must have been a real character. What a shame."

"'Must have been'? A 'shame'? What are you talking about?"

"You haven't heard about Barlow's death?" I watched Percival's deeply tanned complexion pale as my news set in. It was painfully obvious this was the first he was learning of his neighbor's passing. Even Tom Hanks is not *that* good an actor.

Before he could respond, the lady at the cash register motioned him forward so she could tally up his purchases. He glanced around frantically before asking me, "Is it all right with you if I let the customer behind you go ahead of us?"

"Absolutely! I'm in no big rush," I replied. I probably came across as too anxious. I would have been delighted to have the next four customers behind him cut in line in front of us, as well. The longer we talked, the more information I was apt to garner. Percival and I both stepped aside to let the elderly man pass.

"What happened to Barlow?" Percival asked the second the man had cleared him. He sounded more curious than upset about the news of Mr. Barnaby's demise. But then, Barlow didn't appear to have too many fans on Flamingo Road.

"I was actually the person who discovered his body. When I peered through the glass, I saw him hanging by a rope from the big cross beam in his living room."

"Oh, no! That's awful! Have they identified the killer yet?"

"No. Not yet. I'm certain they're closing in on the perp though." I noticed Percival's eyes widen in response to my remark, as though genuinely stunned at the news of Barlow's death. "I got the impression they're convinced the killer is the same individual who abducted Reilly Reynolds. You see, my husband is the former sheriff of Aransas County, and is still friends with many of the officers on the local police force."

"Oh, that's right." Percival's head bobbed up and down like a bobble-head doll. "Milo told me his father-in-law was Sheriff Ripple. Mister Ripster, he calls him."

Mister Ripster? I wonder what Milo calls me behind my back? Oh, well, Mister Ripster's better than what I occasionally call Rip. In fact, my husband might actually like the fact his son-in-law had concocted a unique nickname for him, so I'll let that remark slide for now.

The customer we'd let cut in front of us had only ten or twelve items in his basket. With Percival on deck to check out next, I knew I didn't have much time. He didn't seem prepared to wave another customer ahead of us. While I could, I asked, "You must be having a guest for supper, huh?"

"What makes you think I wasn't planning to eat both steaks and baked potatoes myself? I most definitely would have no problem polishing off this wine on my own. Add a case of Modelo, and it'd be the perfect last supper." His response had been made in a joking manner, so I laughed politely before he continued. "Just kidding. You know the lady who owned the house you were just referring to that had the entire top floor ripped apart? Well, I thought it'd be neighborly of me to invite her over for dinner. I'm renting a fully-furnished condo here in Portland, and I'm anxious to try out the grill on the back deck. She's had a bad go of it, and I feel sorry for her. Thought it might be therapeutic for her to have someone to talk to and a treat to have a home-cooked meal, as well. She's living in a Motel 6 room right now. To be honest, I thought my eyes could use a treat, as well. And JJ is definitely easy on the eyes."

"JJ?" I was floored. My top dentures clamped down so hard in shock, I nearly bit clean through my tongue. It smarted like the devil. "Excuse me for being frank, sir, but asking a good-looking woman over for supper is not going to score you any points with your estranged wife."

"I won't tell if you don't." Percival laughed out loud at his smart remark. He had no idea I not only knew his estranged wife but had also ridden to the store with her.

I opened my mouth to say something, but nothing came out. For one thing, I was stunned at having just learned the JJ who'd left a note for Walker might be another one of the residents on Flamingo Road. Secondly, I was even more shocked that the man who'd just proclaimed to feel terrible about cheating on his wife with one neighbor was clearly hoping to do so with another.

"I was just joshing you, lady. You see, my intentions are to keep my relationship with JJ purely platonic."

"That's good." His words sounded sincere, but the wink he'd given me when he'd said his dinner date was easy on the eyes indicated differently. "Just remember that good intentions often go awry. Weird thing is, I'd just heard JJ got married recently and moved to Austin."

"Nah. You're thinking about the chick who used to work at the bait stand down at Fulton Harbor. That JJ never lived on the island, much less on our street. I'm referring to J.J. Wallinski. She's an independent accountant."

"I see." What I saw was there were actually two young, beautiful ladies in the area with the same nickname. This JJ was the neighbor Regina had referred to on the phone as Jo Jo, which is obviously from whence the moniker, JJ, was derived. Now I had a fix on the one who'd likely left the message for Walker Reynolds to meet her. Just then the clerk hollered out, "Next!" I don't know if I was more upset about the fact there was blood pooling in my mouth from nearly biting my tongue off, or excited about the fact I now had a lead on the mysterious buxom blonde named JJ who might've been mixed up in the disappearance of the young woman who lived next door to Regina and Milo.

According to Percival's estranged wife, he had horned in on Walker's wife. Was he now horning in on Walker's mistress, as well?

After checking out, and exiting the store, I began to sprint to Suzanna's car, which I only recognized because I remembered where she'd parked—in a designated handicapped spot she had no legal right to park in. I'd felt obligated to limp all the way to the entrance of the store when we'd arrived. If I hadn't been certain she'd parked in the closest spot to the front door for her own benefit, I'd have told her being seventy does not make an individual handicapped. In my defense, I'd tried valiantly to talk her out of parking in the spot meant for people with actual physical handicaps.

As I raced through the parking lot, three bags of groceries swung wildly from each arm. By rights, the weight of the six bags warranted being pushed to the car in a shopping cart. But you know how adrenalin can help a mother lift a car off her child? I was so pumped up, I had that same kind of adrenalin pumping through my veins.

As I approached the car, I noticed Suzanna was scrunched down behind the wheel so Percival wouldn't spot her when he'd exited the store. Fortunately for her, there were at least four other light silver Jeep Cherokees in the parking lot nearly identical to hers.

As I reached for the passenger door, my heart skipped a beat. For it was at that very moment, I realized Percival might have made a truly petrifying Freudian slip after all. When I'd told him I'd witnessed his neighbor hanging by a rope in his own living room, he'd immediately asked if the killer had been identified. Given this was supposedly the first Percival had heard of Barlow's death, and I'd not said anything to indicate it'd been a murder, I thought his query should have been more along the lines of, "Did he leave a suicide note?"

If Percival already knew Barlow had been murdered and his body staged to reflect a suicide, what else had he lied about? What more did the man know? He was obviously a much better actor than I'd give him credit for. I suddenly wasn't so certain I wanted to tell Suzanna her estranged husband wanted to patch things up. After all, reconciling with Percival could prove hazardous to the woman's health. Conversely, if I told her I'd just caught him in an incriminating, or at least puzzling, fabrication and it somehow got back to him, my life could be in danger as well.

To calm my fears, I reminded myself the man could have spoken before realizing his question didn't make sense. He was hyped up for his dinner date that evening, and perhaps a little distraught at the news of his neighbor's death. A mix-up like that could just as easily been an indication of inattention as it was of guilt. No different than me asking Regina if she'd heard who the anonymous tipster was.

I made a quick decision to say nothing about my conversation with Percival to Suzanna on the trip back to Rockport. I'd put the exchange I'd had with him in my back pocket for now, so to speak, and maybe I'd dig it out for a future discussion with Suzanna if and when the situation called for it.

As I fastened my seat belt, Suzanna said, "Looks like Percival's cooking dinner for some new woman. Did you happen to notice what he had in his arms before I pulled you around the corner? Steak, baked potatoes, and wine is the exact meal he cooked for me on our first date."

I didn't think it'd be wise to tell her he'd informed me he'd invited her neighbor, Jo Jo Wallinski, over for supper, because, according to him, he felt sorry for her. Repeating Percival's statement about keeping his relationship with JJ strictly platonic would hardly ease Suzanna's angst. The stark evil in her eyes was absolutely chilling as she turned to gaze at me. It was as if I were peering into her core, searching for a soul and finding nothing. Nothing but a vast void, like a black hole in our solar system. I was unable to respond to her remarks.

161

As she resumed speaking, she turned to stare out the windshield again. Her tone made the hair on my arms stand straight up. I felt as though she'd forgotten I was even in the car. Her vehemence made it seem as if she was making a vow to herself. "You'd have thought he'd have learned his lesson the last time. I refuse to be cast aside like leftover meatloaf and replaced by some cream-filled cupcake. I'll find out who she is, just like I did last time, and make sure she doesn't——"

Suddenly she stopped speaking and glanced over at me as if I'd just jumped into her Jeep with the intention of carjacking her. Without speaking, Suzanna then turned and watched intently as Percival maneuvered his Subaru out onto Wildcat Drive. He'd parked in the far corner of the large parking lot. After he was out of sight, she asked, "Do you mind if I go back in and grab a few things? I'm completely out of butter and eggs and don't have a single tablespoon of bath dust left."

Although I was confused about her need for bath dust, assuming it must be similar to bath salt, I nodded. "Of course I don't mind. Is it all right if I wait here?"

It was, so I completed a word puzzle on my phone while I waited for her to purchase the items she needed. She returned in about twenty minutes, carrying two bags of groceries. "I was lucky enough to get the last bag of bath dust."

"How fortunate."

"I also picked up a copy of James Patterson's latest. You can borrow it after I've finished it, if you'd like. Once I start one of his books, I can hardly put it down."

"Thanks, but I'm more of a cozy mystery enthusiast. I guess it's because I can relate to amateur sleuths solving murder cases." I hoped Suzanna didn't put two and two together following my last comment. I quickly changed the subject. "Did you know Walker is having the construction crew add on a small library to their house for Reilly? He's holding out hope she'll return home safe and sound, and wants to surprise her with it if she does."

"Ha! That's a good one!" It was the first time I'd really seen Suzanna laugh so heartily that she snorted in amusement.

"What do you mean?" I asked. "What's so funny?"

"Reilly would get as much use out of a library as I would a home gym. I doubt she's read anything since she dropped out of high school, except maybe a *Victoria's Secret* catalog."

"Oh. That's interesting." I wasn't sure what to make of Suzanna's comment. Why would Walker want to surprise his wife with a library if she wasn't an avid reader?

"She does have a huge selection of CD's though. Always fancied herself a rock star on the brink of making her big break into the music industry. She always acted as if she was the next 'American Idol' just waiting to be discovered. Maybe it's supposed to be a music library, because it sure isn't for her book collection." Suzanna's remarks cleared up my confusion because they seemed reasonable.

As Suzanna exited the grocery store's parking lot, she reached toward the dash, hit a button, and soon a country song filled the air. The song seemed to be the perfect segue for her to change the subject. She sounded eerily cheerful as she said, "Speaking of music, you can see George Strait's vacation home on Curlew Drive from my back deck. Sometimes you can see George himself, which is why I leave a pair of binoculars on the counter."

"That's nice," I said. *And totally creepy*.

I avoided the subject of Suzanna's missing neighbor for the return trip. Instead, as we rode along, we chatted about our pets. I shared a few humorous stories about Dolly, before she told me how she'd accidentally acquired Rascal at a rummage sale.

"I assumed the box marked 'chinchilla' referred to a fur coat, not an actual hyperactive rodent. I guess I should have questioned why the box had small holes in it." Suzanna chuckled as she explained.

I laughed in response, not sure if she was pulling my leg or not. However, it would explain the strange creature I thought I'd seen scurrying out from under her marble-topped table the first day I'd met her. "Is the bath dust for Rascal?"

"Yes. Chinchillas bathe by rolling around in it just like they would roll in volcanic ash in their native South America. They have oily skin and the dust absorbs the dirt."

"I see. How interesting. The idea of rolling around in dust or ash to get clean seems very peculiar to me." *But then, the idea of keeping a large rodent as a pet seems even stranger,* I could have added. "Do chinchillas make loving pets, like our Dolly does?"

"Oh, hell no!" Suzanna replied. "If you tried to cuddle with Rascal, you'd likely get your ear bitten off. The one and only time I attempted to pet him, I ended up at the urgent care center getting thirteen stitches under my armpit."

"Ouch!"

"No kidding. I don't think most chinchillas are as antisocial as Rascal, but he's loving in other ways. Just not physically."

"That's good," I replied. I wasn't sure what other ways a pet could be loving, but decided not to ask. Maybe Rascal was her emotional rock.

"Did you know a chinchilla can live as long as twenty years in captivity?"

"Really?" I asked. "I had no idea."

"It's true. That damned nuisance might actually outlive me. Or, more likely, he'll be the death of me."

"Maybe you should have a rummage sale of your own and try to unload Rascal on some other unsuspecting bargain hunter." We laughed together even harder at my suggestion.

"You are a hoot, Rapella!" Suzanna reached over and

slapped my hand in a friendly fashion. "I'm so glad you showed up on my doorstep peddling MRE's."

"I wouldn't exactly call it 'peddling', but I'm glad we've gotten to know each other too." I couldn't help but like Suzanna. She had a wonderful sense of humor and appeared to sincerely enjoy having me tag along. Before long we were turning right onto Flamingo Road. I thanked her for letting me ride with her so I could pick up the food items that I hadn't added to the grocery list I'd given Regina a few days earlier.

Suzanna smiled as she came to a stop in her driveway. "You are most welcome, Rapella. I appreciated the company."

The truth behind Reilly's disappearance seemed to be growing more curious all the time. Although I prayed she wasn't involved, Suzanna had a motive to eliminate Reilly Reynolds. She'd even voiced a thinly veiled threat against any woman her husband took a fancy to. She didn't really seem the type capable of violence. But then, neither did Rip, and I'd just recently witnessed him whacking a vole on the head with a shovel after he'd caught it chewing on the leather shoe he'd left by the front steps to the trailer. I supposed anyone could become violent if push came to shove, with the rare exception of a saint like Mother Teresa. If she'd found a vole chowing down on her footwear, rather than beat it to death with a lawn tool, she'd have been more likely to bake it a loaf of fresh bread to nibble on.

I wasn't sure who I could trust at this stage in my investigation. So, until I could eliminate Suzanna and her estranged husband as suspects in Reilly's disappearance, I vowed to keep mum about my desire to get to the bottom of the situation. Better to be conservatively cautious than recklessly share information with people who might have skeletons in their closets I'd yet to discover. Although I didn't know it at the time, I actually would find something alarming in someone's closet before long.

SEVENTEEN

At what seemed like the middle of the night, I was jerked awake by the sound of a loud rapping on the trailer door. I instinctively reached over to feel for Rip, only to discover he was already out of bed. I glanced over at the alarm clock and sat straight up when I saw it was nine-fifteen. I couldn't recall the last time I'd slept so soundly or so late in the morning.

As I'd gotten older, I'd noticed a large percentage of senior citizens tended to take great pride in being early risers, as if getting up with the chickens was worthy of a badge of honor. Most of them, however, failed to mention they were in the sack before eight each evening, while younger folks were just sitting down to supper or curling up on the couch for several hours of primetime television viewing. I almost hate to admit that Rip and I fall into that early-to-bed, early-to-rise category except, of course, on Friday nights when Rip thinks watching *Blue Bloods* is worth burning the candle at both ends. As a career lawman and loyal fan of Tom Selleck, it's my husband's favorite show.

Just for the record, I'm more of a *Jeopardy* enthusiast. I can manage to exude a tremendous amount of smugness after coming up with the correct question to the final jeopardy answer even though I've just yelled out twenty-seven consecutive wrong responses during the first two rounds of the show. Rip usually leaves the room before Alex Trebek has even introduced the three contestants.

I slipped on a cotton shirt and blue capris over a pair of stretched-out white undies and one of the two bras I owned that were purchased in the last decade. Our sex life was way beyond the buying of sexy lingerie that made me feel like Raquel Welch but probably made me look like Pee Wee Hermann in a bikini. At this stage of my life, if my undergarments were comfortable and bleachable, they were good enough. Suddenly, I heard Rip's deep baritone voice through the bedroom door as he questioned a visitor in the living room. "I'm sorry. Who'd you say you are?"

In response to Rip's query, I recognized Suzanna's much higher-pitched tone as she replied, "I'm the next-door neighbor. I'm here to see Rapella."

I cracked the door open. "I'll be right out. Give me just a moment."

After applying lipstick and running a comb through my salt and pepper hair a few times to tone down my bed-head appearance, I walked out like I'd been up and about for hours to find Suzanna alone in the living room. It was not typical of Rip to leave a stranger by herself in our personal living quarters. I can't think of anything in the Chartreuse Caboose anyone would want to steal, but he had a tendency to act as if he was responsible for protecting the crown jewels, which were being stored in our food cabinet between the Cheerios box and a jar of dill pickles.

"Good morning, Suzanna," I greeted my guest. "Did my husband happen to say where he was going before he left? I didn't hear the door close behind him."

"You should have," Suzanna replied. "He left three times. The first time he told me to make myself comfortable and walked out. The next couple of times were to retrieve his car keys off the counter and then to retrieve his wallet off the end table. He didn't mention where he was headed, but he drove off in the old truck."

"Yep! That definitely sounds like my Rip. What you just witnessed was a preview of coming attractions. You have roughly three decades before you begin spending half your time searching for the pair of glasses perched on the top of your head. And most likely no more than four or five years before you need those same spectacles to read the expiration date on a carton of milk. Oh, and FYI, don't ever refer to that hunk of junk he drives as an old truck in his presence. He likes to think of it more as a classic automobile."

Suzanna smiled once again, but the amusement didn't quite reach her light green eyes. Her eyes looked red and weary as if she'd been up half the night crying. She appeared anxious. Something definitely had the pretty woman feeling out of sorts.

"Is something wrong, Suzanna? You look upset."

"My mother had a stroke early this morning."

"Oh, I hate to hear that, my dear."

"Thanks. I've been rushing around getting ready to head home to be with her. My sister and brother will be meeting me there as well. But I am Mama's medical power-of-attorney, so I need to be there to make any important decisions regarding her health." I thought it sweet she still referred to her mother's residence as "home", even though she was probably within a year or two of turning forty and had undoubtedly been out on her own for many years.

"With the assistance of your siblings, I hope. You surely won't have that responsibility heaped solely on your shoulders, will you?"

"I'm the youngest of three children. If it were up to Claire and Daniel, they'd have the hospital staff pull the plug at the first sign of trouble. They are more concerned about what they stand to gain from her death than whether she can get past this unexpected setback."

"That's too bad. I'm so sorry your mama has taken ill and pray she pulls through this health crisis with no permanent damage." I didn't want to say anything negative about her siblings, because when it came right down to it, blood truly was thicker than water. I knew I might call my four brothers every name in the book, but heaven help anyone else who spoke poorly of them. "Is there anything I can do to help?"

"Would you mind keeping an eye on my place while I'm gone?"

"I don't mind at all. For as long as you need me to. I can water your plants too, if necessary, and anything else you need me to take care of while you're away." *Wrong answer*, I realized too late.

"Oh, thank goodness!" Suzanna exclaimed. "I was worried about what to do with Rascal. You only need to feed him a tablespoon of pellets every day, along with a small handful of hay, which I keep in the garage. He likes an occasional raisin or two for a treat. And, since he'll be upset that I'm gone, it'd be nice if you stopped by with a treat a few times each day. You'll need to make sure his gravity-fed water bottle has fresh water in it. Rascal's very prickly when it comes to stale water. He uses a litter box, which will need to be cleaned out every day because he's also quite fussy about having a clean place to do his business if you know what I mean. You'll need to make sure his cardboard box maintains about two inches of fresh dust. As I explained yesterday, it's used for bathing. Also, he tends to——"

"Hold up a minute," I cut in. I suddenly felt like I was going to be pet-sitting a champion racehorse, and wasn't sure I wanted to be responsible for the animal's well-being. I'd once killed my brother, Rusty's, pet guinea pig, while taking care of it for two weeks one summer as he attended church camp. He'd never let me forget it either. As badly as I wanted to, however, I didn't have the heart to tell Suzanna I couldn't take care of the chinchilla. It wasn't her fault she'd found herself in such a tight spot. I set aside my reluctance, and said, "Maybe I should be writing these instructions down. You know what I said earlier about a person's memory as they get older. I wouldn't want to feed Rascal two inches of pellets and only have a tablespoon of dust in his bathing box. Let me grab a pen and something to write on."

"Yes. That's probably a good idea," she replied.

Out from underneath a seven-year-old Atlas we kept in a drawer in the coffee table, I pulled the notebook I'd been using to keep track of any useful information I gathered concerning the woman Suzanna was convinced her husband had cheated on her with. I quickly flipped it open to a blank page before she could read anything I'd scribbled down. She might not have approved of my desire to uncover the truth behind the unusual state of affairs. It was reasonable to assume Suzanna was not praying nightly for the safe return of the suspected home-wrecker. In fact, to her, I'd imagine it really was a "good riddance" kind of situation, as Suzanna had actually stated the previous day. To be perfectly honest, I hadn't determined yet that it wasn't she who was behind Reilly's disappearance or death.

I wrote down the instructions she'd given me about Rascal and the security code for her alarm system, while Suzanna dug around in her large satchel. Before long she handed me a key on a key chain that depicted a whooping crane with a crab in its beak. The highly endangered species wintered in the nearby Aransas Wildlife Refuge, which to my dismay had also sustained a lot of damage during the hurricane.

"What a pretty keyring," I said. "Did you buy it here in town?"

"Percival bought it for me at the Oysterfest in Fulton last

year." She looked sad at the memory. "Said the whooping cranes' beauty reminded him of me."

"That was sweet." I felt bad I'd brought her down even further. She was already gloomy about the news of her mother's sudden illness. I changed the subject immediately. "Are you planning to head out right away?"

"Yes. I hope to be in Austin by three. The hospital there is only minutes from Mama's house, so I'll drop off my stuff at her place on the way."

In Austin? Didn't you tell me you stayed with your mother in Horizon City while you waited for power to be restored to the island after the hurricane? I wanted to ask. I knew Horizon City to be as far west as you could get in Texas, save for El Paso. The small, but rapidly growing, border town was a long way from Austin's location in central Texas. I realized you might tell people you were from Austin because it was the closest city they'd recognize to your actual hometown of Ding Dong, Texas, one of many strangely-named towns in the state. Then again, if that was your actual hometown, you might just not want to admit you were a Ding Dongian.

My point is, you'd hardly say your mother was from a city nearly four hundred miles away because whoever asked wouldn't know where Horizon City was. You'd have told them you were from the El Paso area, which was just minutes west of Horizon City. In any event, Suzanna had either lied to me about where she'd stayed after the hurricane or where she was headed today. I thought it best not to question her about it. Instead, I asked, "Where do you keep Rascal's cage?"

"Oh, no!" Suzanna exclaimed, shaking her head as if I'd just asked her how many times a day I was expected to thump her beloved pet on the head with a rolling pin. "He has complete run of the place. I could never keep Rascal pinned up in a cage. He *is* one of God's creations, after all."

Even the creator of the universe should be allowed one mistake, I wanted to say, but managed to resist the urge. "I see."

What I saw more than anything was that I shouldn't have been so quick to offer to do anything Suzanna needed done while she was away. Not only was I hesitant to enter the house with the suspicious black trash bag in a chest freezer in its basement, but I also didn't like bugs, snakes, or creepy crawlers of any sort, let alone furry rodents. I hoped I could slip in each day, put a tablespoon of chinchilla pellets and a small handful of hay in the bowl, water in the bottle, dust in the box, and remove from the litter box all the chinchilla poop Rascal found so offensive before slipping back out without ever laying eyes on the critter.

I should have known that was too much to hope for.

EIGHTEEN

"Anybody home?" I shouted as I eased Suzanna's front door open the following morning. Rip was right behind me. I hadn't been able to get the key Suzanna gave me to open the lock, so I'd asked Rip to break into the house for me. He could unlock nearly any lock, as long as it wasn't a deadbolt. He'd brought along his "breaking and entering kit," which consisted of an expired credit card, a paperclip, and a tiny screwdriver used for repairing eyeglass frames. He had the lock open within seconds. I thanked him, and asked, "What good is a locking door knob anyway?"

"Not much. It's rarely a deterrent if someone really wants to get into a home." Rip turned to exit Suzanna's house and return to the trailer. "You need to suggest she get a deadbolt installed, particularly if she lives alone."

"She told me she recently had a state-of-the-art security system installed."

"Even so. A deadbolt will help prevent the intruder from getting inside to set off the alarm in the first place. There's no such thing as being too safe."

"That's true. I'll make the suggestion to her. Honey, if you aren't in a big rush, I'd like you to stay with me. I've never had to take care of a chinchilla before."

"And I have?" He laughed at the fearful expression on my face. "Don't worry. I'll stick around to protect you from the big bad—Agghh!"

Rip's outcry startled me, and when he followed it up with a violent shake of his left leg, I was even more alarmed. He shook his leg a few more times before a ball of fur slid out of his pant leg. He proceeded to boot the trespasser over the coffee table onto the couch.

"Oh, my!" I stood frozen in time. I was torn between two reactions: grabbing Rip, racing out the front door and slamming it shut behind us, or rushing to check to see if the chinchilla I'd been placed in charge of was still alive. At that moment it looked harmless as it lay motionless, sprawled out on top of a sofa cushion. "I think Rascal just wanted to play. I noticed there are a number of small balls scattered across the floor that must be his toys."

"That may be," Rip said, "but he ain't gonna play in my pants. He can play with his own balls all he wants, but he damn well better leave mine alone."

I couldn't restrain a snicker because Rip was still shaking his leg, as if afraid an army of varmints had invaded his private space along with the chinchilla.

Just as I was wondering if I was going to have to give Suzanna's pet mouth-to-nasty mouth resuscitation, Rascal began to squirm, which was a great relief and terrifying at the same time. I wasn't sure how an animal that'd just been drop-kicked across the room would react. Would it run and hide or be more prone to retaliate? Either way, I had to make sure it didn't need medical attention. Didn't I? I surely didn't want to have to explain to Suzanna how Rascal had suffered an unfortunate incident that had rendered him dead the very first time I'd checked in on him.

Naturally, I'd have been vague about how the tragic accident occurred, mentioning neither my husband nor the unplanned flight across the living room her pet had taken. I'd have recalled Rascal appearing desperately lonely the first time I came in to feed him. Sadly, the second time I'd found him deceased on the dining room floor. Who'd have ever thought the poor little guy would miss his owner so badly, he'd take a suicidal leap off the top of the china hutch? Or, sadder yet, die of a broken heart? Okay, maybe the word "vague" was a gross understatement. To be perfectly honest, I would have out-and-out lied through my false teeth if I'd had to.

Fortunately, Rascal came around, and after shaking it off, barked at us several times before scurrying under the couch, where he remained until we'd departed. He appeared to be none the worse for wear. I put pellets and hay in his bowl, then verified there was still plenty of water in his bottle and more than enough dust in his bathing container. Finally, I scooped what seemed like thousands of small pellets out of his litter box.

The evening before, I'd Googled "chinchillas" and read up on keeping them as pets. Among other things, I learned they could poop up to 250 times a day. I couldn't imagine how the chinchilla could get more than a few yards from its litter box before he needed to use it again. I could certainly see the wisdom in litter-box training one you intended to keep as a house pet. Otherwise, walking through your home would be akin to navigating a minefield.

I was relieved it seemed as though Rascal would survive his traumatic experience that afternoon. Had he died, I'd have been tempted to buy a replacement. Regina had owned four identical goldfish named Gus as a child. She never once questioned Gus's record-breaking lifespan. However, goldfish could be replaced for two bucks and I'd read chinchillas cost around $150 at the pet store.

Before we left, Rip showed me how to pick the lock on the front door, in case he wasn't available when I returned to take care of Rascal. Something told me he'd never be available. I could foresee nightmares in his future featuring a mad chinchilla trying to gather up nuts—in Rip's nether regions.

That afternoon I decided to traipse next door to the Reynolds's house to have a look around. It was Sunday and there was no sign of anyone in the house. No vehicles sat in the driveway. Perhaps Walker was out and about, visiting his neighbor, J.J. Wallinski. Did Walker know Percival was making a play for her in the same way he had Reilly? It seemed to me Flamingo Road would've been more aptly called Peyton Place.

As I stood on the Reynolds's front porch with a glass of lemonade in one hand, I rapped loudly on the door with the other, yelling out, "Anyone home?" I waited for a response for at least thirty seconds before repeating the process. Convinced no one was home, I decided to go inside and take a quick look around. The home was under reconstruction, and most of the furniture and personal items that survived the hurricane had been locked up in a construction trailer in the driveway to avoid being pilfered by looters. I didn't really feel as though I was tres-passing. After all, who, out of pure curiosity, doesn't walk through new homes being constructed in their neighborhood? Instead of using the lock-picking kit Rip had lent me on the Reynolds's front door—which could be construed as "breaking and entering"—I stepped through a floor-to-ceiling window that'd had the glass broken out by flying debris during the storm. The way I saw it, this was basically just "entering". And I'd never heard of anyone who'd ever been arrested for merely entering a structure.

Before continuing on into the house, I hollered out again. "Hello? Anybody home? Walker? Jessie? Hello?"

When no one responded, I took a few tentative steps inside, scanning the living room as I entered it. I saw nothing that raised any red flags. I had to laugh when I walked through the kitchen and saw a couple of rinsed-out storage bags on the kitchen counter with a post-it note stuck to the top one that read, "Return to cookie lady."

Next to the cookie bags was a stack of receipts and photos. A post-it note on top of that pile read, "Give to JJ" The photos were of furniture and household items, and the receipts pertained to the same items. I mused as I skipped through the pile. *Is Walker's neighbor helping him with his insurance claim? It seems as though she might be helping him compile proof of damaged personal property, which would explain why she'd left a note on his kitchen table for him to meet up with her. I recall Percival telling me she worked as an accountant. I take care of all the bills, taxes, and miscellaneous paperwork in our household. Perhaps Reilly had been in charge of those tasks in the Reynolds's home. With his wife missing, it made sense he'd hire someone to perform the daunting task for him. Perhaps JJ isn't a romantic interest of Walker's, after all, and he truly is grieving the loss of his wife. The change in his appearance indicates that's the case.*

Most of the photos were of water-stained tables, soggy beds and recliners, a severely damaged leather sofa and items of that nature. The only picture that really drew my attention was a family photo of Walker, Reilly, and Scrappy. They were sitting around a teal-and-white patio table in matching Adirondack-styled chairs. I recognized the set to be one of the nearly indestructible, outdoor furniture made from old plastic milk cartons that wouldn't rust, fade, mildew, or blow away easily. Regina and Milo had a nearly identical set in orange. I was appalled to think that, according to the Reynolds's receipt, Regina and Milo had blown over twenty-two hundred bucks on their nearly indestructible patio set. And here I'd thought Rip and I had thrown caution to the wind when we'd paid five-hundred bucks for an outdoor patio set from Lowe's. We'd given the set to Regina and Milo when we retired, but I'd noticed the patio furniture had been relegated to the trash pile on their curb.

This particular photo caught my attention for two reasons. One: the pure sweetness of it. The couple looked totally in love, gazing at each other with adoring expressions, while the cute little dog stood between them with a rag doll clenched between his jaws. And second: I'd noticed when I spoke to Walker and Jessie in the back yard a couple of days earlier, the furniture was still there, looking as if it had just been delivered by the store where it'd been purchased. *If the set hadn't been destroyed or blown away by the storm or stolen by a looter, why does he have a photo and receipt for the furniture in the pile?* I had to wonder. Not that everyone was totally honest when it came to insurance claims, I knew. It just seemed like an awfully big and noticeable item to claim as a loss, when it clearly was not even damaged.

I knew I couldn't waste time standing around musing about such trivial things. I hastily went from room to room, finding nothing of any significance. I noticed Bruno had finished drywalling the new library, which Suzanna had surmised was for her collection of music CD's. I had originally thought the thicker-than-normal wall dividing the library from the living room was odd-looking, but now I saw the reason for it. A two-sided electric fireplace had been installed. The thickness of the wall had allowed it to be inset, with glass doors on both sides, which would make for a cozy library and a warm ambiance in the living room, as well.

The library niche now had a wall of shelving, where anything from a full set of the *Encyclopedia Britannica* to all sixty, or so, of

George Strait's number-one hits could be stored. *Very nice*, I thought. I could see myself curled up on a chaise lounge with a good book while a flickering fire kept me toasty warm on one of those rare cold winter evenings in south Texas.

"Oh, crap!" I whispered, coming out of my reverie in a snap when I heard someone entering the house from the front porch. The last thing I wanted was to be caught snooping around in the neighbor's house. My eyes darted around the living room, looking for a place to hide since I knew I didn't have time to escape out the kitchen door to the back yard. I noticed a closet in the hallway. It was probably designed for brooms and mops. There were no shelves or clothes rods, and thankfully, it was currently empty except for a red-stained crowbar and a large metal toolbox with "Torres" written on the top with a black permanent marker. I was able to get inside just in the nick of time. There wasn't a lock on the door, so I could only pray whoever had entered the home wouldn't need to place anything in the small closet.

"I just need to grab my toolbox," I heard as I eased the closet door shut. I recognized Tony, the demolition contractor's, voice and should have been trying to come up with a believable excuse for being inside the closet of a home I didn't own. However, because the words, "Oh, $@#&!" were echoing in my head, I couldn't hear myself think.

I believe in divine intervention, and that's the only thing that can explain why Tony decided to use the Reynolds's restroom before snatching his toolbox out of the closet I was currently cowering in. When I heard the bathroom door close, I scampered out of the closet faster than Rascal could have run from a red-tailed hawk. I made it out the kitchen door before Tony completed his business in the john, only to realize I'd left my lemonade glass on the kitchen counter where I'd set it to rummage through the photos and receipts on the table.

I stood behind a large palm tree in the Moores' yard,

pretending to be interested in the flowering Jatropha plants growing around its base. I stepped behind the palm tree's trunk when I heard the Reynolds's front door open about ten minutes later. For some reason I can't explain, because I'd never considered any of Walker's subcontractors as suspects in Reilly's disappearance, I used my phone to begin videoing the man as he exited the house. Without even glancing my way, Tony walked to his truck, set his toolbox and crowbar in its bed, and drove away. A man I didn't recognize occupied the passenger seat. Though his head was barely visible over the dash, as if he was scrunched down in his seat, I thought I'd captured a decent likeness of him in the video clip I'd taken, if it was ever needed for future reference.

Tony had either been constipated or had done something else in the Reynolds's house besides retrieving his toolbox for that much time to have passed. I then realized another possibility was that someone else had stowed his tools in the closet, causing Tony to have to search around for his box.

Once the TNT Demolition truck was out of sight, I went back in through the broken window to collect my drink. As I walked through the kitchen, I noticed water pooled on the counter next to the sink. A filthy rag was draped over the faucet. I was almost positive neither the rag nor the pool of water had been there before. Apparently, Tony had used the rag to wash something, which explained why it'd taken longer than expected for him to leave.

I briefly wondered what he'd decided was necessary to clean up, but I had learned my lesson and didn't stick around to think about it. I hastily grabbed my glass and vacated the premises.

Once I'd returned to the Caboose, I sat at the kitchen table, sipping on what remained of the lemonade. I'd worked up a sweat, either from the heat outside or nervousness from nearly getting caught trespassing in the neighbor's house. Rip was helping Milo on a project, and Regina had driven to a salon in Robstown, claiming a "nail polish emergency". I didn't know from whom Regina had inherited her high-maintenance trait, but it wasn't from me, and it definitely wasn't from her father, who would be content wearing the same outfit until the fabric rotted and fell off his body. If you looked "low maintenance" up in the dictionary, you'd see a photo of my bald, slightly overweight husband dressed in a solid white t-shirt that'd been bleached a thousand times, and a pair of worn-out denim pants. In another year or two, when the most threadbare areas of his blue jeans began to rip, his jeans would be right in style and worth ten times as much money as we'd paid for them a decade ago.

I looked down at my own fingernails and decided maybe I shouldn't brag too much about not being high maintenance. Low maintenance could also be construed as meaning that one didn't give a rat's ass about their appearance, and that was nothing to boast about. I was actually proud my daughter took the time and made the effort to keep herself looking good. Rip and I should both aim to be a little more like her.

While I had the time to myself, I reviewed the video I'd taken of Tony Torres and his mysterious companion. By taking a screenshot of the dude in the passenger seat and then enhancing the image, I realized it was not a man, but rather a woman. I couldn't make out any of her facial features but could tell she had very blond hair. With a start, I realized she resembled Reilly Reynolds, who had been short and had long, nearly white, hair. I'd only met the woman once, but I was sure Regina would be able to figure out if the woman in the video was her missing neighbor. I thought the chances were remote. A woman trying to stay hidden from the public wouldn't ride boldly around her old neighborhood in the front seat of a pickup truck belonging to the man she'd run off with. Or, at least, one wouldn't think so.

Then I noticed something else disturbing in the video. The

crowbar Tony had been carrying no longer seemed to have a large red stain on it, which I had originally assumed was paint. I took another screenshot from the video to enhance and was unable to detect any paint on the metal bar. I couldn't be certain, however, as the image was extremely grainy when enlarged. *Is that red stuff what Tony washed off in the sink?* I wondered.

The dirty rag draped across the faucet *had* appeared to have a red tint to it, but could dried paint be washed off with water? I wasn't certain but knew Rip would probably know. Milo would if Rip didn't, for sure. *What if the red stain was blood?* I asked myself. *If the woman in Tony's truck was someone other than Reilly, could the missing woman have been bludgeoned to death with the crowbar? Was that why Tony wanted it removed from the house? What motive could Tony have to want the woman dead? Surely he hadn't been having an affair with Reilly too. Would he even consider accepting a job at the victim's house after killing her? How could he look her husband in the eye without giving away his guilt? I know I couldn't have pulled it off. I'd cave like a wet tent the second my victim's spouse laid eyes on me. If Reilly's disappearance truly was due to a homicide, and the crowbar had been the murder weapon, why would Tony ever leave it in his victim's house, where it could be readily discovered by homicide detectives?*

Had the authorities even processed the house for trace evidence after Reilly went missing? I wondered. *It sounds to me as if the local authorities have just dismissed her disappearance as a freak accident that occurred during the peak of the hurricane. Their investigation of her case has been so limited in nature. I'm sure they've come to the conclusion nobody could have withstood the 140+ m.p.h. winds while chasing a dog down a narrow pier, much less a petite woman like Reilly. Or did she not actually attempt such a ridiculously dangerous stunt? That story was based solely on what her spouse said, after all. Could Walker have been wise to the fact his new wife was cheating on him with their neighbor, Percival Pandero, and possibly Tony Torres? If so, could he have used the hurricane as the perfect opportunity to do away with her and make it look like an accident?*

It was questions like these that made me realize I needed to discuss the situation, and everything I'd seen and heard, with Rip. I wanted him to get more involved. I needed his help to continue my quest to discover the truth behind Reilly's disappearance if I hoped to ever get a good night's sleep again. As the former sheriff of the county, Rip had access to everything the local police department knew about the case, if anything. Because he was a generous, giving man, nearly everyone in the local police department owed him a favor, as well.

Whether or not he'd be willing to use his access or cash in on any of those favors owed him remained to be seen.

NINETEEN

R ip and I were sitting outside in our lawn chairs that evening, drinking our daily highballs. I had found the nerve to bring up my concerns about the missing neighbor again.

"I understand your desire to bring what you've discovered to the attention of the Rockport Police Department, honey, but I'm afraid you're overestimating how much pull I have there," Rip said. "I've been retired more than seven years. I don't even know half of the officers working there now. I can guarantee you that Sheriff Peabody's not going to be happy to know you're still looking into the situation on your own. He has his ways, and I had mine."

"So, what are you saying? Are you going to forbid me to keep looking into Reilly's disappearance?" I asked.

Rip raised his eyebrows at me. "Forbid you? I would never forbid you to do anything you wanted to do. You should know better than that. I treasure my life too much to try to enforce my will on you."

I laughed along with him before asking, "Will you help me?"

"I suppose. As much as I can, anyway. I'm sure I can get

Chuck to send that rag you told me Tony used to the lab for testing. If it *is* blood, they'll be able to run the DNA through the
database to see if there's a match."

Chuck Beatty, the medical examiner, was still one of Rip's
closest friends. I knew he would do anything Rip asked of him if
there was a way to do it without overstepping his authority
and/or doing something unethical.

"That'd be awesome!" I exclaimed. "I'll go get it right now
before it gets washed or thrown away."

"You need to slow your roll, dear." Rip stuck his jar in the
drink holder of his chair and turned to me. "Don't push your
luck. You don't want to get arrested for breaking and entering.
I'm sure I could get Joe to drop the charges, but it would be very
embarrassing for me."

"Is it still considered breaking and entering if there's no glass
in the window and you can step right into the house through the
window frame?" I asked.

"Technically, yes. Any way you look at it you are trespassing
on private property."

"I can always say I was just collecting my Ziploc bags off the
kitchen table."

"Your what?" Rip's expression made it clear he thought my
mental capacity had slipped another notch. "Why do you have
Ziploc bags on the neighbor's table? More importantly, why
would you want them back?"

"Long story. Suffice it to say, there's a post-it note on the bags
to remind the general contractor Walker hired, Jessie Garza, to
return the bags to me."

"I'm confused. I don't get it."

"We had way too many cookies left over from my last batch,
so I dropped some of them off over there. I figured they wouldn't
go to waste in a crew of construction workers."

"I guarantee they wouldn't have gone to waste here either,"

Rip said. "But it's just as well you gave them away since I have an appointment to see Dr. Heron while we're here. She badgers me about my weight every time I go in for a checkup."

"Exactly!" I nodded in agreement. We both had appointments to see our primary doctor in Corpus the following week. I'd gained a few pounds, too, and wasn't looking forward to the lecture I was undoubtedly going to get from the no-nonsense physician. "Neither of us has any willpower. That's why I didn't want the cookies sitting on our counter, enticing me to grab one every time I walked through the kitchen. Sugar-free or not, they're still loaded with carbs and calories."

While Rip was distracted by the abrupt change in subject, I took my drink inside and set the glass on the kitchen table. I exited the trailer and walked at a fast pace past Rip. "Be right back."

"Where do you think you're...?" I heard Rip begin to ask, but I'd rounded the corner before he'd gotten his question completely out. I didn't stop or even slow down to respond.

The neighbor's house was still empty. A loose shingle flapping on the roof made an eerie and repetitive sound that gave me the willies. I was disappointed to discover the rag was no longer draped over the kitchen faucet, nor could I find it anywhere else. The sink was spotless as if it had been cleaned with bleach since I'd last seen it. The fact someone would go to such effort to clean it up when everything else in the kitchen was a royal mess made me suspicious.

The way I saw it, there was only one thing to do. I'd have to make a trip over to the Reynolds's house the following morning to retrieve my valuable plastic bags. I might look to the construction workers as the cheapest, chintziest broad in the world, but I wouldn't let something like that stop me. I didn't care what they thought of me if it could help bring closure to Reilly's loved ones.

She deserved justice, and I was going to stop at nothing to help her get it.

———

"Good morning, Bruno!" I greeted the drywall specialist who had just pulled into the neighbor's driveway as I headed next door the following day. I reached Bruno's truck as the diminutive fellow climbed down out of the driver's seat. And, no, this was no coincidence. I'd seen his truck coming down the street and had hid behind the large palm tree until he got closer.

"Good morning!" Without saying anything to prolong our conversation, he dropped the tailgate on the back of his truck and headed to the front door.

"I'm surprised to see you. Jessie told me you were taking a few days off."

"Yeah, I was going to. Luckily, it only took one day to accomplish everything I needed to get done. Now I've taken on another job I need to get going on right away. I just stopped by Walker's to pick up some stuff I left behind." He walked past me as if I were a lawn ornament.

"Did you finish the library niche you told me about?" I asked as I fell in step behind him.

"Yep." Bruno still seemed as if his thoughts were miles away.

"Would you mind showing it to me?" I wasn't going to be dissuaded by his lack of interest in carrying on a conversation with me. "I was so impressed with your clever idea and I'm curious how it turned out."

"Yeah, sure. I'd be happy to show it to you. I think it came out awesome. I decided to add a two-sided fireplace at the last minute, and Walker loves the result." I'd hoped buttering him up might be effective, and it was. There weren't too many people who didn't like to talk about themselves, especially when someone was complimenting them on their work and ingenuity.

I admired the library and fireplace and acted as if I hadn't already seen his handiwork. Bruno beamed with pride as I laid it on thick. "You are amazing! This is beautiful and looks so cozy. Walker was lucky to get you for his reconstruction project. If Reilly does happen to show back up, she'll love having the library to store either books or CD's. Do you know whether her passion is literature or music? My guess is music."

With neither a yea nor a nay to my query, Bruno simply replied to my lavish praise on his work. "Thanks. I'm really pleased with the way it turned out."

"I should think you would be. I imagine the house will be full of workers today, won't it?"

"No. Like I said, I'm headed out to get started on my new job. TNT finished up all the demo work that needed to be done here, and Tony's got a dental appointment this morning. I think Jessie might stop by later on, but that'll be the extent of it. And Walker's at work, so he won't be home until later on this afternoon."

"What does Walker do?" I asked. I hadn't realized until that moment I had no clue what the man did for a living.

"He's a private detective."

"Private detective? Really?" I was floored by this news. I could picture him as being involved in any other occupation other than detective work, from a deck hand on a shrimp boat to CEO of a private firm. Wouldn't a private detective be turning over every stone, searching every nook and cranny in search of his missing wife? "Walker must be doing some investigating on his own about the loss of his wife. Isn't he?"

"Not that I know of," Bruno replied. He had picked up a five-gallon bucket of joint compound and a roll of drywall tape and was heading back out the door. "Mostly he does contract work for the Social Security Administration. He recently caught a man on video windsurfing in Little Bay while on disability for a disabling back injury. If the dude can windsurf, he should have no problem serving up burgers at McDonalds."

"That's for sure. Good for Walker for tracking down folks who are working the system. But what about his wife? Doesn't he want to find out what happened to her?"

"There really ain't much to investigate when it comes to Reilly. It's pretty much a foregone conclusion that she was a victim of Harvey. If her body somehow got wedged under submerged debris from the storm, it might never resurface."

"That's true." It was also true that the first time I met Bruno, he'd told me Walker was the only one holding on to the hope Reilly would turn up alive and well. Why the change? In the last few days, had Walker accepted the fact Reilly was most likely dead or had Bruno altered his story, forgetting what he'd told me previously? I followed the elfin-like man out the door, feeling like Big Foot trailing a newborn fawn. The bucket of joint compound he hoisted up into the bed of his truck looked as if it weighed more than the man lugging it. "Where's your new job?"

"Barlow Barnaby's house."

You mean that half-witted goofball up the street who was just killed by someone who tried to make it look like a suicide? I wanted to ask, using the insulting characterization Bruno had used to describe the murder victim. Instead, I said, "Oh, really? What happened to him was just dreadful."

"Yes, it was," Bruno replied. "No one deserves to die like that. I know the family, so I offered them a good rate to get Barlow's house back up to snuff so it can be sold."

"That's very thoughtful of you. I'm sure they're apprecia-tive." *I wonder how they'd feel about the charming way you refer to their recently deceased family member?*

"It was the least I could do. Tony's agreed to help me out on the side. He'll be joining me at Barlow's after his dental appointment."

"That's great." It was nice to know where the two men could be found, should Rip and I want to question them later. "That must be why I saw him picking up his toolbox and a crowbar here yesterday."

"Yeah. We'll definitely need to use some of his tools at Barlow's house today."

"Hmm. How about that?" I said nonchalantly. I didn't want to seem overly focused on the crowbar. "You got him working on a Saturday even?"

"Yeah. Tony's a hard worker and a dependable guy."

"Handy for you to know so many tradesmen to help out in a pinch, isn't it?" It was also handy to know where I might find the crowbar I'd videoed Tony removing from the house, even if the rag had been disposed of. It was possible that, in his haste to clean up the crowbar, he'd missed a speck of blood, which I knew would be all the crime lab would need to get a DNA sample. To my knowledge, there'd been no soap or bleach on hand at the time, even though it looked as if someone had returned to scour the sink. I hoped Tony hadn't used any bleach on the crowbar itself. Because the potential murder weapon was in his custody, he'd likely be less concerned about blood on it than on his victim's sink.

Although I still couldn't fathom a motive Tony Torres might have to eliminate Reilly, I couldn't overlook the fact he'd been so diligent about removing evidence from the crowbar and then the crowbar itself. Returning to the scene to retrieve the rag he'd used to clean it, and to scour the sink with bleach he'd likely have had to bring with him to the Reynolds' home, only added to my suspicion that the red stain was indeed blood, not paint.

I now had to come up with a way to get back inside Barlow Barnaby's house without breaking and entering. Rip could be so persnickety when it came to his wife breaking the law. But first, I had to go take care of the little furball from hell. I'd never have guessed something weighing in at less than two pounds could scare the holy crap out of me. I wanted to get the necessary tasks accomplished as quickly as I could and keep as much distance between Rascal and myself as possible.

I wonder if Milo would consider it weird if I asked to borrow the neoprene chest waders he uses for wade-fishing so I can wear them while feeding the neighbor's pet? If that rodent were to run up my pants leg the way it did Rip's, my heart would stop mid-beat. I'd be the next person from Flamingo Road Chuck Beatty would be hauling away in a body bag.

TWENTY

I stepped into the mudroom, also known as Rascal's room, which was located near the rear deck door of Suzanna's stilt home. The deck looked out over the bay and offered a beautiful view of the sunset and Rockport's annual firework displays. Sure enough, as Suzanna had boasted, you could see the backside of George Strait's house on Curlew Drive.

I froze when I saw Rascal had crawled up on the table where his food pellets, snacks, and dust containers were stored in airtight plastic containers. After a brief stare-down, Rascal looked away and purred, reminding me of Dolly when she was trying to manipulate Rip into giving her a handful of feline Greenies, her favorite snack. Dolly was nobody's fool. She knew Rip was an easier target than me, and she was more apt to get what she wanted out of the weakest link. Animals were definitely smarter than we sometimes give them credit for.

In this case, I was easily manipulated by the chinchilla—out of fear, not weakness. I'd have been willing to hand over my wallet and the gold-and-jade ring Rip had purchased for me on our golden wedding anniversary if that's what it took to protect myself from Rascal. I'd have even stripped down to my underwear and handed my clothes over to the varmint to keep him from putting me in the emergency room the way he had his owner. I was in no mood to have my ear bitten off, so I placed six raisins in Rascal's food bowl to keep him occupied. While he gnawed on them, I refilled the water bottle, spooned pellets into his food bowl with the raisins, added more dust to the bathing box, and scooped minuscule poop pellets out of the litter box. The last thing I needed to do before departing was water the golden pothos plant on the window ledge behind the kitchen sink. I'd noticed the leaves were beginning to droop as they wrapped around the beautiful copper pot the plant was potted in.

I knew Suzanna's houseplant, also known as "devil's ivy", could be hazardous to pets, like cats and dogs. I didn't know if that held true for chinchillas, but I did recall from researching the animal that they like to chew on plants. To help ensure her pet didn't die on my watch, I decided to place the copper pot on top of the refrigerator and would warn Suzanna about its hazards when she returned home.

When I lifted up the pot, I discovered a business card underneath. The card had "Bloomers Nursery and Landscape" on the front, a local nursery on West Fourth Street I was familiar with. There was a phone number scribbled on the reverse side that was different from the one listed on the front. I assumed the number was a direct line to the business from which she'd purchased the plant.

I took a photo of the back of the card with my phone so I could call the number later and inquire about the plant's toxicity, and whether or not it was dangerous to chinchillas. Chances were, I realized, the nursery was temporarily closed due to storm damage, but the direct line might be to a staff member's personal cell phone, so it'd be worth the effort.

As I turned to leave the kitchen, the sound of ice dropping

into the tray inside the freezer startled me. I was tense, worried that Rascal might decide to terrorize me. My mind quickly went from being ravaged by a crazed rodent to the ice I'd heard drop. The thought of ice reminded me of the ominous big black bag in the chest freezer downstairs. I glanced around for anything that resembled a security camera, nanny cam, or monitoring device of any type and saw none. Her newly installed "state-of-the-art security system" must have been less elaborate than Suzanna had let on. Either that or merely a fabrication to keep me from snooping around and possibly discovering something incriminating inside her home.

Praying I wasn't being monitored by some well-hidden recording device, I hurried down the stairs to the garage and made my way to the basement restroom. Luckily for me, the door was propped open with an old iron anvil being used as a doorstop. Suzanna must have become tired of having to punch in a security code to enter the room, which consisted of nothing more than an old chest freezer, non-working toilet, sink, and a tub full of tools.

Stopping in front of the freezer, I noticed the two boxes of MRE's Suzanna had decided to hang on to and the oil-stained bedspread she'd lain over the top were gone. The unit no longer appeared to be running. I distinctively recalled a loud humming noise coming from it the first time I'd seen it, along with a thick layer of frost covering the black bag inside.

I lifted up the lid tentatively, not sure what I'd find inside. I was both surprised and disappointed to find nothing. Suzanna had been serious when she'd said she was going to get right on the task of defrosting and cleaning out the old appliance. *Why had cleaning out the freezer been such a top priority?* I wondered. *Was there something inside it she was afraid someone would discover if she didn't dispose of it immediately? And, if so, what was it? Scarier still, **who** was it, if the bag contains what I feared it had?*

My number one suspect seemed to change with every rotation of the Earth, if not more often, and my list of people with possible motives to kill Reilly continued to grow. I wished I could begin eliminating a few of them. I was beginning to feel discouraged because I felt no closer to the truth than when I'd first decided to investigate the situation.

I went back upstairs in order to lock the front door, and as I walked down the front staircase to the driveway, I glanced at the pile of debris in front of the Panderos' house. Their home had received remarkably little damage from the storm, but almost no one was completely spared. Their debris pile contained mostly broken lawn ornaments, a few uprooted bushes, the two boxes of MRE's she'd decided not to donate at the last moment, and some banged-up guttering that had been ripped from the roofline by the extreme winds. That was pretty much the extent of the items in the pile, except for one thing I hadn't expected to see—the ominous big black trash bag I'd last seen in the homeowners' chest freezer! It was half-buried under the oil-stained blanket and a couple of dead hibiscus plants.

As I approached the debris pile, I could detect an unpleasant stench. I was surprised I hadn't smelled it earlier. I was hesitant, but decided to check out what was in the bag. The closer I got to it, the more odorous it became. By the time I was a few feet from the pile, I was afraid of what I might find. It smelled like something was not only dead inside the bag, but also overcooked in the scorching mid-September heat.

I stopped short of opening the bag because I was about to gag from the stench. I decided I needed Rip's help to investigate what the stinky bag contained.

Rip was gone when I returned to the trailer, almost certainly helping Milo with a project. I made myself a cup of herbal tea and tried the phone number scribbled on the nursery's business card. I still wanted to find out if Suzanna's houseplant was dangerous to have where Rascal could chew on it, as rodents are wont to do.

"Hello."

"Hi. I hate to bother you, but I just have one quick question."

"Go ahead." The male voice on the other end of the line sounded familiar. I must have dealt with the individual at the nursery on one of my many visits there in the past. As I had a black thumb and a tendency to kill every plant I bought with kindness, I was often buying new plants to replace dead ones. One thing I was a stickler about was not letting a live plant in my home make a dead pet out of our chubby tabby.

"Do you know if golden pothos plants are hazardous to chinchillas?"

"No."

"No, they aren't, or no, you don't know?" I asked.

"Lady, if this is a joke, I don't find it particularly humorous," the man sharply replied.

"I'm not kidding. I need to know what I should do with—"

"Wanna know what you can do?"

He told me what I could do and ended the call before I could respond. As you can imagine, I can't repeat his suggestion. Suddenly, I realized why I'd recognized the voice. It wasn't an employee of the nursery. It was Walker Reynolds. At first, I was baffled about why Walker would be answering the phone at Bloomers Nursery. Then I realized I hadn't called the nursery at all.

Clearly, Suzanna had scribbled Walker's number down on the first thing she could find. I guess she'd thought his professional services might come in handy when trying to determine if her husband was having an affair with Reilly. Or perhaps she had formed an alliance with Walker. After all, their spouses were both cheating on them with each other's spouses. How far they'd take that conceivable alliance was anybody's guess.

"If you recognized Walker's voice, then he might have recognized yours, as well." Rip looked at me pointedly after I told him about the phone call.

"I hadn't thought of that," I admitted. And now that he'd brought it to my attention, I was worried. "I don't think he did though. Hope not, anyway."

"Why'd you call him in the first place?"

"I didn't call him intentionally, Rip. I thought I was calling the nursery advertised on the front of the business card and was surprised when he answered the phone instead. You see, I found the card under a potted plant."

"You must have been doing some heavy-duty snooping to find something under a pot." Rip sounded disgusted with me, and for good reason.

"I wasn't snooping at all. I was moving the plant to the top of Suzanna's fridge because I recognized it as one that is toxic to animals and didn't want Rascal to get sick."

"After the traumatic experience he put me through, I'd have chopped up a few leaves and fed Rascal a golden pothos salad for lunch." Rip clearly felt no affinity for the chinchilla.

"Oh, hush, Rip! I have no real fondness for Rascal either, but I need to keep the damned thing alive until Suzanna gets home. That's why I called the nursery. I wanted to find out if the plant was dangerous to chinchillas as well as cats."

"Why would she hide the phone number under a potted plant?" Rip asked.

"We can't know for sure she intentionally hid it."

"What do you mean?" Rip asked. "Of course she hid it. Under a pot is not a normal place to keep a business card with a phone number written on it."

"Nor is a sugar canister a normal place to keep a grocery list under."

"Huh?" Rip looked at me as if I'd just told him I stored live grenades in the undercarriage storage compartment of the Chartreuse Caboose.

I walked over to the kitchen counter, lifted up the orange, brown and olive green ceramic canister shaped like a mushroom that I'd been gifted in the seventies, and exposed a piece of paper with brown sugar, paper towels, and malted milk balls written on it. I set the canister back down before Rip had time to read it. The last thing on the list was not intended for his consumption. It was exclusively for mine when my sweet tooth was too powerful to ignore. If he thought I kept my grocery list in an unusual place, he should see where I hid the candy. I knew the very last place he'd ever look was behind the laundry basket.

"I don't get it." Rip looked both hurt and confused. "Why do you keep your grocery list hidden under the sugar? Are you afraid I'll look at it for some reason?"

Yes, I am, but that's beside the point. "Of course not, sweetheart. Don't be ridiculous. Why should I care if you looked at our grocery list? It's just that women sometimes sweep the dirt under the rug, so to speak. The list isn't *hidden* there, it's just that we have a limited amount of counter space in this trailer. I keep it under there so the kitchen doesn't look messy. It's the same reason I leave the can opener in the cabinet, despite the fact I have to get it out nearly every single day to use it. Perhaps Suzanna put the card under the pot so it'd be handy without cluttering up her counter, or not be accidentally pitched out with junk mail or blown off the window ledge by a gust of wind."

"I suppose." Rip sounded dubious. But then I realized it

wouldn't bother him if every pot, pan, dish, utensil, and small appliance we owned was out in the open, stacked halfway to the ceiling on the kitchen counter, table, and stovetop, where they'd all be handy when needed. What I considered clutter, he considered a convenience. Rip shook his head. "I guess I'll never understand women."

"No, probably not. And we'll never understand you men, either."

"Well, I need to go help Milo install a couple of new windows in their sunroom pretty soon. Let's go check out the contents of that trash bag and we'll continue this conversation later."

"All right." As I agreed to his suggestion, I thought, *While he assists Milo, I need to find a new hidey-hole for my grocery list, like maybe inside my box of Swiffer duster refills or under an unopened container of hummus in the refrigerator. If he knew I was buying one of his favorite candies and hiding it from him, he'd be tearing the trailer apart looking for it. And malted milk balls are definitely not on his diet these days.*

"Since you couldn't locate the rag used to clean the crowbar, I guess taking it to Chuck to see if he can get it tested for blood is out of the question," Rip said as we exited the trailer.

"It's not entirely out of the question, but we'll discuss that later too."

"Okay, although I'm not sure I like the sound of that."

I just smiled at Rip in response. I had a feeling the window project might get delayed after we discovered what was in the black bag in the debris pile, and I was right. The reason for the delay, however, was not at all what I'd anticipated.

TWENTY-ONE

With wet rags held up against our noses, Rip slashed open the black garbage bag with his pocketknife. When the contents spilled out onto the ground, we both jumped back in shock—and a bit of fear, as well. The last thing we expected to find was a passel of venomous snakes. Dead, but still alarming.

"There must be two dozen rattlesnakes in this bag!" Rip exclaimed. "Why in hell would Suzanna's husband hunt and freeze rattlers?"

"Beats me. But at least it isn't something that'd put one or both of the Panderos behind bars for the rest of their lives."

"Maybe not for the rest of their lives, but a few years is not beyond the realm of possibility," Rip said.

"What do you mean?"

"These are timber rattlesnakes. They're the only venomous snake in Texas that's protected and illegal to hunt, kill, sell, or have in one's possession. I'll need to notify Sheriff Peabody right away. Take a couple of photos with the phone in the meantime."

"Okay." I snapped two pictures as requested. For about the zillionth time, Rip had impressed me with his knowledge. For a guy who'd never been much on reading, he seemed to be well-versed about a lot of random things. "Will Suzanna be in legal trouble if she was aware of what was in the bag?"

"Yes, I'm afraid so. It's referred to as 'aiding and abetting a criminal'."

I suddenly felt awash in emotions—mixed emotions, to be precise. I was certain Percival was behind the bag of snakes, but not so certain Suzanna was unaware of his gruesome hobby. She'd definitely acted as if she didn't want me to know what was in their freezer. I was appalled that Percival would kill a protected species, even though I've always maintained the only good snake was a dead snake. Was he aware the species was classified as protected? Or like me, was he totally in the dark about the subject? Either way, he should have used his phone to research the topic before killing the snakes. I wasn't sure ignorance would carry enough weight in a court of law, and who doesn't carry a wealth of information in their back pocket these days?

Along with disgust, I also felt remorse. The neighbor I'd bonded with was trusting me to take care of not only her pet but also her home, a major investment. Instead, I was responsible for potentially getting her estranged husband incarcerated, or at the very least, in deep doo-doo. Suzanna's fate was up in the air, as well, depending on how much she knew about Percival's illegal activity. On the bright side, their beloved rodent was still alive and kicking.

While Rip was busy talking with the sheriff in front of the Panderos' house, I hoped I could find a way to track down Tony's crowbar. With any luck at all, there was still enough of the red substance left on it to be tested. Bruno had said earlier that morning he and Tony were working on Barlow Barnaby's house as a favor to the deceased man's family. Chances were I could find the two men still there, trying to get as much done as they could. With so much rebuilding going on around town, time was definitely of the essence.

Rip walked into the trailer just then. "Joe needs to track down the snake dude. Didn't you tell me you ran into the man who lives next door at the grocery store in Portland?"

"Yes. He told me he was renting a fully-furnished condo there." I hesitated before giving out any more information and then decided I'd only be prolonging the inevitable if I didn't spill it all. "He was having dinner with the lady who owns the house up the street that was nearly demolished. Her name is Jo Wallinski, but she goes by JJ She's currently staying at the Motel 6 in Portland."

"That's great, honey! This JJ lady can probably lead Joe to Par—"

"Percival."

"Percival's whereabouts." Rip grabbed an energy drink out of the fridge and headed for the door. "After I give Joe a call, I'll go help Milo with the windows. He had to go to the Home Depot in Corpus to pick up the materials, so he's getting a late start."

"Percival told me the lines there were really long."

"Wow! You and he had quite a chat, didn't you?"

"Well, we were stuck in a lengthy line at the grocery store at the time with nothing else to do to pass the time." Rip gave me a look that spoke volumes all by itself. "I can't help it if I'm sociable. Being friendly's not a bad thing, you know."

"I'm just amazed at the coincidence of you ending up in line directly behind him." I read the sarcasm in his voice and gave him an icy glare. After studying my expression, he laughed and enveloped me in a bear hug. "I was just kidding, sweetheart. I applaud you for your quick thinking. And your outgoing nature is one of the many things I love about you.

Now I need to get going. You should relax this afternoon and take it easy."

"That's what I'd planned to do."

As you can well imagine, that's not *all* I had planned to do. As soon as the Chevy truck was out of view, I slipped on my shoes and began walking up the street. I'd come up with an excuse to pop in at the Barnaby house. It wasn't a great plan, but it was all I could think of at the time. This was one of the occasions I wished I had Lexie Starr with me. Her ruses were rarely without peril, but they were usually effective.

"Hello, again," Bruno said as he opened up Barlow's front door. "What's up?"

"The other day when I found Barlow's body hanging in the living room, I'd been touching up my lipstick when I passed out. I haven't seen that tube of lipstick since then, and it's my favorite color. Thought I'd drop in while someone was here and look for it."

"I haven't seen any lipstick, Ms. Ripple." Bruno was gazing at me in a peculiar way. Perhaps he couldn't understand how a woman could unexpectedly stumble across a nude man hanging from a ceiling and her first thought was to touch up her lipstick even though she was on the verge of fainting. What's not to understand about that?

"Hmm…it must be here somewhere. I can search around for it while you and Tony continue your work." I hadn't spotted Tony, but I saw his toolbox on an end table in the corner of the living room. His crowbar was lying directly behind it. I hoped to be able to snatch the bar up and sneak out of the house before Tony returned to the room to get it or something else out of his toolbox. Later, when he couldn't locate the crowbar, he'd likely think he'd mislaid it or left it in another room. He'd surely never suspect me of taking it. After all, why would I want to pilfer something like a crowbar when I'd only dropped by to look for my missing tube of lipstick?

"Tony's not here yet. His dental appointment must be taking longer than he expected. I doubt he'll feel like working this afternoon."

That's awesome! I thought. "Oh, I'm sorry to hear that."

"He was in such pain this morning, his girlfriend had to drive him to Corpus to find a dentist who took emergency cases on Saturday."

"Oh, you mean that pretty lady with the long blond hair?"

Wearing a bemused expression, Bruno replied, "Yeah, Judy Goetz. She's a looker, for sure. They're engaged to be married on Valentine's Day."

"How romantic." That was one question answered. The blonde I'd seen in his passenger seat was his girlfriend, not the missing neighbor. "I hope Tony's back to work soon. I know work goes much faster when you have an extra hand helping out."

"That's for sure," Bruno muttered. "Holler if you need anything. I want to finish getting the sheetrock up on the bedroom wall today so I can get started on the living room."

He'd barely left the room when I rushed over, pulled a latex glove out of my pocket, put it on, and picked up the crowbar. I was surprised to see there was still a decent amount of the red-colored stain on it that I hadn't been able to see in the video I'd taken. I hastily made for the front exit. As I opened the door, I shouted, "Found my lipstick! Thanks, Bruno!"

I didn't wait around for a response. As I hustled up the street, holding the crowbar to my chest so it couldn't be seen from the windows of the Barnaby home, I wondered about Tony's reaction to finding it missing. If it truly was the murder weapon and still had proof of his victim's blood on it, he might experience a feeling of pure panic. I know I would've keeled over for the third time in a matter of days if something like that happened to me.

Maybe this sudden habit of passing out is something I should bring to Dr. Herron's attention at my appointment next week, I thought. *If nothing else, maybe it'll be a good enough distraction to keep her from lecturing me about the weight I've gained since my last checkup. Note to self: scratch malted milk balls off the grocery list.*

"What do you mean, you took it when no one was looking?" Rip was livid. I'd expected a high five, not a look of condemnation. Rip and Milo were standing in the front yard with their hands on their hips and sweat rolling down their foreheads when I walked up the driveway from Barlow's house with the crowbar. "Are you intentionally trying to make any evidence the crime lab might find on it inadmissible in a court of law?"

"Well, no. No, of, course not. I, I, just…" I was stuttering, trying to justify my impulsive actions. "I was just thinking—"

"No, you *weren't* thinking. That's the problem."

"But, I, I just—"

"You need to take that crowbar back right this minute. I'll call Chuck and have him get a search warrant to pick it up at Barlow's house. If we have proof to arrest a perpetrator for murder, we don't want him getting off on a technicality. Do we?"

"Of course not. I'll go return this thing right now." Rip was right. I hadn't thought about the legal aspects of how the evidence was obtained. I needed to get the crowbar back where I'd found it before Bruno discovered it missing or finished the bedroom and started putting up sheetrock in the living room.

I was back in Barlow's driveway in record time, hurtling over anything in my path, including a kid on a Big Wheel bike. Did my speed and agility spare me the embarrassment of returning the crowbar? No, it didn't! Did it cause me to injure my ankle from an ill-timed leap onto the front porch? Yes, of course it did! I didn't not pursue a career as a ballerina out of choice, but rather because of my ability to stumble over things that aren't even in my way. I once tripped over the shadow of an overhead power line on a sidewalk and wrenched my knee. What can I say? The wind was causing the electrical line to sway and I thought the undulating shadow it cast was a snake. And not a dead one, either!

That recollection made me wonder what was going on behind the scenes regarding the bag of rotting timber rattlers. *Has Percival been arrested?* I wondered. *Would he be told who'd discovered the snakes and turned him in? Was I in the process of making sure I was on the top of everyone in the neighborhood's shit list?*

That was my last thought before my ill-timed leap onto the front porch landed me on my rear end in a crumpled heap at Barlow's doorstep.

TWENTY-TWO

"What the hell?" Bruno asked when he responded to my tapping on Barlow's front door with the crowbar. He looked down at me as if eyeing a circus clown stuck in a wooden barrel. "What happened?"

"What do you think happened?" I asked, feigning indignation. "I tripped over this damned crowbar someone left on the top step!"

"Oh, crap! I'm so sorry. Tony must have set it down as he was leaving last night and forgot to pick it up. Are you all right?"

"Not really. I think I broke my ankle." I was trying not to smile at this fortunate turn of events. Not that my ankle might be broken, mind you, but that Bruno hadn't noticed the crowbar lying behind Tony's toolbox earlier when we were talking in Barlow's living room.

"Should I call for an ambulance?" Bruno looked genuinely concerned, which touched me. "No. But could I use your phone to call my husband? I left ours with him. I'm beginning to think we both should have our own phone, like the rest of the world."

"Not a bad idea. And of course you can use my phone. Give

me the number." He dialed and handed his phone to me. "Can I get you anything while you're waiting for your husband?"

I smiled and shook my head. After speaking with Rip, I handed the phone back to Bruno. "Thank you. I'm going to set this crowbar against the railing so no one else trips over it."

"No. I'll take it inside to make damned sure no one else gets hurt because of it."

"Good thinking." I was concerned about any trace evidence on the crowbar being compromised and wanted to suggest he wear my latex gloves to handle it but knew that'd look suspicious.

As I waited for Rip, Bruno did everything he could to make me comfortable. He brought me a bottle of water, gave me a cushion to sit on, and a second one to prop my throbbing ankle on. He went back inside to retrieve a third cushion to wedge behind my back as I leaned against the porch railing. It was hard to imagine he'd harm anyone. But I had to keep in mind you couldn't judge a drywaller by his cushions.

After a trip to an urgent care center for x-rays, I was back home with my left leg elevated and a bag of frozen peas resting on top of my black-and-blue sprained ankle. While I rested on the couch, Rip went over to take care of Rascal. He looked as if he'd rather go into a bear's den and offer to give it a free colonoscopy.

He returned twenty minutes later, smiling and all in one piece. As he walked into the Caboose, he said, "I've got great news!"

"Really?" My spirits perked up immediately. I'd been feeling kind of low since the accident on Barlow's front porch. I hoped the medical examiner had called Rip with results from the crime lab on any trace evidence they might have found on the crowbar, even though it didn't seem as if enough time had elapsed for the results to be available. My spirits perked right back down at the "great news" Rip had to report.

"Yes. I never even laid eyes on that pint-sized devil while I was next door, so we don't have to make a second trip to the urgent care center today."

I'd been napping on the couch, but woke up when someone lifted my foot and placed something cold next to my skin.

"You're supposed to have that ankle elevated," Rip said. "I don't want it swelling up on you, so I brought you a fresh pack of frozen corn. The peas are thawed and nearly ready to eat from the heat of your body lying on top of them."

"I was wondering what that lump beneath me was."

"I also have some news for you."

"Oh, Rip, stop it." I knew he'd gone back over to give Rascal a couple of raisins as a mid-day snack and figured the fact he'd come home unscathed was the news he was about to share. Not only was my foot throbbing, but now my head was, too. "I'm not in the mood for your nonsense right now."

"You must have misheard me, honey. I didn't ask you if you wanted to fool around."

"Be serious!" I whacked him on the head with the bag of corn he'd so thoughtfully placed on my ankle.

"I am. Chuck just called me with the results of the DNA test."

"Wow! That was quick. So it *was* blood, and they were able to run a sample?" I asked excitedly. "Was the blood Reilly's?"

"Yes and yes. As you expected, the DNA test on the blood matched hers. When the detectives picked up the crowbar at Barlow's house today, they also had a search warrant to pick up a brush belonging to the missing woman at the Reynolds's house.

They got a DNA sample from a few strands of her hair in the brush."

"Great thinking."

"Thanks! It was my idea." Rip was deservedly proud of his suggestion to the sheriff.

"I'm not surprised." I was fully awake now. Even my headache had suddenly abated. "Have they arrested Tony?"

"Not yet. They're still trying to put the case together. It's just now gone from a missing person case to an official homicide investigation. Finding Reilly's blood on a tool in her house doesn't prove without a doubt she's been murdered. It points a finger in that direction, but it certainly doesn't point it at any particular suspect. On another front, your friend's husband is now behind bars."

"Percival Pandero?"

"Yep! Detectives Morris and Collins found him at the Motel 6 in Portland with his girlfriend. Good job on extracting that information out of him, Rapella."

"Thanks, although he told me it was just a platonic relationship."

"Yeah? Then why were the two entangled in the bed sheets when the detectives arrived?" Rip asked derisively.

"I should've known that rake was lying to me. What about Suzanna? Have they got a warrant out for her arrest, as well?"

"Mr. Pandero swore his wife knew nothing about the snakes. In fact, he said if Suzanna had had any idea there were rattlesnakes in that bag—dead, or not—she'd have never had the guts to pick it up and haul it to the curb. He'd told her it was meat from a small feral hog he'd trapped, which *is* legal, and was surprised she'd even drag a bag containing part of a dead hog to the debris pile unless she had a huge incentive to do so."

"The stench of the bag was all the incentive most folks would need. That's good news about Suzanna, though." I breathed a sigh of relief and hoped Pandero was telling the truth for once. I would hate to be responsible for having Suzanna thrown in jail, even if what she'd done was wrong. I suspected she knew full well what was in the black bag in her chest freezer, but I'd never say so out loud. If that was the case, it was considerate of Percival to lie to protect her, considering they were on the brink of divorce. "Did he say why he had a bag of dead timber rattlers in his freezer in the first place?"

"A friend of his owns land in Refugio and runs about a hundred head of cattle on it. A couple of years ago, the friend wanted to relocate the snakes on his property to open grassland because the aggressive rattlers were striking his livestock. He paid Pandero to do the job. Pandero claims the rancher had no idea they were relocated to a chest freezer in Pandero's basement. Pandero couldn't come up with a logical explanation of why he froze them rather than relocate them. The rancher in question was shocked to hear what his friend had done, and the sheriff is convinced he had no part in the crime."

"That's good news about the rancher, but the killing of a protected species is despicable." I wasn't overly fond of snakes— or anything else that creeps or crawls and can inflict great bodily harm. But protected species are protected for a reason. I didn't particularly condone the killing of anything, with the exception of a few annoying nuisances like mosquitoes and flies. "Can a rattler kill a cow?"

"It's rare, but they can. Often, the bite results in dead or damaged tissue, which can cause infection. If the infection becomes systemic, it can cause blood poisoning and potentially kill the cow. Calves are the most susceptible."

"That's interesting."

"And, Rapella. Just FYI, Perch—"

"Percival," I supplied when Rip hesitated.

"Percival. What the hell kind of name is that anyway?" he asked in disgust.

"Probably more common than Rip, and not much rarer than Clyde." I teased Rip because of his distaste for his given name. He'd been happy to be nicknamed Rip in grade school and even happier when the name stuck for his entire life. "And to answer your question, I think Percival is a French name. And, of course, one of the knights of the round table was named Percival."

"Round table?"

"Yes. Percival, like Lancelot, was one of the knights in King Arthur's Court who sought the Holy Grail."

"Oh. *That* round table." I couldn't tell by Rip's response if he actually knew what I was talking about or had just tired of the conversation. As I've mentioned before, he wasn't exactly an avid reader. The only thing I'd ever known him to peruse religiously was the TV guide.

"Get back to what you were going to tell me about Percival."

"Oh, yeah. He was questioned about the missing neighbor lady, and he had an alibi for the entire window of time in which she disappeared. It was easily confirmed."

"Really? What was his alibi?"

"He was in Christus Spohn Hospital in Corpus Christi throughout the storm. Two doctors and numerous nurses confirmed it, along with a disgruntled roommate who was being treated for a sexually transmitted disease."

"That's weird," I said.

"I thought so too, being the roommate was in his eighties *and* a Catholic priest."

"Okay, that *is* strange, but that's not what I was referring to. Suzanna told me Percival came to their house to seek shelter from the storm and she wouldn't let him in."

"That's kind of cold, don't you think?" Rip replied.

"My thoughts exactly. Clearly, however, her story was a lie."

"Not necessarily. He might have requested shelter there well before the storm actually made landfall. According to Chuck, he was being treated in the hospital for a collapsed lung and several broken ribs, injuries he sustained in a car wreck in the early morning hours of August 25th. The storm didn't hit until late that evening."

"I see. So what happens next regarding the murder case?" I asked.

"Nothing happens next as far as you and I are concerned. The case is in the detectives' hands now." Rip grabbed a throw blanket off the back of the couch, laid it over me, and tucked in the edges. "Now, you need to rest. Keep that foot elevated, too. I'll wake you up in an hour or so for our evening cocktails. Okay, honey?"

"Sure. Thanks for all you do for me, sweetheart."

"I said I would, didn't I? When I said 'I do', I meant I'd do everything. Even put myself in harm's way to feed some satanic weasel you agreed to pet sit."

I threw my bag of corn at him but missed. I also missed a treasured heirloom——an antique porcelain statue that had belonged to my mother——but only by a hair.

"Ball one!" Rip laughed, picked the corn up off the TV stand where it'd landed, and lovingly placed it back on top of my sore ankle. "Sleep tight, punkin."

I wasn't able to get back to sleep because too many thoughts were racing through my head. I couldn't quite figure out why Tony would want to harm Walker's wife. He had a beautiful girlfriend he was scheduled to marry on Valentine's Day. What possible motive could he have had to kill Reilly? Not merely kill her, but brutally beat her to death with a crowbar? He seemed like such a laid-back, sweet guy. Or, at least he was when he wasn't drinking, according to Rip.

Even though Rip had said the case was now in the hands of the homicide detectives, I found it hard to put it out of my mind. I kept sensing I'd overlooked something important. Something that had been dangled right in front of my face. When it finally hit me, I sat up straight on the couch. My injured leg jerked up instinctively, causing the bag of partially-thawed corn to fly across the trailer and hit Rip in the chest. He bolted up out of the recliner he was napping in as if he'd been reliving his close encounter with the 'satanic weasel' who'd scurried up his pants leg.

"What the——?" He yelled.

"I'm sorry, Rip. Something just came to me."

"So you threw this bag of corn at me, *again?*"

"Well, kind of. But not intentionally this time."

"Okay," Rip said with a sigh. "What just came to you that excited you enough to 'unintentionally' almost cause me to have another heart attack?"

"You didn't have an actual heart attack. Dr. Murillo said it was just a heart 'event'; a precursor to a heart attack if you hadn't have had the triple bypass he performed on you."

"Well, that 'event' led to having my chest split open like a watermelon a few days later." *Men can be such drama queens sometimes*, I thought as Rip spoke, *and my husband is no exception. I didn't complain half as much when I gave birth to our nine-pound daughter, which was like passing a kidney stone the size of a Thanksgiving turkey.* "But enough about my near-death experience. What's up, Rapella? What just came to you?"

"I was thinking about Barlow Barnaby dangling from his living room ceiling. Chuck told you the signs pointed toward homicide but were technically inconclusive. Because murder couldn't be ruled out, the department opened up a homicide investigation. Right?"

"Yeah." His one-word response was accompanied by a questioning look.

"That means it could have been a suicide, even if it wasn't likely. Correct?"

"Yes, I suppose," Rip replied. "But what does that prove?"

"Nothing, other than if it truly was suicide, it's possible Barlow killed himself because he couldn't live with the guilt from something atrocious he'd done."

"I assume you mean guilt about something like killing the lady next door."

"Exactly. What if Barlow killed Reilly for some unknown reason and initially called in the tip about seeing her get into a car in order to lead the investigators on a merry chase that pointed away from the truth? Suzanna told me he's not only a terrible drunk, but he's also been treated several times for mental illness. She also said he's always 'seeing things', which might mean he has hallucinations. It could have been nothing more than one of those hallucinations that caused Barlow to kill Reilly. In the midst of something terrifying, like Hurricane Harvey, I'd guess someone who's prone to having visions could easily suffer horrible and vivid figments of their imagination that might bring on an episode of violence from fear or in retribution for something."

"That sounds a bit far-fetched, but I suppose it's possible. However, I'd like to have a little more evidence to base that conclusion on before I take it to Sheriff Peabody." Rip wore a pensive expression on his face, and I was relieved he seemed to be taking my supposition seriously.

"Bruno Watts, the drywall subcontractor working on the Reynolds's house, is now also working on Barlow's house to get it ready for his family to sell. He told me he took on the project because he was close to the family. He probably knew quite a bit about Barlow if he's close to the Barnaby family. Why don't we talk to him about the late gentleman and see if he has any insight into the situation?" I suggested.

"Not your worst idea, but I promised to help Milo again today. At least this time I won't be swinging a hammer and sweating like a whore in church. Pardon my language, but I'm just not cut out for that kind of work anymore."

"You shouldn't be swinging anything." I was not happy Rip was exerting that kind of energy. "I'm surprised Milo even asked you to perform manual labor in your condition."

"What do you mean 'in your condition'? I'm in pretty good condition for the condition I'm in. Besides, he didn't ask me to do it. I insisted. Now he wants me to drive to Home Depot in Corpus to pick up a list of materials he needs to replace the floor in the master bathroom."

"He needs supplies at Home Depot again? I swear he goes there every day."

Rip laughed. "Not all that surprising, considering how many projects he's got going on at the same time. In this case, however, I think Milo's trying to keep me busy so I *don't* try to pitch in with the strenuous stuff."

"Good for Milo. That boy's got more sense than you do sometimes."

"I'd have to argue that one. Honey, why don't you wait until I get back to go speak to Bruno so I can go with you?" Rip offered. "Or at least wait until some of the swelling has gone down in your ankle."

"I've gotten to know Bruno fairly well and feel safe when I'm alone with him. I'll wait to go speak to him until tomorrow. Regina found me a pair of crutches somewhere."

"Yeah, Milo said she went next door and borrowed them from a neighbor who recently had knee surgery." I recalled Milo saying Walker had undergone surgery for a torn ligament in his knee just prior to the hurricane. I raised my eyebrows at Rip's remark, but he didn't comment on my reaction. Instead, he was focused on me and my injury. "Don't push it. If you aren't up to questioning the guy tomorrow, wait another day or two."

"Of course." Rip should have known me well enough after over fifty years of marriage to realize I would be going up to the Barnaby home to speak to Bruno the following morning if I had to crawl there on my hands and knees.

TWENTY-THREE

Following an unexpected shower overnight, the road was still wet the next morning as I hobbled up Flamingo Road on Walker's crutches. Wet pavement posed no obstacle for me. From the curb in front of the Reynolds's house, I could see Bruno's truck parked on the far side of Barlow's driveway. However, when I reached Barlow's house, a man on a forklift was unloading lumber from a truck owned by a lumber company out of Kingsville and stacking it on the near side of the driveway. As I approached the area, the man driving the forklift stopped me.

"Sorry, ma'am, but you'll have to go through the yard. It's against company policy to allow you to get so close to moving equipment. We can't be responsible for your safety, and it looks like you've already got a bum leg."

I waved but didn't respond verbally. I soon discovered that negotiating a soggy yard with crutches was more difficult than one might expect. With my full weight on the crutches, they sank several inches into the softened ground. After a couple of embarrassing falls, I decided to cover the rest of the distance on all fours before a sprained ankle was the least of my troubles. I glanced toward the driveway to see the man on the forklift and the truck driver both pointing at me and laughing. I was tempted to give them the finger but knew that would only make them find my humiliation even more hilarious.

The fifteen or twenty yards I crawled to Barlow's front porch, dragging the pair of crutches behind me, felt like the length of a football field. Finally, I reached my destination. I took a few moments to catch my breath and pull myself together before ringing the doorbell.

"Good morning, Ms. Ripple. How are you doing this morning?" Bruno then looked down at my muddy knees. "Oh, no! Have you fallen again?"

"No. I just had to kneel down to pick something up, and the lawn is wet."

"Uh-huh. That's your story and you're sticking to it?" Bruno chuckled and opened the door to allow me inside. He had a half-eaten peanut butter and jelly sandwich in his right hand, and a tiny glob of wiggly jelly embedded in his mustache. "So was the ankle broken?"

"No, just sprained, and please call me Rapella. I think we know each other well enough by now to be on a first-name basis. I've been calling you Bruno since I first met you."

"All right. Rapella it is. What brings you up here?" *Again,* was his unspoken implication.

"I was thinking about having a small memorial service for poor Mr. Barnaby. Just a celebration of life kind of thing for his neighbors and nearby family members, if there are any. I wanted to see if you could help me come up with a list of folks to invite. After all, you said you were tight with the family."

"You'd be wasting your time, Ms. Ripple——"

"Rapella," I reminded.

"Yeah, whatever." Suddenly, Bruno's friendliness faded like a colorful sunset. "Ain't nobody gonna come to a memorial service for Barlow. He wasn't well-liked in the neighborhood, and he has no real family in the area. Not that his family cared much for him, either. He was an all-around miserable S.O.B."

"But, but——"

"Look, lady. It's a bad idea. I'm sorry the old coot's gone, but there's not a lot of grieving going on by anyone who knew him. Trust me."

"Okay. I just thought it'd be the neighborly thing to do. So, why are you making the effort to get the house up to snuff as quickly as you can?" I asked.

"Not for Barlow, I can tell you that. I'm doing it for the family's sake." Bruno was speaking quite brusquely. I was puzzled about what I'd said that had upset him. I found out the reason when Bruno next spoke. "Now I need to get back to work. Oh, and by the way, the police stopped by and confiscated the crowbar you tripped over. I'd had Tony borrow that crowbar for a project we worked on yesterday. I had to go to Portland to buy another one first thing this morning because the cops said we wouldn't be getting that one back anytime soon. Did you have anything to do with that?"

"Well, um, well, kind of, sort of," I stammered.

Bruno's gaze bore through me like a diamond-head drill bit. He was squeezing his sandwich so hard, excess jelly squished out of it and dropped to the floor next to the glob that had finally fell from his mustache. The man looked so on edge I didn't know what to say. Honesty was always the best policy, so I told him the truth, or, at least a slightly revised version of the truth.

"You see, my husband is the former sheriff of Aransas County and I just happened to mention I'd noticed a crowbar in Walker's house the other day and wanted to take some solvent over to clean the red residue off of it for him. I'm a little anal about stains, you see."

"Uh-huh." Bruno didn't appear to be buying my story any

more than he'd buy a unicycle for his pet bunny. He confirmed as much with his next remark. "I'll agree with one thing. You do seem to be anal about a *lot* of things."

"I don't appreciate your attitude, Mr. Watts." I was ticked off because he had no right to insult me. "Are you denying the crowbar had some sort of residue on it?"

"I'm sorry if I was offensive. I was only messing with you. And, no, I'm not denying that the crowbar had something on it. Tony *was* using red paint in Walker's living room the other day. He not only does demo work, he also does some painting on the side. I suppose he could've gotten some of the paint on the crowbar, but I don't know how. It's not like he'd stir the paint with it."

"Exactly! That was what I was getting at before you interrupted me with your nasty remark."

"Again, I apologize. I was only——"

"Messing with me. I know. You said as much." I'd cut him off. I had no desire to hear him try to claw his way out of the crater he'd dug for himself. "Before I could attempt to remove the stain, someone else already had. I'm almost certain it was Tony who wiped it down and disposed of the rag he'd use to clean it. Rip brought the crowbar to the current sheriff's attention, thinking it could contain critical evidence in the event Reilly was murdered rather than being a victim of the storm, as they'd first suspected. They both thought the stain could've been caused by blood rather than paint. If that was the case, they suspected there was still trace amounts of it on the crowbar. Sheriff Peabody decided it would be remiss not to have it tested." I studied Bruno's expression. He seemed fixated on every word I spoke. After I finished speaking, he silently stared at me for an uncomfortable length of time before responding.

"That's ridiculous! There's no way Walker would've ever hurt his wife. He loved her with all his heart." I hadn't mentioned Walker's name as the suspect in question, but the victim's spouse had evidently been the first to come to Bruno's mind. Or was he deliberately trying to avert suspicion away from himself, or his buddy Tony? Once again, Bruno spoke about Reilly in the past tense, as if aware she was no longer among the living, even though she was still classified as a missing person.

To test his reaction, I replied, "I don't think they were looking at Walker as a potential killer, but rather at whoever was using the crowbar at the time."

Bruno's expression didn't change. He showed no reaction at all to my remark, which told me he was either not involved in Reilly's disappearance or was doing his damnedest to hide any emotion he might be feeling. I suspected the latter, due to the irritation he'd displayed earlier. I'd been going to ask if he thought Tony or Barlow capable of harming Walker's wife, but changed my mind when he'd begun acting so defensively to my questioning.

When it became apparent Bruno was not going to respond to my statement, I said, "I'd better let you get back to your work."

As I approached the front door, I was surprised when Bruno stopped me. "Rapella, wait."

"Yes?" I was almost afraid to turn around and face him again.

"What did they conclude when they examined the crowbar?" Bruno asked intently.

"They determined there *was* blood on the crowbar. Reilly Reynolds's blood to be precise." I watched as the color drained from his face, as if all of his own blood had gravitated toward his work boots. "You seem shocked, Bruno."

"I guess I *am* a little stunned."

I so desperately wanted to ask him if he was surprised by the news Reilly's blood had somehow found its way to the crowbar—which he'd inferred earlier he'd borrowed from Walker, or perhaps Jessie—or shocked that her missing person status had just been updated to possible homicide when he'd thought he'd successfully staged her "death by hurricane". Maybe he'd intentionally used the crowbar owned by his victim's spouse in the event it was determined to be the murder weapon. *Did I have a new number-one suspect?* I wondered. I wasn't sure. But knowing the potential killer now had a brand new shiny crowbar in his possession, and I was not in any shape to challenge him in a foot race, I remained silent.

I'd come to the house thinking Barlow, the homeowner, might have had a hand in Reilly's disappearance. But after visiting with Bruno, a man I'd never have thought could harm even an irritating fly flitting about his face, I wasn't so sure he wasn't the guilty party. Bruno's resentful attitude convinced me he needed further attention and interrogation by the homicide detectives.

"I think I'd better get going now," I said. My voice quivered in apprehension.

Is it also possible Bruno lied about the owner of the crowbar to protect himself from what might be found on a tool that actually does belong to him? If so, how far would he go to protect himself? This new conundrum made me tense, and right then the source of my anxiety was glaring at me as if I'd just told him he was denser than the sandwich he was gripping like a vise. When Bruno stepped toward me as I was backing toward the door awkwardly with the crutches, I felt my pulse quicken. When he sat his sandwich on a sawhorse and put his arm around my waist, I tried to swing one of my crutches at his crotch to protect myself. He easily grabbed the crutch in mid-air.

"Easy, Rapella," he said. "I'm just trying to help you. I'll support your left side so you can make it to the street all right. The lawn is really mushy right now, and the lumber deliverymen won't let you use the driveway. I don't know how you made it to the front porch on those crutches to begin with."

I didn't want to tell him that, in my determination to do some interrogating on my own, I'd crawled the last twenty feet, so I just flashed him a forced smile. "Thank you. I appreciate your help."

I let Bruno, who probably weighed at least a stone less than I did, support much of my weight all the way to the curb while the forklift and truck drivers stopped working long enough to watch. I was confident Bruno wouldn't wallop me in the head with one of my crutches with two witnesses looking on in amusement. What I really wanted to do was use a crutch to whale away on the two disrespectful onlookers until the smirks on their faces were replaced by expressions of remorse. Naturally, that was just a pipe dream I'd come up with in a fit of fury.

I thanked Bruno as he released my arm once I was on solid ground. I laughed and said, "I'd probably have had to crawl through the yard without your assistance."

"Like you crawled through it earlier to get to the front porch?" When I glanced at him, he winked. I felt my face burn in mortification.

"Oh. I was hoping you didn't see that."

"I just happened to be looking out the window to see if the lumber was being stacked in the right place. No worries. I admire your 'can do' attitude. I also saw the doubt in your eyes as we were speaking earlier. Just for the record, Ms. Ripple—I mean Rapella—I would never lay a hand on a woman. No woman. No matter how angry I was with her. To be perfectly honest, I've only struck another man once in my life. And he had it coming after insulting my little sister in a bar one night. Unfortunately, the dude was much larger and much drunker than I was, and he hit me back. Five times, in fact. Maybe more, because I blacked out after the fifth punch."

"Oh, dear. Even though you were on the wrong end of that fight, it was gallant of you to defend your sister."

"Thanks. Stupid, but gallant." Bruno grinned broadly after

his remark. Maybe he really *was* denser than his sandwich. "Have a good evening, Rapella."

"I will. You too, Bruno." I returned his smile and began to hobble back down the street to the travel trailer. Bruno's last remarks had been spoken so sincerely, so tenderly, and so emotionally that I wanted to believe him. I really, really did. But could I? As easy as it was to be distracted by a show of kindness, I couldn't let myself forget that people could often put up a believable front—even bad, evil, and *guilty* people.

Later that afternoon, I recited a *Reader's Digest* version of what had occurred at Barlow's house to Rip, who seemed unimpressed with my observations and suspicions. He did at least assure me he'd relay what I'd said to the sheriff. I'd hoped for more enthusiasm but had to be content knowing the information would be passed on to the authorities.

For supper, Regina invited us over to their motorhome for a light meal of grilled salmon and arugula salad. Behind our daughter's back, as she'd issued the invitation, Rip had pretended to gag at the mention of arugula. I knew from past experience he'd rather munch on grass clippings. Salmon was pretty far down on the list of his menu preferences, as well. I shot him a look that changed his tune immediately.

"Salmon and arugula salad sounds perfect, Reggie," he replied to our daughter. *Perfect for a grizzly bear and a rabbit*, I knew he was thinking.

"Good. See you at six." Regina smiled lovingly at her father before winking at me. She was under no illusion. Her wink made it clear she knew her menu choices were not her father's favorite foods. Like me, she was worried about his health. His cholesterol level had likely not been within the normal range since before she was born.

"Anything we can bring?" Rip asked hopefully. *Like rib eye steaks and baked potatoes*, I sensed he wanted to add.

"Nope. Just yourselves."

"Swell." He smiled at Regina and then turned to me and rolled his eyes. I could foresee an entire bag of pork skins being consumed on our couch in the next hour and forty minutes.

"The salmon is cooked perfectly, Regina. It just melts in your mouth." I glanced over at Rip, who clearly did not agree. He was politely trying to choke down a mouthful of the salad. He looked like he was consuming his last supper before being shackled and led to the execution chamber.

"Thank you," she said.

"I'm curious, Reggie," I began, using her father's nickname for her, "how well did you know Barlow?"

"Not all that well, but I know Bruno was living with him and they argued all the time, almost as frequently as Mr. and Mrs. Willming across the street from them."

"Bruno?" I was floored by her remark. If Bruno had been living with Barlow, why had he not mentioned the fact to me when I'd spoken with him earlier that afternoon?

"Yeah. He's the guy I told you used to date Jenavieve Jacobowitz. He does drywall and is working on Walker's house right now. One time as I was driving up the street, I saw Bruno walk out Barlow's front door. Barlow followed, hollering so loud I could hear him with my windows rolled up. He picked up a paving stone and threw it at Bruno."

"Good Lord!" Rip exclaimed. "Was Bruno injured?"

"No," Regina said. "Barlow missed him by a mile, but it wasn't for lack of trying."

"Thank goodness!" Rip replied. I was unable to speak as I tried to process the information she'd just given me, so I was glad Rip had stepped in to carry on the conversation. "Why was Bruno living with Barlow?"

"Barlow was Bruno's stepdad, but they didn't see eye-to-eye on much of anything."

I was still musing over what I'd just learned, when Milo added, "However, as luck would have it, Bruno's probably going to end up with Barlow's house."

As luck would have it? Was it luck, or motive to kill? No wonder he's so motivated to get the place repaired. I pondered what Bruno had told me. I recalled him saying, "No one deserves to die like that. I know the family and offered them a good rate to get Barlow's house back up to snuff so they can sell it." *He knows the family, all right. He **is** the family. **He's** the one who wants to get the house sold.*

As if reading my mind, Milo added, "And he needs to get it fixed up and sold soon. From what I've heard, Bruno's house is a complete loss and he had no insurance. After Harvey hit, he had nowhere else to go except to stay with his stepdad, whom he despised, until he could get back on his feet. Barlow's untimely death was probably a stroke of luck for Bruno."

"A stroke of luck or the result of a devious plot?" I asked. "Do you think Bruno could've had something to do with Barlow's death? The authorities *are* looking into it as a possible homicide."

Rip gave me a look, reminding me I'd promised not to mention the case's recent status change to anyone, including Milo and Regina. I mouthed a "sorry about that" to Rip, who rolled his eyes in response. He should know by now that my keeping a secret was about as likely as him finishing the arugula salad he was moving around on his plate.

Although I didn't say it out loud, I was wondering if Bruno killed Barlow out of vengeance. Perhaps Barlow knew of Bruno's involvement in Reilly's disappearance and had been coerced by his stepson to call in the anonymous tip to lead the authorities astray. Then, later, in the midst of one of their disagreements, Barlow had threatened to rat him out. Killing his stepdad would've been a win-win solution for Bruno. First and foremost, he'd eliminate the threat of Barlow turning him in, and secondly, he'd inherit his victim's house.

My musing came to an end as I listened to Milo's response to my last question. He seemed to confirm what Bruno had so earnestly told me a couple of hours prior.

"No. I can't believe Bruno would devise some devious plot. I really don't think Bruno has a mean bone in his body. I can't see him intentionally hurting any—" Milo's remark was interrupted by Rip's phone ringing. It was Chuck Beatty on the other end of the call.

"No, I'm not busy. I just finished eating," Rip said, as Regina glanced at his half-eaten salmon and barely-touched arugula salad and rolled her eyes. I didn't have the heart to tell her he'd filled up on pork rinds and a can of Vienna Sausage before we'd joined her and Milo for supper.

The three of us continued to eat quietly as we listened to Rip's side of the phone conversation. I considered an idea that'd been percolating in my brain all afternoon. I thought long and hard about where Reilly had ultimately ended up, when this idea hit me out of the blue. I was ready to suggest the homicide detectives do an x-ray of the over-sized wall separating the Reynolds's living room from the new library, a wall that had been Bruno's brain child by his own admission. The fireplace insert had been a last-minute inspiration, he'd told me. I had a sneaking suspicion it'd been a clever, and well-thought-out, ploy to hide his victim's body. Reilly was slender and very short, I recalled. Bruno could have dismembered her, and wrapped each piece in plastic or

228

drywall tape. Then he could've stuffed her body parts in one large, thick plastic bag the same way Percival Pandero had hidden his illegal snake harvest. After which, he could have wedged the bag, or bags, between the studs supporting the wall and then, finally, sheet-rocked the wall around her. He'd then installed the fireplace insert to explain the thickness of the wall. Last-minute inspiration, my well-padded behind!

Granted, my imagined scheme would have been a long shot, but it would explain the necessity for a wall that otherwise seemed unnecessary. Building a library for a person who was not only a non-reader but who was also missing and presumed dead, seemed implausible, if not downright ridiculous. Who needs an entire room to store their music CD's, unless they happen to be a music producer like David Foster or Clive Owens? It was even conceivable that Walker was in on the killing of his own wife, whom he'd known was cheating on him with Percival Pandero. They could have been co-conspirators, I realized.

If my notion was spot on, I should think Bruno, and/or Walker, would be concerned about another hurricane in the future, or a house fire, or anything that could expose Reilly's body at some point down the road. If Bruno was the sole perpetrator, he might've thought, if that were to happen, Walker would likely be the prime suspect, not him.

Just then, Rip ended the call with the medical examiner and sat his phone on a table behind him before relaying what he'd just learned to his three dinner mates. The tox screen had come back negative. Extensive testing had been done in conjunction with the autopsy, and Barlow's cause of death had officially been ruled a suicide. Supporting this conclusion was a note the detectives had uncovered inside a bible in Barlow's nightstand. Ironically, the note was inserted on the page that contained two Bible verses.

So that I would choose strangling and death rather than my bones. I loathe my life; I would not live forever. Leave me alone, for my days are a breath. Job 7:15-16

Being that the short message penned by Barlow contained the exact words from the bible verse, the authorities determined it to be a suicide note. It seemed to me to be an odd thing to write as a suicide note unless it was in conjunction with a more personal message, which it wasn't. The bible verse constituted the entire note.

"Oh, yeah!" Rip said, as he remembered something else Chuck had told him during their short phone conversation. "And another thing. Bruno also had a good alibi. Two days before the hurricane, he flew to San Francisco to visit an uncle who was dying from throat cancer. The uncle passed the next day, and Bruno stuck around another few days to attend the funeral."

"I'm sorry to hear he lost a close family member," I said in a solemn voice. "But glad to hear Bruno has a verifiable alibi."

What the medical examiner had reported to Rip blew a big-ass hole in my latest theory, but at least I could finally mark a suspect off my list. On one hand, I was relieved to know Bruno wasn't responsible for Reilly's disappearance. But on the other hand, I was disappointed to know I was back to square one in my quest to determine who *was* responsible for the woman's fate.

As if to change the subject to something more positive, Regina said, "Before I forget to tell you guys, Chase is throwing a thirtieth birthday party for Tiffany in October. We probably won't be able to get away, but she'd be so happy if you two could make it. She hasn't seen her grandparents in a while, and I know she's missed you."

"We've missed her and Chase too," I said. Tiffany was our oldest grandchild and lived with her husband in Albuquerque, New Mexico. We hadn't seen her in over two years. "Is it to be a surprise?"

"No, or I wouldn't have told you, Mom," Regina said with a snort. "You and secrets are hardly a match made in heaven."

"Ain't that the truth?" Rip said. "Your mother never could keep a secret."

"Whatever." I was offended by both Regina and Rip's remarks, but I really couldn't argue the point. In fact, I'd just proven they were right. "We'll put it on our schedule, sweetheart."

"Good. She'll be thrilled to hear you're coming," Regina said.

"Why don't we keep the fact we'll be there for her party to ourselves so we can surprise her? I'll show you both I can keep a secret." I wanted to prove it to them and myself, too.

"Are you sure you and Milo won't still need us in October?" Rip asked. His expression showed concern, but his tone made it clear he'd be ready to head somewhere else by then.

"Yes. Tiffany's birthday is the twenty-second, so we should be fine if you guys take off in mid-October." Regina's expression was one of gratitude, but her tone also made it clear she'd be ready for us to head somewhere else by then, too.

I'm not sure if being able to read voices and facial expressions so accurately was a blessing or a curse.

TWENTY-FOUR

After a fitful night of tossing and turning, I finally dozed off in the wee hours of the morning. I awoke at six to find Rip already up and about. From the bedroom, I could hear the coffee dripping into the carafe. I donned a pair of denim dungarees and a sleeveless cotton top and hobbled to the kitchen for a cup of strong Columbian brew.

"What's up, buttercup?" Rip greeted me. "How's your ankle feeling?"

"A little better, I suppose." I gave him a quick peck on the lips. "But I didn't sleep well last night."

"Yeah, no kidding." You kicked me a total of sixty-seven times throughout the course of the night, and several of those kicks were made with your injured ankle."

"You were counting?" I asked playfully.

"Sixty-seven was a guesstimate. I lost track at forty." Rip laughed and then grew serious. "Why couldn't you sleep, honey?"

"There was a pea under my mattress."

Rip looked at me in puzzlement. I could tell he thought I'd

slipped three shots of tequila into my coffee cup. "Do you mean you stuffed that frozen bag of peas under the mattress instead of on top of your swollen ankle?"

I should have known my reference to *The Princess and the Pea*, by Hans Christian Andersen, would fly over Rip's head like a seagull trying to catch a bread crumb. "No. It was a reference from a classic children's book where the princess in the story is tested by the prince to see if she's a true princess before he marries her. He places a pea under her mattress. She feels the pea under the mattress and can't sleep. The prince keeps stacking more mattresses on top of the pea, but the princess still keeps feel—"

I stopped talking when I noticed the expression on Rip's face. He didn't have a clue what I was talking about, and clearly didn't give a flying fig whether the princess passed the pea test, or not. "You lost me at 'classic children's book'. Were you awake half the night because you're still upset about the missing neighbor?"

"Yes. I couldn't stop my mind from racing. And 'murdered neighbor' seems more probable than 'missing neighbor' at this point."

"Yeah, but I assumed that from the beginning. Reilly's body would have resurfaced by now. With the constant movement of the water from tides, boat traffic, and the ever-present wind, it would have eventually jarred loose if it was hung up on something. The presence, and magnitude, of her blood on that crowbar is damning evidence of murder, as well."

"Absolutely." I got up to get the coffee carafe and refilled our cups. Rip turned the television on to catch the morning news, which gave me an opportunity to let those thoughts begin to race through my mind again.

Now that I knew the murderer wasn't Bruno, I wondered if he'd be open with me about everything he knew about Reilly and her relationship with Walker and the other men in the construction crew. I'm sure they all used each other's tools on a regular basis. If the murder was spur of the moment, a crime of passion *and* opportunity, the killer might have grabbed the handiest thing available that would suffice as a weapon. If a coconut had been the closest item, Reilly might have been bonked to death with it rather than the crowbar.

Bruno had shown kindness to me and genuine concern when I injured my ankle. He had even helped me to the street so my crutches wouldn't sink into the saturated yard from the force of my weight. Maybe if he knew I was dabbling in Reilly's disappearance, he'd be willing to share anything he knew that might aid me in getting to the truth of the matter.

As it would turn out, he didn't willingly offer me any useful information. But unbeknownst to him, his remarks led me straight to the perpetrator behind Reilly's untimely death.

"I'm going to make a run to Corpus for some materials. Again." The way Rip added "again" told me he wasn't thrilled about having to make the long trip back to Home Depot. "Milo forgot to put screws on the list, and his current project will come to a standstill soon without them. Speaking of screws, sometimes I think that boy has a loose one."

I smiled and gave Rip a warm hug. I had a feeling Milo had all the screws he needed and was just trying to keep Rip occupied. "Have patience, my dear. I know Milo and Regina really appreciate all your help. Both the kids have had their lives turned upside down and are understandably on edge. It'd be easy to forget something like screws. Besides, how many trips do we make to the hardware store every single time we take on a do-it-yourself project?"

It was nearly always Rip who forgot at least two or three items at the hardware store, but so as not to willingly hand him a bone to chew on, I'd included myself in the remark.

"Yeah, Rapella, I guess you're right. Well, I better get on the road. Rest that ankle while I'm gone. All right?"

"I will. I have no plans to leave the trailer today." *Except maybe once. I need to walk up the street and talk with Bruno one more time.*

I watched as Rip drove our truck out of the Moores' driveway, and was delighted to see Bruno pull into the Reynolds's driveway almost simultaneously. I saw Rip wave at Bruno and the other man return his wave absentmindedly. It was pure habit on both men's part, I knew.

Still hindered by the crutches, I thought this was the perfect time to approach Bruno. I'm sure he'd suppress a groan when he saw me coming. I know I'd be plumb sick of me by now if I were him.

As expected, Bruno greeted me in a joking manner. "I'm beginning to think you're stalking me."

"It probably seems like it," I said. "I promise I won't keep you long. I just want to ask you a few questions about Reilly's disappearance. I'm doing a bit of personal investigating to see if I can help the authorities nail down the killer, if she actually *was* murdered."

"Yeah. I figured that out when you called the police to have the crowbar you thought belonged to Tony tested for evidence of Reilly's death." He laughed, but his tense demeanor suggested he hadn't found my meddling at all humorous.

"Yes, well. I never seriously suspected either of you could be involved in her disappearance." I smiled but sensed Bruno hadn't bought the bull crap I'd just fed him. "You see, I helped solve the truth behind the death of Milo's former business partner last year."

"Cooper?" he asked. "That was a terrible deal. I liked him a lot."

"I never got a chance to meet him, but I know the loss of Cooper Claypool was hard on my son-in-law—as his business partner and closest friend."

"Yeah, I know. Milo mentions him every time we get the chance to chat. As far as Reilly's disappearance, I doubt I'll be able to answer any of your questions. I was in California throughout Hurricane Harvey. I had planned to evacuate the area, but going to San Francisco was a last-minute thing after I learned my uncle had been placed in hospice care. I arrived at his bedside just hours before he passed."

"I'm so sorry to hear about your uncle. I can only imagine how hard that was. Particularly not knowing what the storm was doing to your home while you were away."

"Yeah, it was probably the worst week of my life. I came home to find my house literally in a zillion pieces." I tried to suppress a smile as Bruno spoke solemnly about the loss of his home. Like Jessie, Bruno didn't know the true meaning of the word "literal". At least in this case, his estimation was probably closer to the mark. "It was totally uninhabitable. I've since had it razed and will break ground on a new home as soon as I can scrape up the money."

"I'm so glad to hear you'll soon be moving forward on a new place." I was genuinely happy for the man. I knew his home had been uninsured and, like so many other local residents, moving on was easier said than done. "It shouldn't be too long before you can get your stepdad's house sold. That should give you enough funds to at least begin construction."

"How did you know Barlow was my stepdad?" Bruno appeared to be momentarily taken aback by my comment. "Oh, never mind. Nothing you do or say should surprise me by now. Actually, you know the uncle I just mentioned, whose funeral I attended in California?"

"Yeah."

"His wife was my stepdad's sister. Barlow left his entire estate to her, which I wholeheartedly agree with. Barlow's two daughters are livid, but that's what they get for practically disowning him when he got older and began to have behavioral issues. My stepsisters haven't offered to help with arranging his services or anything, but that was to be expected."

"Sounds like the stepsisters are a little on the self-absorbed side."

"Truer words were never spoken," Bruno replied. "Barlow and his sister, my Aunt Sofia, were always very close, and she is the sweetest lady ever. It's not her fault her brother became so disagreeable and mean to everyone he came into contact with in his later years. What my mother ever saw in the guy is a mystery to me. After Mom passed a few years ago, Barlow became even more unbearable. He loved my mom, but sure had a funny way of showing it."

"I'm sorry to hear about the loss of your mom, and more recent loss of your aunt, along with all the other family issues you're dealing with."

"Thanks," replied. "But who doesn't have at least some level of dysfunction in their family?"

I started to say, "Me!", then I remembered my brother, Howie, who once had three women pregnant at the same time: a drug-addicted prostitute, our first cousin, Carla, and the local Methodist's preacher's wife. It's probably no surprise Howie passed away from a potent strain of syphilis a few years later. "I can't think of anyone who doesn't have at least one 'free spirit' in their family."

"Me neither," Bruno agreed. "Aunt Sofia's the reason I'm

trying to get Barlow's house ready to sell. Now that she's a widow, her already tight budget is about to get even tighter. I want to ease her financial worries by helping her get the house sold quickly and for a decent price. I took some personal time off this week to make Barlow's funeral arrangements and speak with a realtor on Aunt Sofia's behalf. I don't have much left to do here at Walker's place before I can donate all my time to Barlow's."

"That's so sweet of you. I'm sorry I misjudged you," I said, contradicting my earlier statement of never having seriously considered Bruno as a suspect. "I know now you're truly too kind a gentleman ever to harm a woman or anyone else who hasn't insulted your little sister."

Bruno laughed. "Yeah, I really showed that guy, didn't I? I bet he's still smarting from me punching him in the fist with my face."

We both chuckled at his quip. When our laughter died down, he said, "I appreciate the fact you're trying to get to the bottom of Reilly's disappearance. Whatever happened to her, she didn't deserve it. However, I don't know if you should put your neck on the line. It could put you in danger. If someone killed Reilly, they'd have nothing to lose by killing someone who's trying to nail them to the cross for her murder."

"I know. I've considered that possibility, but Reilly didn't deserve what happened to her. Nobody does. I feel driven to get to the bottom of this mystery."

"All right. Please be careful, though. Have you spoken to Walker about who he thinks might have had a motive to kill his wife? He may have some kind of inkling."

"No. Not yet." I hesitated to tell Bruno that the man he suggested I speak with was actually the person I now suspected of Reilly's death. I'd lost count, but Walker had just become my fifth, or perhaps sixth, number-one suspect.

"I know he was heartbroken when he heard she was running around on him with some guy who lives in the neighborhood, and he was absolutely crushed when she asked for a divorce. Shortly after that, he tried to kill himself. About a week after finding out about Reilly's affair, Walker swallowed around two dozen pain pills, but luckily his best friend showed up just in time. He'd stopped by to drop off some beef jerky he'd made with his new dehydrator, but instead found Walker lying on his bed and unresponsive. He was able to perform CPR until the EMT's arrived. His actions saved Walker's life."

"Thank goodness!" I exclaimed. "Sounds like divine intervention. I didn't realize Reilly had plans to divorce Walker."

"He doesn't talk about it much." Bruno snapped his fingers. "I just remembered something I've been wanting to tell you, but keep forgetting. The day you discovered my stepdad hanging in his living room, it should have been me."

"It should have been you hanging in his living room?" I asked. I was baffled at his remark.

"No." He looked both amused and sad at the same time. "It should have been me who discovered his body."

"How's that?"

"I stopped by Barlow's in the middle of the day to grab something for lunch because I'd driven straight to Walker's that morning after spending the night with my new girlfriend. I rushed in the back door, which opens right into the kitchen, and grabbed an apple and a Coke from the fridge. Before I left, I stepped into the pantry to grab a bag of chips and some of the beef jerky Jessie had given me. I froze when I heard you come in the back door. You muttered a few curse words and I recognized your voice."

"Why didn't you step out to say hello?"

"For one thing, I was afraid I'd scare the holy hell out of you, and no offense, but I was afraid you'd want to chat. I was in a hurry to get back to Walker's so I'd be there when the supplies I'd ordered were delivered. That's why I didn't take the time to step into the living room. If I had, I'd have been the one to discover Barlow. I have to say, I wasn't surprised by him taking his own life. He threatened to kill himself about every other day. Naturally, I thought he was bluffing. Guess I was wrong about that one, huh?"

"Dead wrong, it appears. However, to be honest, I'm still not convinced he *did* take his own life. But that does answer one question I had. The back door was open when I left the kitchen and closed when I returned after finding Barlow's body, so I knew I hadn't been alone. Thinking about it later sent chills down my spine."

"I can imagine. Sorry about that, Rapella."

"That's all right. Did you not even wonder what I was doing in your stepdad's house?"

"Not really. From what I've seen the last few days, you don't hesitate to enter any house, whether you own it or not." Bruno chuckled, probably trying to take the sting out of his remark.

"Yes, well," I began, blushing a second time from one of Bruno's comments. "I'm glad you explained to me what actually happened. I also understand now why you and Tony rushed up to Barlow's house when you saw the emergency vehicles outside, even though you weren't allowed inside."

"Actually, I was. Because I was living there, and Barlow was my stepfather, they allowed me in. Tony was told to remain outside and I joined him on the front lawn shortly after speaking with the sheriff. I certainly hadn't anticipated the scene that greeted me when I entered the house."

"No, I'm sure you were shocked to see your nude stepdad swinging from the ceiling."

"That didn't surprise me as much as finding you sprawled out on the floor with paramedics tending to you. I'm not surprised you didn't notice me until later when we were all outside on the lawn. Like I said, Barlow threatened to kill himself frequently. Although I *was* concerned when I saw a fire truck pull up, I thought he might have forgotten about something he had roasting in the oven and started a kitchen fire."

"From the number of emergency vehicles at the scene, you'd have thought a terrorist bomb had gone off in Barlow's oven." I shut up when I realized I'd sounded flippant about the death of Bruno's stepdad. "Sorry, Bruno. I should have been more respectful."

Bruno waved off my apology and seemed completely unmoved by his stepfather's death. I wondered if he'd treated his stepdad any better than his stepsisters had, even though Barlow had opened up his home to him in his time of need. I couldn't judge the man by his cold-hearted attitude, however. I hadn't walked a mile in his shoes and had no clue what had transpired between him and Barlow in the past.

I didn't want to keep Bruno from his work any longer, so I thanked him and returned to the trailer. If I hadn't been a little hurt by his remarks about my excessive chattering and trespassing, I'd have told him about another question he'd answered for me. He'd put the thinly veiled insults into nicer words, of course, but that's what he'd meant.

I'd been confused by the medical examiner's deduction that Barlow had been dead for nine to ten hours when I discovered his body. At the time, I'd thought perhaps the man's death was actually a homicide and I'd been in the house with the killer for a short while. Now I knew the person who'd exited the house was Bruno, who'd been hiding in the pantry from the trespassing chatterbox. Bruno told me he'd spent the night with his girl-friend, so his stepdad had been alone in the house all night and the following morning. That meant the nine-to-ten-hour estimate was undoubtedly correct.

As I stepped into the Chartreuse Caboose, a light bulb went off over my head. Literally. And I *do* know the actual meaning of that word. But another went off over my head figuratively, too. I suddenly had a very clear picture of what had happened to Reilly's body, and who was responsible for her death.

TWENTY-FIVE

"You want me to call Joe Peabody and have him meet us at the Reynolds's house?" Rip sounded skeptical. You'd have thought I'd asked him to call Pope Francis and invite him over for pizza and a beer.

"Yes. I think I know who killed Reilly and where her body can be found."

"Pray tell." His tone now took skepticism to a whole new level—a highly sarcastic level. "Who and where?"

"I'll go through all of that when the sheriff arrives." I made it clear I wasn't going to give Rip an opportunity to shoot holes in my theory. I was convinced I'd figured out the entire deplorable scheme behind Reilly's death, and I didn't want Rip trying to make me second-guess myself.

"All right," Rip agreed. He was clearly reluctant, but knew if he didn't call Sheriff Peabody, I would. "Just don't embarrass me. Okay?"

"Have I ever embarrassed you before?" I asked, daring him to answer my question. Wisely, he didn't. I glared at him and handed him the phone to dial the sheriff's direct line. I've never before seen anyone take so long to punch seven numbers into a cell phone.

"Under this?" Sheriff Peabody asked an hour later when he joined Rip and me on Walker's back patio. I could tell he wanted to add, "Are you frigging nuts?" Lucky for him, just as Rip had been earlier, the sheriff was wise enough to keep the thought to himself.

"Yes, under this new concrete. And, no, I'm not crazy!"

"I would never accuse you of being crazy, ma'am." The sheriff said, although I could tell he was wondering if he'd accidentally voiced the thought out loud.

"Well, I'm certain you were thinking it. When I was talking to Bruno earlier, he referred to Walker's best friend, and it hit me who had killed Reilly. Everything added up all of a sudden. Let me tell you what I know and why I'm convinced her body is under this concrete patio we're standing on."

The three of us sat down in the teal patio furniture that had been reported as a loss on Walker's insurance claim. I then went on to explain how I'd come to the conclusion that Jessie Garza had killed Reilly Reynolds out of loyalty to his best friend since high school, using the horrific storm to stage the murder to look like a terrible accident.

"It seems as though it had come to Walker's attention that his wife was having an affair with Percival, the man you just arrested for killing the protected timber rattlers. That arrest was thanks to me, of course." I couldn't help but feel a little arrogant. Or a lot arrogant, to be more precise. "I just discovered Reilly told Walker she wanted a divorce shortly before the hurricane. One day I brought some leftover food over here to give Walker, but found Jessie, his general contractor and best buddy, instead.

Jessie was asleep on the floor from pure exhaustion. He told me it had been a very long morning. He said he'd been working on water lines all morning, but there was no evidence of that. Instead, Jessie's clothes were spattered with fresh concrete and his boots were completely covered with it. He'd obviously gotten up early and begun pouring this patio at or before daybreak. He told me an insurance adjuster was coming to appraise the damage to his home later that day. If Reilly's body had been tightly wrapped in plastic and stored in Jessie's home since her death, he would've needed to find a place to move it where it'd never be found."

Joe Peabody's expression was one of doubt. "What makes you think the killer didn't dispose of her body immediately? With all the destruction in town and uprooted trees, it could have easily been buried in a remote area."

"I realize that, Joe. But I don't think he did. Maybe he was afraid her body would be found when all the trees were picked up by those large trash haulers with the boom truck and those swinging buckets that look like clam shells. I doubt he was thinking logically at the time, having just murdered his best friend's wife. I asked Jessie specifically if he thought Reilly's body would ever be found."

"What'd he say?" The sheriff now showed more interest in my theory.

"He said he did at one time, but at that point, he was certain it'd never be seen again. It was the look in his eyes more than the words he spoke that sent a chill down my spine. It was almost as if he knew without a doubt Reilly's body would never be discovered. Having just poured a concrete patio over it might have boosted his confidence."

"Hmm." The sheriff was cupping his chin with his left hand as he spoke. "That sounds ominously foretelling."

"Yeah. What he said," Rip mumbled when I looked at him in

question, curious if I'd swayed his opinion. With a wink, he added, "It *does* sound ominously foretelling."

I pointed to the portable concrete mixer still in the back yard. "Jessie mixed the concrete himself, and I believe he dug a hole to place Reilly's wrapped body in before pouring the concrete over her. This, I think, he did before daylight, because I vaguely recall hearing the spinning of a concrete mixer early that morning as I was waking up."

"I didn't hear anything," Rip said.

"Of course not," I snapped at Rip. "You don't even wear your hearing aids when you're awake, much less while you sleep."

The sheriff tried unsuccessfully to suppress a chuckle, and said, "Okay. Go on."

"This part is unclear, but I think during the time Rockport was in the eye of the hurricane, Jessie was driving over to check on Walker and his wife. He saw Reilly running around looking for Scrappy, and probably convinced her to get in the car. In any case, he must have hit her over the head with the crowbar then or killed her elsewhere.

"Either way, I think it was a crime of passion, as well as opportunity. He was extremely upset about the way she'd broken his best friend's heart. After all, Walker nearly succeeded in killing himself, except Jessie found him in the nick of time. He basically told me Reilly was promiscuous. In fact, he referred to her as a home-wrecker. I think he actually believed he was doing Walker a favor and giving him the chance to 'move on', as Jessie so callously put it."

"I thought you said the crowbar belonged to Tony," the sheriff said.

"I originally thought it was Tony's, then I thought it belonged to Bruno. But Bruno told me he had borrowed it for a project he and Tony were involved in. Bruno is Barlow's stepson, by the way. Bruno basically implied the crowbar belonged to Walker. Jessie might have even borrowed it from his best friend and was returning it to Walker when he spotted Reilly out by the street."

"Who returns a borrowed crowbar in the middle of the night during a powerful hurricane?" The sheriff asked.

"Oh. Okay. I hadn't thought about it that way. I did tell you that part was unclear. Nevertheless, I believe the crowbar belonged to either Walker or Jessie, who loaned it to Bruno and Tony to use to complete whatever project they were working on together. It probably belonged to Walker, as I'd first seen it in a closet in his house, but it seemed to be freely passed from one worker to another. And I think Jessie wielded it to kill Reilly." I was beginning to question my own theory as I watched the two men share a knowing look. They appeared to be wondering if I hadn't been whacked on the head with something myself, rather than Reilly. The subsequent concussion obviously had me imagining preposterous scenarios involving the woman's disappearance.

"Is that all you have?" Peabody asked. "It sounds as if it's all circumstantial."

"Maybe so," I admitted. "But don't you think the man should be interrogated, his alibi questioned and confirmed?"

"We'll see."

I was seething when Joe Peabody left, convinced my theory would go no further. Imagine my surprise when I woke up the next morning to the sound of jack-hammering next door. Considering the short amount of time it took me to get out of my pajamas and into a shirt and jeans, I could have competed in *America's Got Talent* as a quick-change artist.

Rip stood next to Sheriff Peabody and two detectives when I limped next door as fast as I could, too impatient to use the crutches. I was ticked off at Rip for not waking me. Did he really think I'd rather laze around in bed than watch to see if my theory was confirmed or not? I forgave him when he greeted me with a warm hug and quick kiss. "Good morning, sunshine."

"Good morning. What's going on?"

Rip brought me up to speed as the sheriff spoke to the detectives. "Garza was brought in for questioning yesterday afternoon and told the detectives he was with his mother at her house in Bayside throughout the storm."

"His mother couldn't or wouldn't confirm his alibi?" I asked.

"Oh, I'm sure she would have—if she was alive!"

"She's dead?"

"For the last seven years," Rip replied with a smirk. "Seems she was a heavy smoker and died of COPD in 2010. Her house in Bayside was sold shortly after her death. Kind of shot a big hairy hole in Garza's alibi."

"I'd say so." I tried not to smile at the news Jessie's mother had died an undoubtedly painful death, but I was too gleeful that the verification of my theory seemed to be coming to fruition. Just then Rip and I looked up to see the gentleman using the jack-hammer make a thumbs-up gesture.

We rushed over to see blue plastic peeking through a void in the concrete. Within minutes, part of Reilly's body was exposed. The tightly-wrapped plastic, which had partially preserved the body as if she were a mummy, had been ripped in several places, and the sudden overwhelming stench of decaying flesh was almost unbearable. The sheriff gave some quick instructions to the detectives and ushered Rip and me back to our travel trailer.

"I guess I owe you a big thanks, Rapella. Looks as if you've done it again." Sheriff Peabody looked me directly in the eyes when he added. "I suppose I owe you an apology, too, because I thought you'd gone off your meds or something when you were expressing your suspicions yesterday."

"Thanks. But I only take a thyroid medication, Joe." I was dismayed the man thought I took medicine for a mental illness.

"It's just a saying. I didn't mean it literally," Sheriff Peabody said. *There's that word again*, I thought, *but I'm glad Joe used it properly*. I smiled and urged him to continue. "Anyway, I started thinking about what you'd said and came to the conclusion we had nothing to lose by questioning Jessie Garza. Glad we did, too. To be honest, I was surprised to find out your supposition was right. The man has no priors, not even a speeding ticket on his record. Just what seems to be a no-holds-barred loyalty to his best friend."

I wasn't surprised. My gut feeling had been so strong, I was convinced it was spot on. What did surprise me, however, was when a second arrest was made later on that afternoon.

TWENTY-SIX

We received a call from Sheriff Peabody at three-fifteen. When Walker Reynolds had heard his best friend had been arrested on a voluntary manslaughter charge for the murder of his wife, claiming he alone was responsible, Walker had driven to the police station and turned himself in.

As it turned out, he claimed he'd casually mentioned to Jessie he wished Reilly was dead after she'd asked for a divorce. He really hadn't expected Jessie to take his words to heart and bludgeon her to death with his crowbar. According to Walker, Jessie had driven over to check on the couple during the lull in the storm. Like so many others, he'd thought the worst of the storm was behind them. He saw Reilly out front and stopped to speak with her. She told him she was looking for Scrappy, who'd gotten spooked and run off. Jessie told her to hop in his Ford Explorer, and he'd help her search for the dog.

They found Scrappy a block away and picked him up, but when Reilly made a snide remark about Walker, Jessie's anger exploded. He reached for Walker's crowbar in his back seat and struck her with it, splitting her head wide open and killing her instantly. It had been a crime of passion and opportunity, as I'd suspected, but a crime nonetheless.

According to Jessie, the back side of the storm was just beginning to ravage the area and he knew trying to dump her body at that time was foolish and dangerous. He didn't want to be take the risk of being blown off the road and rescued by first responders with Reilly's body in his trunk. Panicking, he drove Reilly and the dog to his house. Once there, he wrapped her body tightly with the large roll of thick blue plastic he'd purchased in the event he'd need to use it to tarp the roof of his house following the storm. He then hid the wrapped body in a closet in what was left of his garage, where it remained until he received word the insurance adjuster would be coming by to inspect the damage to his home.

The following day, Jessie turned Scrappy loose. The Maltipoo found his way back to Key Allegro and was discovered, hungry and exhausted, by some Good Samaritan on Luau Lane who posted the dog's photo on Facebook, aiding in his safe return.

It took several more days for Jessie to admit to his best friend what he'd done. He'd originally told Walker that as he was driving up to their house during the lull in the hurricane, he'd seen Reilly racing down the pier after their dog. He'd added that since the storm was beginning to pick up again, he'd changed his mind about stopping by and had instead returned to his home.

Walker hadn't actually seen Reilly chasing after Scrappy, but that was the story he told the police, and the one he'd eventually maintained as the truth of his wife's disappearance. Walker was appalled when Jessie finally told him what he'd done, but he felt partially responsible. He reluctantly agreed to help Jessie cover up the crime. Walker had felt both sick to his stomach and relieved beyond belief to know that Reilly, the woman who had shattered his heart into a million pieces, was out of his life forever.

In the month following her death, Walker had been riddled

with guilt. That's why he'd barely eaten and had dropped a lot of weight. His hair had begun to gray and his cheeks had sunken into his face. His appearance had changed so drastically in a matter of weeks that even his closest friends hardly recognized him.

It had been his idea to bury her in the back yard and pour a new patio over the top of her body when Jessie said he had to find a place to bury her body immediately because the insurance adjuster was due to appraise the damage to his house the next day. It was Walker who had prepared the patio for concrete with two-by-four forms and re-bar. Even another Category 4 hurricane would not expose the reality behind Reilly's disappearance, he'd assured Jessie. She would remain on the missing person's list forever. Or so he thought.

Walker hadn't counted on a curious woman with mediocre investigative skills, and—sometimes—uncanny luck, to dig up the truth, resulting in his wife's body being dug up, as well. He actually admitted he was relieved his evil deeds had been exposed. He couldn't eat, couldn't sleep, and could hardly stand to look at himself in the mirror any longer, he'd told the detective. Jessie, on the other hand, was not pleased at all. Lucky for me, he'd never see the light of day again, or I might have ended up being his next victim.

Even if I'd never gotten to the bottom of the case, I have a feeling Walker eventually would have turned himself in, incriminating his best friend Jessie in the process. When I'd come across the two buddies arguing on Walker's back patio, Jessie had been begging Walker not to do something, which I now suspect was that very thing. Walker had backed down and promised to keep silent, but he seemed relieved he no longer had to honor his vow, according to the sheriff.

In his remorseful meltdown in the sheriff's office, Walker also admitted that his accountant and neighbor, JJ, a.k.a. Jo Jo

Wallinski, with whom he swore he had no romantic interest, had helped him file an erroneous insurance claim. The claim included everything from his expensive and nearly indestructible patio furniture to a lot of electronic equipment he hadn't even owned. As it would turn out, JJ's personal claim was even more inflated, as were those of several more of her clients.

During Jessie's interrogation, with no proof whatsoever, the young detective, Chad Morris, who'd given me the impression he had cotton candy for brains, had cleverly asked, "Why did you feel compelled to kill Barlow Barnaby, too?"

Thinking there must be a mountain of proof of his guilt, Jessie had openly admitted to killing Barlow after hearing about the anonymous tip called into the hotline. Chuck Beatty's initial impression had been correct after all. Barlow had been Jessie's second murder victim. Only in this case, Jessie wasn't charged with voluntary manslaughter, but rather, first-degree murder. The killing of Barlow had been premeditated and highly deliberate.

Like everyone on Flamingo Road, Jessie had instinctively suspected Barlow was the anonymous tipster. He was afraid that, given time, Barlow would recall more details about what he'd witnessed in front of the Reynolds's home during the lull in the storm. He had already reported the car he'd seen Reilly getting into was a tan SUV, which Jessie put up for sale immediately after the murder. It was the Ford Explorer I'd asked Jessie about in Walker's driveway. Naturally, he'd lied and told me it belonged to a friend of Walker's who lived out in the country. I guess it was actually a lie by omission, as Jessie had failed to mention *he* was the friend who lived out in the country and wanted to sell his car.

To prevent Barlow from passing on more information to the police, Jessie went to the man's house early in the morning. He knew Bruno was staying over at his new girlfriend's house that night, so the timing was perfect. One punch to the jaw knocked Barlow out cold. Thanks to his size and strength, it was easy to hoist Barlow up to the ceiling and slip a hangman's noose around his neck. He knew Bruno would not be overly grief-stricken about his stepdad's death, nor would anyone else who lived in the neighborhood. He almost felt as if he was doing a great service for Bruno and the residents of Flamingo Road.

"Why did he strip Barlow down before hanging him?" I asked the sheriff.

"He didn't. He said when he arrived at two in the morning, Mr. Barnaby was asleep in bed, naked as a jaybird."

"Eeww, gross."

"That's what Jessie said," Joe said. "But the worst part of it is that Barnaby wasn't even the anonymous caller to begin with. Unfortunately, his reputation for calling the tip hotline on a weekly basis got him killed."

The sheriff went on to explain his remark. It seemed Jessie's instinct that Barlow was the anonymous tipster was misguided; proving yet again that making an unsubstantiated assumption was not always the smartest thing to do. Sheriff Peabody told us only that the tipster had been a female, with an impossibly high-pitched voice. Although he didn't leak the identity of the caller due to confidentiality protocol, I knew without a doubt Suzanna Pandero was the anonymous eyewitness. Suzanna had undoubtedly thought Reilly ran off with her husband, using the ferocious storm to fake her accidental death, and wanted the police to investigate the matter. She'd hoped they'd track the love-struck couple down and punish them. Perhaps even make Percival see the error of his ways and rekindle his relationship with her. I'm sure Suzanna was happy to let all of her neighbors assume Barlow Barnaby was the anonymous eyewitness due to his proclivity for calling the tip hotline. I wondered if she now felt somewhat responsible for the man's death—not that she could've ever foreseen the horrendous fate that would befall him.

Speaking of Suzanna, she returned from Austin on the afternoon of the two men's arrests. Her mother was recuperating nicely from her stroke, and Suzanna had been anxious to return home. I took her house key over to her as soon as I saw her pull into her driveway. I wanted to tell her the key didn't work and that she needed to have a deadbolt installed, as Rip had suggested. She'd already heard about Percival's arrest and was surprisingly torn up about the situation, so I didn't mention to her that it was I who instigated it. She obviously still loved the man, despite his many transgressions.

"How was Horizon City?" I asked, knowing she'd actually been in Austin. I couldn't help but wonder why she'd fibbed to me.

"Oh, you're thinking of my mom's winter home. Her primary residence is in Austin, and that's where I've been the last few days."

"Oh. It must be nice to have a vacation home." I smiled brightly. *And nice, because it means you weren't lying to me about where you went directly after the storm or earlier this week.*

Suzanna's pet chinchilla was delighted to see his owner again. He'd been missing her, I could tell. The little "rascal" had begun to grow on me over the last few days, but not so much that I wasn't happy to be relieved of the responsibility for him. I'd been thankful for not being the cause of his death, any houseplants' death—or Rascal's death due to a houseplant. I even remembered to warn her about the toxicity of the golden pothos plant I'd placed on top of her refrigerator. I advised her to Google what plants were poisonous to pets.

I also got a chance to speak to Tony, whom I saw pull up next door when he came to claim a few of his tools from Walker's house one day. He was blown away by the arrests of Jessie and Walker. He hadn't had a clue about their involvement in Reilly's disappearance. He still could hardly believe the way it'd turned out.

Tony said that later in the afternoon on the day he'd painted Walker's living room, he'd returned to Walker's house to wash his hands and pick up his tool box and Walker's crowbar, which he'd need to use on his project at Barlow's house. Convinced the red stains on Walker's crowbar were caused by the red paint, even though he couldn't imagine how they'd gotten there, he'd decided to try and wash the majority of it off. Fortunately, Tony left enough behind to be tested by the crime lab.

After completing a quick task at Barlow's, he'd returned to the Reynolds's house with a bottle of bleach to scour any paint stains he'd left behind in the sink or on the counter in his haste to get back to the job he'd been working on. Having no clue he'd removed blood, not red paint, from the crowbar, Tony pitched the ruined rag in the large dumpster out in Walker's drive, which had his company's TNT Demolition logo on it. *When we knock them down, they stay down.* Too bad for Jessie and Walker that when you bury them, they don't always stay buried.

Walker would eventually serve time for being an accessory to murder. A lot of time, to be exact. JJ would pay a hefty fine, spend nine months in jail on numerous counts of insurance fraud, and spend many hours performing community service. Jessie, whose crimes were the most atrocious, would be placed on death row for committing two murders. Texas does not mess around when it comes to the death penalty. It wasn't likely that Jessie would spend thirty years on death row before being executed, as was the case in many states. I had no doubt his days on this earth were numbered. It was a realization that like Walker at the time of his arrest, both relieved me and made me sick to my stomach.

Although I'd only been back home in Rockport for little over a week, I'd managed to be instrumental in putting three men and a woman behind bars, including the neighbors on both sides of

Regina and Milo's house, and the accountant a few houses down. This fact didn't go unnoticed by my daughter.

"I'm really proud of you, Mom, but I'm kind of glad you guys are leaving in mid-October to go to Tiffany's birthday party. If you stay here much longer, we won't have any neighbors left on Flamingo Road."

I assured her my sleuthing was over for the time being. I was ready to roll up my sleeves and do whatever I could to help them recover from Hurricane Harvey. The remarkable storm had been a terrible one, but it had also brought out a strength in people they didn't know they possessed. I believe it proves there truly is a rainbow after every storm. Sometimes you just have to look hard to see it.

AFTERWORD

Hurricane Harvey was the second-costliest hurricane on record, following Hurricane Katrina in 2005. It made landfall as a category 4 hurricane in Rockport, Texas, at 10:00 p.m. on August 25, 2017, with winds in excess of 140 mph, heavy rain, and a massive storm surge that swamped coastal areas. It was the first category 4 hurricane to hit the mainland since Hurricane Wilma hit Florida in October of 2005. After causing catastrophic devastation in southern Texas, Harvey moved up the coast, dumping over fifty inches of rain on the Houston area.

The destruction left behind by Harvey was overwhelming. Thousands of power poles were snapped in half in Aransas County alone, and they, along with many miles worth of downed power lines, littered the roadways. The incredible response from electrical companies across the country, that volunteered their assistance, had power restored to the area in a matter of two to three weeks. It was an amazing achievement, considering the pure volume of work required to accomplish such a feat, and greatly appreciated by all of the county's residents.

Clean-up and debris removal had begun by that time, and most of the downed trees, demolished RV's and boats, and general debris from structures, were being stockpiled in the median of Highway 35 Bypass. Years earlier, the wide median had been designed for exactly such a potential disaster, and the inspiration had proven to be very beneficial. The growing mountain of trash seemed to stretch for miles. Two, then three, and finally a half dozen or more smokeless incinerators were set up to burn debris around the clock. Still, they could not keep up with the ever-increasing volume of rubble.

Meanwhile, residents were out working their tails off in the wicked heat and humidity, saving what could be saved, disposing of what couldn't, and doing their best to help out their friends, neighbors, and even complete strangers. It was a prime example of how the worst of circumstances brought out the best in people.

Over one hundred people lost their lives as a result of the massive storm, either directly or indirectly. Incredibly, only one of those deaths occurred in Rockport. That in itself is remarkable because an alarmingly high percentage of residents ignored the mandatory evacuation order and rode out Harvey in their homes. Fortunately, many of the homes in the quaint little coastal town are vacation and/or short-term rental properties. Most of those who stayed behind now claim they'd never ride out another hurricane, as it was a terrifying experience they'll never forget.

Rockport, and other affected areas, continue to recover from Harvey, and the citizens of the Lone Star State continue to stay "Texas Strong". Although *Ripped Apart* is based on an actual event, the story is completely fictional. I hope you enjoyed it.

As for future tropical storms who even think about hitting the Texas coast, please take heed to our state's motto and "Don't Mess with Texas"!

RIPPED OFF

A RIPPLE EFFECT MYSTERY, BOOK SIX

"Surprise!" I exclaimed as I threw my arms around my grand-daughter, Tiffany, in a long-awaited hug. We hadn't seen her and her husband, Chase Carpenter, in two years. My husband, Clyde "Rip" Ripple, and I, Rapella, had traveled from Rockport, Texas to the foothills of the Sandia Mountains in Albuquerque, New Mexico to surprise her for her thirtieth birthday. As full-time RVers, we'd spent the last couple of months in Rockport helping our daughter, Regina, and son-in-law, Milo Moore, recover from Hurricane Harvey.

"Oh, Grams!" Tiffany began to sob as I embraced her at the entrance to her home. "I'm so glad you and Papa are here."

I soon realized Tiffany's tears were not ones of happiness like mine were. She was genuinely distraught. I'd hoped to make her day, not make her weep. "What's wrong, Tiff?"

"Trey is dead."

"Oh, dear, I'm so sorry." I stroked her back as she continued to shed tears on my shoulder. "Who's Trey?"

After a few long moments, her blubbering stopped. "Trey and

his wife, Sandy, are two of our best friends. I met her at work, and she introduced us to her husband."

"I see."

"Trey *was* her husband, I should say." At the thought of having to use Trey's name in the past tense, Tiffany's crying began anew. "Trey was our investment broker, as well. He convinced Chase to invest in an IPO, and we stand to make tons of money."

"That's wonderful." I didn't know what an IPO was, but I would Google it later. I didn't want Tiffany to think Grams was behind the times. The last thing Rip and I invested money in had been our daughter's college education. Regina had majored in marine biology, minored in secondary education, and ended up being a real estate agent. I'm not sure how well that expensive investment had paid off, since her college education had nothing to do with her chosen vocation. "How nice to have a venture pay off so splendidly."

"Yeah. It was a tech stock that soared in its first quarter. Trey was going to sell it for us today. I sure hope he completed the transaction before he . . .well, you know." For a brief second, I saw Tiffany smile; it was that of the rich kitty who'd eaten the solid gold canary. Had I blinked, I would've missed it.

"Yes, I know. But that's neither here nor there right now. The most important thing is that your dear friend lost his life. What happened to this Trey—"

"His name was Trey Monroe." A new round of sobbing commenced after using his name in the past tense once again. "We don't know what happened yet. All Chase heard was that Trey was getting ready to board a plane at the Double Eagle II Airport and he suddenly dropped dead on the tarmac."

"Oh, my! How awful," I said in commiseration. I glanced around, and asked, "Sounds like a massive heart attack or possibly an aneurysm. Where is Chase right now?"

"Chatting with Papa in the garage, I think. Why don't you two get settled into your RV site and return around seven for supper? I'm sure we'll know more by then. I'm having a couple of pizzas delivered because I'm too upset to cook. I hope that's okay."

"That's more than okay. We both love pizza." *Not so much the agonizing heartburn that comes with it*, I could've added. Naturally, I didn't. Both seventy years old, Rip and I suffered from acid reflux. His was so severe I often wondered if he was having another cardiac-related issue. Rip had recently undergone a triple bypass while on our golden wedding anniversary cruise to Alaska, and that was not an experience either one of us wanted to repeat. "We'll pick up the tab for dinner. Order some bread-sticks too, if you'd like."

Tiffany looked truly touched by my offer. "Okay, but you and Papa are our guests."

"Regardless, we'd like to pay for supper. I'm sure we'll eat our share at your birthday party tomorrow night. Chase told us he's having it catered by Bruiser's Barbecue."

"I don't know how we can celebrate anything after this horrible news." Tiffany had a point. To host any kind of party the day after one of your best friends suffered an untimely death sounded cold and heartless. "We'll likely cancel and just have a quiet dinner here tomorrow night."

"We're fine with whatever you and Chase decide," I said. We'd reserved a site in a nearby RV park so we wouldn't be underfoot. Plus, travelling with Dolly, our overweight grey and white tabby, it was always best if we stayed in the Chartreuse Caboose. The unusual name of our thirty-foot travel trailer was based on the color I'd painted the exterior to make it stand out in a crowded campground or Wal-Mart parking lot. "See you in a couple of hours, honey. Again, I'm sorry for the loss of your friend."

As we drove to the campground, I relayed my conversation with Tiffany to Rip, who nodded in response.

"Chase was very upset about his buddy's death." He cocked his head to the side and asked, "What's an IPO?"

"An IPO is an initial public offering." I'm sure I sounded full of myself despite the fact I'd only known what an IPO was for about fifteen minutes after Googling it on our phone. "It's when a company launches into the stock market and sells shares of their company to institutional and retail investors."

"Yeah, okay." Clearly unimpressed with my knowledge, he asked, "What's for supper?"

"Pizza and garlic breadsticks."

"Oh, good grief. I can taste the acid reflux already." Rip clutched his chest in mock anguish. "Don't forget to bring the Tums."

"I won't. Oh, and we're paying for the pizza, too."

"In more ways than one, I'm sure."

That evening, we discussed Trey's death as we sat around the kitchen table and ate Chicago-style, deep-dish pizza. Our conversation stopped when Chase's phone rang. Looking devastated, he listened to the caller for only a few minutes before ending the call. His expression was like that of a man whose favorite football team had just lost the Super Bowl by missing a twenty-seven-yard field goal attempt with one second left on the clock.

"What's wrong, son?" Rip asked.

"I've got good news and bad news. It seems Trey was murdered. Someone injected him with a large dose of fentanyl shortly before he collapsed at the airport." Chase now looked angry rather than upset.

"Oh, no!" Tiffany sniffled. "Who'd kill one of the nicest, sweetest guys we've ever met?"

Chase replied with a shrug. "My guess is there are many possible suspects."

"What?" Tiffany asked, clearly baffled by his remark. "So, what's the good news?"

"That *was* the good news." Chase had all three of us putting our pizza down with that comment. "The bad news is he sold all of our stock two days ago."

"So?" Tiffany had taken the one-word question right out of my mouth. "Isn't that what we wanted him to do?"

"Yes, but Trey sold all of his clients' entire portfolios and now the proceeds are missing. No one at his firm knows what happened to the money, and it hasn't been deposited into any of his clients' accounts. The private charter he was about to board was scheduled to fly him to the Grand Bahamas International Airport in Freeport. The logical conclusion is that Trey was skipping town with all the money when he was killed."

We all sat in a suspended state of shock.

"I don't get it." Tiffany was the first to speak. "What's that mean?"

"It means we've been ripped off!" Now Chase was royally pissed. "And that we're almost broke. I invested every dollar I could scrape up to invest in that IPO."

Tiffany replied angrily, "No-good, slimy rat bastard!"

Wow! Tiffany went from "one of the nicest, sweetest men she'd ever met" to "no-good, slimy rat bastard" in less than thirty seconds. I'd have to check the *Guinness Book of World Records* to see if she'd broken the record for the quickest 360-degree turn-around. Of course, that's assuming she was referring to the man who'd ripped them off and not her husband who'd invested all their money in such a risky gamble to begin with.

I was setting a new personal record myself; my heartburn was already intense, and I'd only taken two bites of pizza. Or maybe that was just my gut telling me Rip and I were in for another bumpy ride. We couldn't just sit back when our only grand-daughter and her husband were in such dire straits. We'd have to do our best to find out where Trey Monroe had stashed the money he'd stolen from his clients. In the process of doing that, we might also discover who killed him. My mind whirled with questions. Had one of Trey's former investors taken getting ripped off just a little too personally and exacted revenge? Only time would tell.

Available in Paperback and eBook from Your Favorite Bookstore or Online Retailer

ALSO BY JEANNE GLIDEWELL

A Lexie Starr Mystery Series

Leave No Stone Unturned

The Extinguished Guest

Haunted

With This Ring

Just Ducky

Cozy Camping

Marriage and Mayhem

The Spirit of the Season

Lexie Starr Cozy Mysteries Boxed Set

A Ripple Effect Cozy Mystery Series

A Rip Roaring Good Time

Rip Tide

Ripped To Shreds

Rip Your Heart Out

Ripped Apart

Ripped Off

The Ripple Effect Cozy Mystery Boxed Set

Soul Survivor

ABOUT THE AUTHOR

Jeanne Glidewell, lives with her husband, Bob, and chubby cat, Dolly, in Rockport, Texas, on Salt Lake, just off Copano Bay.

Besides writing, Jeanne enjoys fishing, wildlife photography, and traveling both here and abroad.

Jeanne and Bob owned and operated a large RV park in Cheyenne, Wyoming, for twelve years. It was that enjoyable period in her life that inspired Jeanne to write a mystery series involving a full-time RVing couple - The Ripple Effect series.

As a 2006 pancreas and kidney transplant recipient, Jeanne is an avid advocate for organ and tissue donation. Please consider the possibility of giving the gift of life by opting to be an organ donor should you no longer need them.

Jeanne is the author of a romance/suspense novel, Soul Survivor, seven novels and one novella in her NY Times best-selling Lexie Starr cozy mystery series, and five novels in her Ripple Effect cozy mystery series. She's currently writing Ripple Effect book six titled *Ripped Off* and expects to have it released in early fall of 2020.

www.JeanneGlidewell.com

www.ingramcontent.com/pod-product-compliance
Lightning Source LLC
Chambersburg PA
CBHW031211020726
47499CB00002B/551